Forever Mine

By

Linda Sealy Knowles

Forget Me Not
Publisher
~ Where stories take flight~

ISBN: 978-1-956654-38-7

Dedication

It is with great joy and privilege that
I dedicate this book to two sisters,

Judy Hartley Callen
And
Elaine Hartley Moore

These two wonderful, lifetime friends have
helped make
my writing journey a success with their loyal
support.
I am blessed to have these sisters in my life.

Chapter 1

Trembling, Jazz Whitmore lay back on a stack of messy quilts inside her covered wagon as a stranger stood over her young body. His knee dug into the middle of her stomach securing her down, while he held a large, cold pistol under her chin.

A checkered kerchief hid his face. With his free hand, he ripped several boxes open. "Where's the money your man stole from his last bank robbery?" After she fiercely shook her head, he pushed the gun harder against her neck. "Listen, little gal, I know he gave you the money before the posse caught up with him. He didn't have it on him when they strung him up to the highest tree they could find."

"That's not true!" She screamed as he slapped her across the face, grabbed her two hands, and tied them together. He stuffed a dirty rag in her mouth and tied another kerchief around her face to secure her mouth.

"What's not true, sweetheart? The part that your man gave you the money, or my telling you all about your dearly departed husband's death?"

Jazz lay perfectly still with tears clouding her eyes. *Don't cry. Don't believe anything he says. Try to remember everything about this horrible creature.*

"If you don't tell me where the money is, you'll have to pay me something for all the trouble I've had to catch you." He took out the hunting knife he wore on his belt and started slicing down the front of her clothes until they gaped open, baring her lily-white skin.

"Even in the dark I can tell you're a beauty." He ran his knife close to her skin, touching her chest, and flipped back her dress, shift, and corset to view her soft breast. "Where's the money?" His foul breath caused vomit to rise in her mouth, and she was sure she might die by suffocation.

"So, you know where the money is?"

Frantically, she shook her head side to side, and he said, "I guess that means no."

Jazz wished with all her heart she could tell the man where the money was hidden, but she didn't know her husband had robbed banks or even had any money. Joe hadn't shared any information about their finances with her. Often, he went on short trips into towns, but he never showed any signs of having extra cash. Never had he brought back any frivolous items for her and only purchased the bare essentials.

Unbuttoning his shirt, loosening his belt, and laying his hat on a box, the stranger started to crawl on top of Jazz when the pounding of horse hooves came from town. Cursing, he grabbed his hat and leaped out the back of the wagon.

"Thank you, Jesus," Jazz said, rested her head on the makeshift bed as tears flowed down her cheeks.

"Miss Jazz, Miss Jazz, where are you?" Tommy Sanderson called as he jumped off his horse and climbed in the back of her wagon. Looking at her, he said, "Gosh, Miss Jazz, what happened to you?" The boy was only thirteen, but he helped drive her wagon and take care of the animals when her husband was gone for a couple days.

Jazz removed the gag from her mouth with her bound hands and coughed. She tried holding her clothes together with one hand while beckoning with the other for Tommy to untie them. "A stranger accosted me. He heard the horses coming and made his escape."

~

Mr. George Sanderson, Tommy's pa, tied his horse to his wagon. The wagon train looked deserted because there weren't any women and children surrounding their fires. "Where are you, son? Where is Mrs. Whitmore?" He asked as he poked at the cold coals in the fire pit.

"Over here, Pa, in the wagon. A man has hurt Miss Jazz."

George lowered the tailgate of Jazz's wagon and climbed inside. Jazz was clutching her clothes together, her lip bloodied.

His hand clenched at the sight. "Did the man do any harm to you?"

"No," Jazz answered as her face burned from embarrassment, "but he intended to until he heard you returning."

"Good. Did you know the man who hurt you?"

"No," Jazz answered. Her eyes looked blank, lifeless.

"Would you recognize the man again if you saw him?" Mr. Sanderson couldn't imagine who would do this.

"He wore a bandana over his face, but I would know him. His foul breath, harsh voice, nice clothes, and even the oil on his hair would be hard to forget. Yes, I will know him."

"Did he want something from you, other than . . .?"

"Yes, sir." Tears flooded her face. "Don't know how much more I can take. My husband's dead. The man I've loved with all my heart since I was seventeen, nearly four years next month. That's what the guy told me."

Mr. Sanderson repeated his question. "What did he want?"

"Money. He wanted money," she sobbed. "He said Joe robbed a bank. Said a posse had caught up with him and . . . hung him." She doubled over in sobs.

Mr. Sanderson was shocked to the core to hear that Joe was dead and that he had been hunted down by the law and hanged

3

without a trial. Joe was one of the nicest young men he had ever met. Now, he was gone, and his young wife left all alone. Words couldn't help her. "Tommy and I are going to leave you now. Pull yourself together and get properly dressed. I will come for you in a little while so you can tell this story to the leader of the wagon train."

~

Jazz cried until hiccups assailed her. With swollen eyes, a bottom cracked lip, and a bruised cheek, she must look like the devil. How could she face the leader of the wagon train and retell this horrific event to him? Would he think that she had invited this stranger inside her wagon?

Jazz climbed down from the wagon, poured herself a pan of cool water, and splashed her face and cleaned her bloody lip. She laid a cool cloth over her eyes and put on a day dress with a clean white apron. With a comb, she untangled her long, blond tresses and twisted them into a tight bun on the back of her head. Jazz wanted to look like the innocent young woman she was.

Mr. Sanderson and Tommy came by the wagon and instructed her to follow them to the captain's wagon. As she trailed behind Mr. Sanderson with Tommy, she witnessed many of the women cooking and children playing. There didn't seem to be any of the menfolk sitting around the fires.

Once, they arrived at the front of the wagon train, Jazz saw why the men weren't in their camp. They were circled close to the big fire.

Jazz stood frozen at the edge of the circle of men. She tightened her hands into fists, then loosened them. Her posture was rigid.

"Come over here, Mrs. Whitmore. No one is going to hurt you." Captain Kildare motioned for Jazz to join him.

Jazz eased into the circle of men and walked over to the tall man who led the wagon train. He offered her a barrel to sit on.

"Now, Mrs. Whitmore, Mr. Sanderson explained to me what you told him happened while all the ladies were down by the creek washing clothes and watching the young'uns play in the water. May I ask why you weren't with the other women?"

"Well, I thought I would cook a good supper for Joe. It takes time to prepare meat and vegetables. After I put the stew over the fire, I went into my wagon to clean up. I wanted to look extra nice, since he had been gone a few days."

"Did you know where Joe had gone?" The wagon master asked.

"Well, he said he wanted to go into town and have an extra wheel made for our wagon. But, he said it would take a few days for the blacksmith to make it, so he would need to stay in town."

"Mrs. Whitmore, did you object to Joe staying away from you while he took care of this so-called business?"

He'd obviously heard about the posse killing him after he robbed the bank. "Object, Captain. I always tried to be a good wife so I never told my husband what he could or couldn't do. Joe was good to me." Jazz wiped away a falling tear.

"I see." The captain glanced around at all the men.

Some of the women had silently eased behind their husbands to hear what they were discussing. The captain didn't tell them to leave.

"So, you had no idea Joe had this secret activity while he was away from you? He never shared any of the bank money with you. Am I correct in stating this?"

"Captain, I would have never believed my sweet husband was a bank robber. He had no reason to steal. We always had plenty of money for our needs." Although now she wondered where Joe acquired it since he never worked. The realization made her feel suddenly faint.

"You never questioned Joe about money? He always handled everything? Joe bought all the supplies, horse feed, and whatever was needed?" Captain Kildare was obviously trying to ascertain whether she was guilty by association.

"That's right. Does your wife purchase your supplies?" Jazz quizzed the captain, her chin lifted.

"No, I handle all that for us," he said, his eyes darting to his wife. "Mrs. Whitmore, I am sure you are innocent when it comes to Joe's activities, but this stranger who entered your wagon, did you know this man?"

"No sir," Jazz responded. She had gained some of her backbone, and she wasn't going to let them accuse her of being a Jezebel that invited men into her bed. Her mother used to call her *little jezebel* when Mama had been drinking, which was most of the time. Jazz remembered her mama saying that when she grew up, she was going to be a beautiful lady, not like her. She shook her head trying to remove those awful memories as the wagon master plied her with more questions.

She peered into his face. "Captain Kildare, I would never invite a total stranger into my wagon. I never saw the man before. He wanted money that he said Joe had stolen from a bank. I didn't know what he was talking about." Tears threatened to take over. "Then, he told me that my husband was dead. After that I couldn't think straight. I wanted to die and . . . I still do." Jazz hung her head.

One of the wives yelled from the back of the crowd, "She knew no one else was nearby. She invited that man into her wagon. She can fool you men, but we all know how she smiles and sways her hips in front of our young men." Several ladies murmured and echoed her comment with a *yes, she does that*!

Tommy couldn't be quiet. "That's not true. There's no nicer lady on this wagon train. They are telling lies."

Mr. Sanderson grabbed Tommy by the arm and sat him down on the ground with a stern look that said, be quiet. Tommy looked over at his mother who stood as silent as a mouse. She was looking down at the ground.

"As you can see, Mrs. Whitmore, you are a lovely young

widow now. You don't have a man to hunt meat for you, or care for your wagon or your animals." He peered around at the families that had gathered. "Once we arrive in Yellowstone, you will have to leave our wagon train. You can sell your rig, take the money, and travel back to your hometown, or you can stay in Yellowstone and find a job. Mrs. Whitmore, you are young and strong, and I'm sure you can take care of yourself."

He eyed the faces of his fellow travelers. "Does anyone have anything to say before I adjourn this meeting?"

"Good riddance," Another wife shouted. Several ladies made nasty comments under their breath but loud enough for Jazz to hear.

"Men, control your wives' comments. We still have three days before we reach Yellowstone. I will not have Mrs. Whitmore abused by their ugly attitudes or tongues. If you can't control your wives, your wagons can be left behind, too."

Jazz remained on the barrel. She watched the men and their wives quietly walk away from the bonfire. As she stood, Tommy moved beside her. "Miss Jazz, I will walk you to your wagon."

"You'd better not. Your mama might get mad at you."

"No, ma'am. Mama sent me to help you," he said smiling.

"Please, thank her for me." Jazz took his elbow to help steady herself.

Chapter 2

Captain Kildare's wagon train circled at the edge of Yellowstone, Texas. Everyone had leaped down off their wagons, stretching and looking toward town. Yellowstone was a fairly large town. At the edge of it was a white church, and judging by the sign on the lawn, it also served as a schoolhouse.

Tommy jumped down off the high bench of Jazz's wagon and held the lead mule's head while she climbed to the ground. Captain Kildare walked over to Jazz and asked Tommy if he would drive Mrs. Whitmore's wagon to the livery stable at the other end of Main Street.

"Yes, sir. Let me tell my pa where I'm going, and I will take it right away."

Captain Kildare and Jazz watched the young boy race past several wagons. "I'm really sorry about this, Mrs. Whitmore. I am sure you will be able to sell your rig for a nice price. If you'd like, I will speak to the owner of the livery for you."

"Thank you, Captain, but I can manage. Please don't worry about me. I am a big girl, and before I married Joe, I always took care of myself. My mama ran off when I was twelve, so I grew up fast."

"I understand. Please know that I still hate this kind of business, but to keep peace on my wagon trains, I have to make decisions that are best all-around for everyone. Women can be vicious and make their husbands' lives, and the lives of whomever they dislike, miserable. Good luck, and if you need any help, go and seek out the town's preacher." He placed his hand on his hat and gave her a nod goodbye.

Jazz watched the captain walk away as Tommy hurried back to her side. "Ready, Miss Jazz? Pa said that I could stay with you until you get settled somewhere today. Mama whispered that she will be praying for you."

"What would I do without you, Tom?"

"Tom? No one has ever called me that. I like it." He smiled.

"Tommy is for a boy. Tom is a man's name, and you are a man around me." Jazz let Tommy help her climb back on the wagon and drive to the livery.

Jazz's head was on a swivel. She couldn't seem to take in all the buildings as Tommy drove down Main Street. "This is a nice town. I believe I will be able to find a job and a place to live. We passed a boardinghouse that looked real nice. After we park this rig somewhere and board the animals, I will go back and see if I can let a room."

Tommy parked Jazz's rig on the side of the livery. A burly man with a black grizzled beard greeted Jazz and Tommy with a friendly smile. "Welcome to Yellowstone," the muscular man said. "My name is Mel Carter. I own this business, and it looks like you need my help with your animals and wagon, right?"

"Yes, sir," Tommy answered, "Mrs. Whitmore wants to talk to you about selling her rig. Isn't that correct, Miss Jazz?"

"Tom is correct, Mr. Carter. I cannot continue with the wagon train, so I must sell my rig. Is this something you can help me with?"

'Where's your man? I don't normally deal with womenfolk."

"Well, sir. I'm a new widow. I know I am not dressed in black, but I just found out a few days ago that my husband is dead."

"Sorry, ma'am. Well, I guess I can help you. If you trust me,

I mean."

"I don't have much choice, Mr. Carter. You have an honest face, and for now that is all I can go on. I don't know a soul in this town."

"What about all the things in your wagon?" Mr. Carter peered in the back of Jazz's wagon.

"The only things I need are my clothes and a few of my husband's personal items. Everything else can go with the wagon," Jazz said.

"Good, all those things will help sell it. It is in great shape and your mules are strong and healthy. I should be able to get a good price for you."

"How much will you charge me for selling it?"

"A businesswoman, after all." Mr. Carter grinned. "If I sell it quickly, I will only charge you ten percent of the total sale. If I have to keep it for a while, I will have to charge you more for feeding the mules." He watched Jazz's expression and asked her, "How does that sound to you?"

"Fair, very fair. I know feed is expensive. We have a deal, Mr. Carter. Do we need to sign an agreement, or do you take my word to pay you?"

"I believe we can trust each other, Mrs. Whitmore." Mr. Carter stuck his large hand out for Jazz to shake on the deal.

"I'm going to walk down to the boardinghouse close to the church. I hope to let a room there. Do you know the place I am speaking about?"

"Yes, Mrs. Browning is a nice lady, and she runs a clean place."

"Thank you. If I rent a room there, I will come back and gather my clothes and other things." Jazz took Tommy's elbow as they headed to the boardinghouse.

"Oh, Tom, look at all the stores. There's a café. Maybe I can find a job there," Jazz said but quickly changed her mind. "Oh no, it's next door to a saloon."

"I see that. Look, there goes Mr. Johnson from the wagon train through those swinging doors. I bet he will hear it from his witch of a wife when he returns to his wagon." He laughed.

"A lot of men like to hang out in those places. I never wanted to marry a man who liked to drink."

"Did your mama drink whiskey, too?"

"Yes, she drank every night after we washed and delivered the laundry to our customers. Sometimes a man would drop by to see Mama, and she entertained him. She locked me outside until he left. One evening when I was twelve, she ran off with a boat gambler, so I left and went from town to town working in cafes or boardinghouses. Finally, I met Joe who was so good to me," Jazz said, and then she smiled at Tommy. "That's enough about me."

"May I ask how you got your name, Jazz? It is so different from any name I have ever heard."

"One of my mama's friends, a regular customer, started calling me that. He was almost drunk when he told Mama that he didn't want her to call me a Jezebel any longer. Call her Jazz, he said. So, it stuck. I like it better, too."

"Your childhood was so different from mine. I guess I should appreciate my folks."

~

Jazz and Tommy stepped on the front porch of the blue painted boardinghouse. Flowers beds skirted the pathway leading to the porch. The place looked homey. Jazz knocked on the tall white door, and after the second knock, the proprietor opened the door and smiled at them.

"How may I help you, child?" she asked, wiping her hands on her apron.

"Are you Mrs. Browning, the owner?" Jazz asked.

"I sure am. This is my boardinghouse, and I let rooms by the week. I don't do just a day at a time. Too much work, if you know what I mean."

"I am in need of a room. Just came in on the wagon train that is headed to California."

"And who is this nice young man with you?"

"Oh, this is a friend of mine who is traveling with the wagon train. They are parked outside of town for a day or two and he is helping me get settled."

"So, you only want a room for yourself? My weekly rate is two dollars which includes three meals a day. I can make you a lunch if you are working somewhere and need one. For that I charge another dollar each week."

"May I see a room before I commit myself for a week?"

Mrs. Browning looked shocked, but she laughed. "You know, you are the first to want to look at your room before agreeing to stay here."

"I didn't mean to offend you, but I have worked in rooming houses before, and some weren't very pleasant."

Mrs. Browning led Jazz up the stairs to the first door on the right. The room was plain but looked clean enough. There was a water closet with fresh towels and clean water every morning.

"If you will have me, I would like to rent your room by the week. I may be staying for a while, if that is all right with you."

"I have house rules: no men in your room, no smoking, no drinking, and no loud conversation. Oh, I don't allow pets, either."

"I understand and will obey your house rules. If I have a caller, may we visit in your parlor?" Jazz said. "I don't know why I asked you that because I don't know a soul in this nice town."

"Well, as pretty as you are, I am sure you will have plenty of callers."

"Mrs. Browning, I failed to mention that I am a new widow. My husband just passed away, and I am all alone. That is the reason I am not traveling on the wagon train. I have no man to help me with my wagon or animals so I was asked to leave. But I am grateful that Yellowstone is a nice town."

"Oh, child, I am so sorry. Don't you fret none. I will be more than glad to help you get settled in our town. We have a nice church and several friendly ladies' groups that meet regularly. You will be very happy here."

"I hope that I can find a job in town soon. After I'm settled here, I will have to start looking."

Chapter 3

Early the next morning, Jazz awakened to a wonderful aroma. The scent of coffee, bacon, and fresh bread floated up the staircase into her room. As fast as she could, she combed her long blond hair into a tight rope that flowed down her back. She dressed in a clean, dark-print day dress and pinched her cheeks to add color to her pale face. She needed to find a dry goods store and purchase some black ribbon to wrap around her arm to let people know she was a widow. Jazz glanced in the mirror. The cut on her bottom lip wasn't as noticeable as before. Her stomach growled, which reminded her to hurry downstairs. She couldn't remember the last time she had eaten.

"Good morning, Mrs. Whitmore," Mrs. Browning greeted her from across the breakfast table. "Come, take this chair. Everyone, this is our new boarder, Mrs. Jazz Whitmore. I hope you will all make her feel at home here."

Everyone smiled and nodded to Mrs. Browning.

"Jazz, you are sitting next to Mabel Crossbow. Next to her is Mr. Joseph Cummins. Across from you are Sylvia Bennett and Amelia Parker. Two of our men boarders left earlier this morning to work in the mines. You will meet them at dinner tonight."

"Hello, everyone," Jazz said.

'Sit down and let me serve you. Coffee?" Mrs. Browning asked.

"This table looks wonderful. I haven't seen this much food

cooked at one time in several years." Jazz took an extra piece of bacon when it was passed to her.

~

After assisting Mrs. Browning with clearing the breakfast table and stacking the dishes near the sink to be washed, she went upstairs and grabbed her small handbag.

Mrs. Browning stood at the foot of the stairs. "Now, Mrs. Whitmore, I want you to know that you do not have to help me like you did after breakfast. You are a paying boarder not a maid here. I do have a woman who comes in after the breakfast meal and helps with cooking and cleaning."

"Oh, Mrs. Browning, please call me Jazz. I enjoyed helping you. You worked so hard preparing the wonderful breakfast, so the least I could do was clear the table. It's been a long time since I have helped anyone in their kitchen. I've been over an open fire, so it feels good to be in a nice home."

"I appreciated the help." She smiled and told Jazz to run along and look the town over. We do have a wonderful dry-goods store."

"See you later," Jazz said, as she walked outside into the bright sunshine and cloudless sky. Joe would love this, she thought, and the thought made her want to sit and cry. Her heart broke to learn that he could steal from people who worked hard for their money. It was hard for her to believe this about him. Thankfully she had found the tin that held several hundred dollars buried in her trunk. Joe had placed the money there for them to use on the wagon train, but now she realized it was stolen money. With the sudden news that he was dead, she decided not to tell anyone about the money until she was able to find a job and support herself. She would keep an account of every penny she spent and replace it before she gave the money to the sheriff.

Music drifted out of the saloon across the street. Standing on the boardwalk in front of the café was a group of the ladies from the wagon train. One of the ladies pointed at her and made a man look her way. He must be the owner of the café.

Continuing on her way, she came to the dry-goods store. The sign above the door read, James and Son Dry Goods Store. Jazz entered and glanced up at the bell that jingled. She stopped and waited for the clerk to come out of the back to help her, but no one came. Stepping into the store, she immediately found a basket of lovely ribbons on the counter. After selecting several, she kept waiting for someone to appear.

As she continued to browse around the store, she heard something like moaning, and she would have sworn she heard the word, help. Jazz eased closer to the staircase and listened. There it was again, moaning. "Hello?" she called up the stairs. "Is someone up there?" She listened closely and there was a response—a weak *help me* came from somewhere.

Jazz looked around the room. She walked behind the front counter and pulled back a curtain. There was a bedroom with a few men's clothes thrown on the unmade bed.

"Help me!" the voice was a little stronger this time. Jazz dropped the curtain and rushed up the stairs. On the floor was an elderly woman sitting with her back propped against the bed. The woman's gown was wet.

Jazz stooped down next to the older woman and asked, "Are you hurting anywhere? Do you think that you might have broken a leg?"

The woman shook her head.

"I am going to try to get you back on your bed. Can you place your arms around my neck?"

The woman murmured, "Yes."

Jazz lifted the frail woman up on her bed and stretched her out. "Let me find you some dry clothes." She opened a chest and pulled out clean drawers and a pink gown. After removing her wet things and drying the old woman, she put on the clean clothes. "Do you have someone living with you?"

"My son, Cole, should be downstairs," she murmured.

Jazz took the woman's hand and held it close to her chest. "I came in to the store, and no one was down there. Maybe he stepped outside. I'll go down and look for him. Will you be all right by yourself for a few minutes?"

The older woman squeezed Jazz's hand.

As Jazz walked slowly down the stairs, a man came through the back door. He stopped suddenly when he saw Jazz. "Good morning, Miss. Can I help you?"

"Are you Cole?" Jazz asked, pretty sure this was the woman's son.

"Yes, my name is Cole James, the owner of this store."

"Your mama needs you. I came in and heard her calling for help. I went up and helped her off the floor. She is waiting for you." He flew up the stair taking two at a time, while she was still talking.

She could hear his voice. "Mama, are you all right? Did you fall off the bed or fall after you got up?"

Jazz stood close to the stairs and listened to the older woman's reply. As she glanced around the room, she noticed a handwritten sign lying on the counter that read, *Help Needed.*

After waiting for Mr. James to come down, Jazz prayed silently that maybe he would hire her to work in this store. She really needed a job, and maybe he could use her help with his mother, too.

When she opened her eyes, Mr. James was standing in front of her. "I want to thank you, Miss, for helping my mama. She told me what you did for her. I had an errand to run, and when I looked in on her, she was sleeping."

"I was glad to help her. She wasn't hurt, just more embarrassed than anything that she couldn't get up by herself."

"Can I assist you with anything? I need to fix my mother a breakfast tray before I get busy with customers."

"I want these black ribbons. Hope you don't mind, but I

already tied one on my arm. I am a new widow, and I don't have any dark clothes to wear…yet."

"Oh, I'm sorry. You just take the ribbons as a thank you from me."

"I noticed your sign on the counter. Is that a new sign, or have you already hired someone to work?" Jazz asked.

"No, it's a new sign. I need help desperately."

"Well, I would like to apply for the job. I have never worked in a store, but I worked in cafes and rooming houses before I married. I can read and cipher and I am a hard worker. I really need a job." Her words flowed out faster and faster.

"Let me cook my mother's breakfast and think about it. I really wanted a man to help me with heavy things."

"Please show me your kitchen, and I will gladly fix her breakfast. I'm told that I am a pretty good cook."

A burly customer came in the door and started spouting out his list of supplies while Cole stood listening. Turning to Jazz he said, "All right, my kitchen is through that room, and you will find everything you need. Let me know when you have it ready, and I will carry it up the stairs."

Jazz walked into the room and smiled at what looked like a dream kitchen. She stood in awe as she surveyed the large wooden cabinet that contained four small drawers with a flour bin on top. The smooth counter had four large drawers under it. Beside the cabinet sat a two-door icebox. Beside the back door was a hand pump placed next to a deep sink. Running water inside the kitchen was something she had only heard about.

Jazz looked under the cabinet and pulled out a black skillet, a small pan, and a cookie sheet. A warm fire already burned in the fireplace. In less than twenty minutes, she fried up some bacon, scrambled eggs, and buttered the bread. She placed a plate of food on a tray and poured a cup of coffee, then prepared a plate of buttered bread, bacon, and eggs for Cole.

Jazz pulled back the curtain and saw several men standing at the counter all staring at the tray of food she'd given to Cole for his mother.

"Cole, when did you start serving breakfast? I sure want a plate of whatever she has cooked."

"Sorry, George. The young lady is helping me with my mama. This food is for her. Please excuse me while I carry this upstairs." Cole took the tray from Jazz and hurried up the stairs.

"Good morning, gentlemen. May I help you with your order?" Jazz asked, as the men stared at her with wide eyes.

When Cole came down the stairs, the store was empty. "Shoot fire, I lost more customers. It seems I can't take care of the store and Mama, too." His mouth twisted into a sour expression.

"I hope you don't mind, but I helped those men. They told me the prices and I took their money or put it on their account."

Cole blew out a breath and scratched his head.

"I cooked enough breakfast and coffee for you. Go into the kitchen and eat, and I will continue to watch the front. Afterward, before I leave, I will see if I can help your mother."

"You've been my angel today." Cole gave her a grin as he disappeared behind the curtain.

Jazz looked at the display in the front window of the store. The glass certainly needed to be cleaned. Everything in the store window held tools for men. Drab and plain. Men, thought Jazz. They don't come into a store to shop. They come to buy what they need. The women are the shoppers. Maybe, if I worked here, I could fill the window with pretty items that ladies would like.

In less than fifteen minutes, Cole came back into the front of the store. "Miss, I know you asked me if I was hiring, and I am. I thought I needed a man clerk, but I really need someone to help me care for my mama. You, I believe, will fill that job. Maybe while Mama is napping, you could help me in the store."

"Yes, I can do that, but may I ask you why your mother is upstairs and not in the bedroom down here? I'm sorry, but I was looking for someone when I came into the store and I looked behind the green curtain."

He shrugged. "I don't know why I haven't moved her down here. She would be easier to take care of if she was closer. I'll ask her if she'd be willing to change rooms with me." Cole smiled, and lines framing his mouth vanished. "You have already been a great help." He looked at the black ribbon on Jazz's arm as the bell over the door jangled.

"Good morning, Mrs. Evergreen, Mrs. Woodard," Cole greeted the two ladies as Jazz returned to the kitchen to clean it up. Later she would see what was in the pantry to prepare for dinner.

Scooting up the stairs as Cole helped customers, Jazz assisted his mother with her attire for the day. She needed to go to the water closet and then have her long hair brushed.

~

After Jazz left the store with instructions to be back around eight o'clock in the morning, Mama said to Cole, "Did you notice that the young lady you hired to help me never smiled? Not once. She is a good worker, diligent, smart, but terribly sad. Do you have any idea why?"

"I didn't notice she was sad. She did say that she became a widow not too long ago."

Chapter 4

The minute Jazz walked out of the dry-goods store, she felt lighter. A heavy load had been lifted off her shoulders. She thanked God for Mr. Cole James' trust in giving her a job. Working in a store in the center of town would help her meet the residents of Yellowstone. It had been many months since she'd left her last hometown of Logan City, near Houston, Texas. She had worked fourteen-hour days in a rooming house and made enough money to pay for her board and eat two meals a day, but there was no time to linger outside in the sunshine or even go to church.

Then she met Joe who married her and carried her away from that drudgery. Several years later he wanted to travel to California, so, they joined the wagon train. She was thrilled for the first time in her young life. Joe was so good to her, but the ladies on the wagon trail would not have anything to do with her. She was labeled trash. Trash because she worked in a rooming house that rented to men. Joe was her only companion until she met the Sandersons. Their young son, Tommy, was her only friend.

Jazz had decided that she wouldn't talk about her past life with Joe, except to tell about the good times. She hoped people didn't find out that her husband had robbed banks and hanged for it. The only people who knew of this were the travelers on the wagon train, and they had left Yellowstone early this morning. Now she could make a fresh start.

As she ambled along the boardwalk toward the rooming

house, she bumped into a well-dressed older man wearing a black suit and hat.

"Pardon me, Miss. I wasn't watching where I was going." The man removed his hat, revealing the cleric collar he wore.

"No sir, it was my fault. I'm afraid I was daydreaming as I strolled back to my room."

"Please, let me introduce myself. I am Reverend Harrington, the minister of Yellowstone Baptist church. Are you new to our town?"

"My name is Jazz Whitmore and, yes, I am new to town. I came on the wagon train a few days ago."

"I don't want to step out of line and asked personal questions, but I see you are wearing a black ribbon on your sleeve. Are you in mourning for a loved one?"

"Yes," Jazz said, feeling like she was on trial. "I am a widow."

"I see," Reverend Harrington responded.

"I am living at Mrs. Browning's boardinghouse, and Mr. James hired me to work at the dry-goods store. I will be helping with Mrs. James."

"That's wonderful. He has needed help. Cole nearly runs himself dizzy taking care of his farm, the store, and caring for his mother. I am sure you will be a great comfort to Mrs. James."

"I am going to try. Well, I'd better hurry now. So nice meeting you."

"Please, if you like, I would love for you to attend our church Sunday. You will be more than welcome."

Jazz lowered her head and said, "Thank you."

Hurrying inside the boardinghouse, Jazz noticed a small child sitting on the floor in front of the fireplace. An old man was poking his cane at her to make the little girl get up.

"Move out of my way before I hit you with this here stick."

Jazz moved to block her from man's cane. "Sir, if you hit that child, I will break that stick over your head. Don't you dare speak to this little girl like that again." Jazz reached for the little girl's hand and moved her closer to her.

"Well, I wouldn't have hit her. I just wanted to sit in this rocker, and she was in my way. I would never hit a small child, even one like her."

"Really? I'm happy to hear that."

The grumpy old man shuffled to the rocker and lowered into it.

Sighing, Jazz looked down into the little girl's wide eyes and sweet smile.

"Hello. My name is Miss Jazz. Please show me where the kitchen is located." The little girl pulled on Jazz's hand, leading her out of the lobby, bypassing the dining room, and led her to the kitchen.

"Here it is, and that's my mama." The child pointed at a small Black woman who had the biggest brown eyes Jazz had seen.

"I'm Georgia Crandall. What trouble have you been into now, little missy?"

"She hasn't been in any trouble at all. I asked her to show me the kitchen." Jazz glanced at Mrs. Browning, who stood at the counter cleaning off dishes with a spatula.

"Mama, she told Mr. Morris that he'd better not hit me with his cane," she said, her chin lifted.

"What were you doing to cause that old man to get riled at you?"

"Nothing, ma'am. I was in the room when he came in wanting to sit in the rocker. Your little girl was sitting on the floor, and he demanded she get out of his way. Is he always so mean talking?"

Mrs. Browning shook her head. "He doesn't know how to talk nice to anyone. I will threaten to throw him out of my house if he can't be nicer."

"Please, don't do that. Lily can just stay out of his way." Georgia walked over, picked up her little girl, and placed her in a chair near the window. "Sit and behave yourself while I finish these biscuits."

"Please let me help. I love to bake. Let me roll out the biscuits while you do something else." Jazz walked over and took the rolling pin from her.

Mrs. Browning spoke up, "Jazz, you need to go and rest before the dinner hour. Georgia and I will cook the food. You are my house guest, so now you run along."

Jazz hung her head down and sighed. "Please let me help. I have spent so many hours alone, and it feels so good to be in this room. I don't want to go and sit in my room when I can be of some help here."

Mrs. Browning sighed. "Well, If helping out in the kitchen will bring a smile to your face, so be it."

Jazz immediately went to work kneading and rolling out several dozen biscuits. Once they were in the oven, she placed cups of flour in a large bowl. After stirring all the other ingredients in the bowl, she rolled the dough out on the counter, kneaded it, and set it to rise. Over and over, she did the same thing until she had made six loaves of bread.

"Mercy, child," Mrs. Browning said when she reentered the kitchen. "Look at all that bread. I always buy my bread from the café. You will save me some money." She laughed as she peeked at the rising dough.

"I worked in a café when I was a young girl, and the cook taught me to bake a lot of different things. After I married, I cooked for my husband. But this past four months, we traveled on a wagon train, and it was hard to cook fresh bread without an oven. It felt good handling the dough again."

"Well, child, you can come into my kitchen and cook all the bread you want," Mrs. Browning said.

Jazz poured melted butter over the hot biscuits and set them in the middle of the dinner table. All the boarders raved about how light and fluffy the biscuits were, and one man asked Mrs.

Browning if she had changed her recipe.

"No, sir, Miss Jazz cooked them tonight."

"Well, Miss Jazz, I might have to propose marriage to you."

Everyone laughed at the boarder's comment.

Chapter 5

Early the next morning, Jazz donned one of her nicest dresses, tied the ribbon on her arm, and brushed her long blond hair into a soft rope to hang down her back. She rushed down to the kitchen and helped Georgia slice several loaves of her fresh bread. After she warmed butter in the oven, she poured it over the loaves and sprinkled them with sugar and cinnamon. The kitchen and dining room smelled heavenly.

She quickly set plates and silverware on the table and carried two pots of hot coffee to a side table. While the bacon and eggs were being cooked, the boarders were taking their places at the table.

Jazz poured cold water over the hot boiled eggs and began peeling them. She rinsed the fresh strawberries and cut off the green stems. After the eggs and bacon were ready, she carried all the food into the dining room and placed it in the center of the table.

Mrs. Browning laughed. "Jazz, tomorrow I am going to sleep in. You don't need me at all in this kitchen."

"Don't be silly. This is a big job, and all hands are needed."

"You are like a whirlwind. I never peel the boiled eggs." Mrs. Browning smiled. "You are going to spoil my boarders."

"Oh, I am so used to rushing around where I worked before."

"Please don't apologize. You haven't even made a mess for Georgia to have to clean up." Mrs. Browning took Jazz's hand and led her to the table, then insisted she sit and eat.

~

Jazz entered the store at 8:00 a.m. Cole glanced at her and smiled. "Good morning, Mrs. Whitmore."

"If we are going to work together, please call me Jazz."

"If you are sure. You can call me Cole." He smiled as he walked around the counter. "I spoke with Mama about moving downstairs, and she agreed. So, before we get busy, let's do that first thing. I have already carried my things to her room. Mama doesn't have many things—mostly her personal items and clothes. I thought you could bring those while I carried her down the stairs."

"Good plan. Let me check the bed in your old room. I want it to look inviting. Can she sit up in a rocker?"

"Yes, if you can convince her to do it. The doctor thinks she is lying around too much." Cole peered upstairs. "Don't tell her I said that."

"She will never improve if she doesn't get out of bed. I will work with her first thing." Jazz entered the downstairs bedroom and was satisfied with how the bed looked. "Let go upstairs and bring her down. Then I will cook breakfast for you both."

Mrs. James cooperated with Cole as he carried her downstairs and placed her in his double bed. "This is a nice bed," she said. "Thank you, son."

Jazz placed her personal items in the dresser and hung her clothes on several pegs next to the water closet. After Cole left the room, Jazz asked Mrs. James to sit up on the side of the bed so she could remove her gown and put on a soft day dress.

"No, I want another gown. I don't need to wear a dress."

"Sorry, Mrs. James, but later after breakfast, I want you to sit in a rocker near the door of the store so you can see some of the customers. It is not good for a person to be lying in bed all the time."

"Who do you think you are? You are not my doctor. I will do as I please." The old woman's lips pursed.

"I am following your doctor orders. Now, let's don't fight about what you will or will not do. I am here to help you."

"Cole," Mrs. James yelled as loud as she could.

"What in the world, Mama. Why are you screaming? Don't you know I have customers?"

"Tell that girl that I will do what I want to do. I want to wear a gown, and she is trying to make me dress in that." She pointed at Jazz, who held a dress in her hands.

Cole stared at both of the ladies and turned around and left the room.

"Well, he is not my boss either."

"What would you like for breakfast?"

"Oh, do you mean I get to choose what I want to eat?"

"Yes, after you get dressed and I fix your hair, but not until." Jazz stared down the older woman without a smile on her face.

In less than an hour, Jazz was removing the breakfast tray from Mrs. James' room. "I'm tired now. I want to take a nap," Mrs. James said to Jazz.

"All right. A morning rest will be just fine. Should I pull the curtains too?" Jazz watched as Mrs. James stretched her body out on the bed and sighed heavily. "You have worn me out, girl, and I don't like you. "

"I'm sorry, Mrs. James. I had hoped we might be good friends. Maybe later, you will change your mind, for your son's sake. He really needs help with you and the store." Jazz pivoted and pulled the heavy curtains closed as she walked into the store.

Cole looked at Jazz and then at the backroom. "Mama resting?" he asked.

"Yes, for now. But she doesn't like me, so I will probably have to look for a new job soon." She headed into the kitchen. Jazz warmed a bucket of water and spent the morning washing the kitchen walls with borax to combat insects that might come indoors.

"I didn't hire you to kill yourself cleaning." Cole stood with his hands on his slim hips. "You look like the rag you're using. If the walls and floors need scrubbing, I will hire a man to come in after store hours to take care of that task."

"This is part of my domain, and while I'm working here, I want everything to be clean." Jazz strode out on the porch and emptied the bucket of dirty water.

After a long day at the store, learning all the items and prices, preparing lunch and cooking a meatloaf with mashed potatoes for Cole's and Mrs. James' supper, Jazz was ready to walk home. Darkness fell and lanterns lit the streets around the town. The air was cool and crisp and the breeze felt good on her face. She hoped that most workdays wouldn't be as long as today. Mrs. James was a tyrant, which made helping her almost impossible. She would pray for her tonight.

As Jazz entered the boardinghouse, the boarders were just leaving the dining area. After a sweet greeting from several of them, she rushed into the kitchen where she found Georgia and Lily sitting at a table in the corner. "Good evening," Jazz said. "May I fix myself a plate and join you for supper? I'm starving."

"Now, Missy, you just sit down, and I will bring your supper. I put a plate of food in the oven for you," Georgia said as she jumped up.

"I can get it. You just sit and eat," Jazz said. "You don't have to wait on me hand and foot." Jazz opened the oven door and took out her plate of food. It smelled delicious. She grabbed a knife and fork and sat down next to Lily. "How was your day, Miss Lily?" Jazz asked.

Lily hung her head down to her chin.

"Answer Mrs. Whitmore, child."

"Good, I guess. I don't have anyone to play with."

"Now, Mrs. Whitmore doesn't need to hear any complaints from you," Georgia reprimanded her daughter with a sharp tone.

"It's all right. I know how she feels. When I was a small girl, I had no one to play with either. I stayed locked inside while my mama slept. I was very lonely until I grew old enough to go to school."

"I won't have no school to go to when I get bigger," she mumbled under her breath, but Jazz understood. There weren't school for her kind in Yellowstone, or in the South for that matter.

"This food is delicious, Georgia. Thank you for saving me a plate. Where is Mrs. Browning tonight?"

"She went to her prayer meeting at the church. Mrs. Browning goes once a week." Georgia said, as she went to the sink and started washing dishes.

Jazz took an apron off a hook beside the pantry door and wrapped it around her waist. "While you wash, I will dry, and you can show me where everything goes."

"Oh, no, Miss. I can't let you help me. Mrs. Browning would not like it one bit."

"You let me handle Mrs. Browning. After we clean off this counter, I am going to set some bread to rise for tomorrow."

Jazz and Georgia made fast work of the dishes. What kept the dishes from not being dropped and broken was hard to say, as they both laughed when Jazz told Georgia how Mrs. James acted when forced to sit in the rocker for an hour or more.

"If looks could have killed, I would be one dead woman. She pouted until Mrs. Goldworth came into the store and told her how good she looked. Mrs. Goldworth apparently is the town gossip."

Before long, Jazz had four pans of dough set to rise for loaves of fresh bread. Georgia and Lily said goodnight and let themselves out of the back door. Later, Jazz went upstairs to her room, dressed for bed, and brushed her hair. She put on her robe and hurried downstairs to punch the rising bread for the last time. As she was covering the bread to set until morning, Mrs. Browning came in the door.

"Mercy, child, what are you still doing up? I figured with

your first day at work, you would be exhausted."

"I wanted to set this bread to rise before I retired for the evening. All you have to do with this dough is place it in a warm oven, and you'll have four loaves of fresh bread."

"You are something. I can't thank you enough. Did you arrive home in time for dinner? I had to leave early so I let Georgia set the food on the table for the boarders."

"No, I was late, but Georgia saved me a plate so I sat and ate with her and Lily."

"You sat at the table in my kitchen and ate with my maid and her child?"

"Yes, but I don't think of Georgia as a maid. Is there something wrong?"

"You cannot eat with . . . them. Understand?"

"Them? Who is them?"

"Why, my maid and her child. It just isn't done, and I don't want this to happen again." Mrs. Browning tucked her Bible under her arm and started for her room.

"Wait," Jazz said. "Mrs. Browning, I don't understand you. You allow Georgia to clean this house, cook the food the boarders and you eat, yet I can't sit with her and have my supper? Am I understanding you correctly?"

"She is my servant, my maid."

"To me, she is a very nice woman with a precious child. They are both God's children, and we are all alike in his eyes. She's a hard worker and a Christian woman. I am sorry to tell you that I *will* eat with her, talk, and laugh, too. I will never treat her any different than I do you."

"Do you want me to fire her? I will, you know." Her jaw clenched.

"Do you want me to move out?" Jazz wrapped her arms across her chest.

Mrs. Browning stood and glanced around the spotless kitchen. She sniffed the fresh bread rising. "No, I don't want you to move out, but you cannot let anyone know that you eat with my help. Understand?"

Chapter 6

Jazz hurried to work during a terrible rainstorm. She was thankful for the small parasol Joe had given her for one of her birthdays. The only time she had used it was when she sat on the wagon's bench to keep the direct sunshine from blistering her pale complexion. Jazz jumped over mud puddles and tried to walk on the boardwalk as much as possible until she reached the store. As she closed her parasol, she noticed an older man curled in a ball at the end of the store's porch. His poor body was shivering from the dampness.

Once she entered the store, she noticed the front room of the store was cold. Jazz hurried to the potbelly stove in the men's boot section and struck a match to the wood that had been placed inside. She rushed into the kitchen and placed wood in the stove and tucked a sheet of paper in it to make the wood catch quicker. Finally, she removed her wet coat and hung it on a peg by the back door.

What was going on? She hurried to the back of the store, grabbed a small quilt, and went outside onto the front porch. The old man was still there. Jazz bent down and tapped the man on the shoulder. "Please stand, Mister, and let me wrap this quilt around your shoulders."

Wide-eyed and shaking so hard his teeth were chattering, he nodded. "Thank you, Miss," he said weakly.

"Please follow me into the store, and I will pour you some

hot coffee to warm you up."

"No, I can't do that. The owner will shoot me."

"Cole wouldn't harm a soul."

"Not him. That woman who runs the store."

"What woman?" Jazz couldn't image Mrs. James being strong enough to hurt anyone.

"The owner. She's a mean old woman."

"Now, you listen to me. I work here, and no one is going to harm you. I want you to dry off before you die of pneumonia." Jazz took the old man's arm and led him inside to the back of the store. She pulled up a straight chair and pushed him down in the seat. "Now, don't you dare move. I'm going to bring some hot coffee for both of us. I'm chilled from my walk from the boardinghouse."

The old man removed the chair and stretched out on the floor in front of the potbelly stove. He rested his head on his hands and was sound asleep in a few minutes.

Jazz peeked in Mrs. James' bedroom, and fortunately she was still asleep. As fast as she could, she put the ground beans in the coffeepot and put it on the stove. She sliced ham, a fresh loaf of bread, and scrambled nearly a dozen eggs. Later today, she would make something sweet for Cole to enjoy with lunch.

As she prepared a tray for the old man, she wondered what was keeping Cole. He was always working in the store whenever she came in at eight in the morning.

"Jazz?" Mrs. James called from her bedroom. "Jazz, I need you."

Opening the heavy drape, Jazz hurried to Mrs. James' bedside. "Good morning, Mrs. James. Did you sleep well?" She asked. "Do you hear the storm? It is raining buckets. I love to wash my hair in rainwater."

"Water is water. Doesn't make no different a 'tall," Mrs. James spouted.

The old woman was going to be difficult today, so Jazz kept

her voice cheerful. "I have some coffee already made. After you go to the water closet, would you like a cup and a tray of food in bed?"

"You're going to allow me to stay in bed this morning? Why?"

"It's such a dreary day. I just thought you might want to relax while it's storming outside."

"Help me get up and then bring me a tray. I smell fried ham, which is my favorite."

Once Mrs. James was settled back in bed, Jazz prepared her a breakfast tray and a small pot of hot coffee. She placed the tray on her lap and put a large napkin under her chin. "How's that?"

"Fine. Where's Cole this morning? He usually comes in to see me before he gets busy."

"He hasn't made it in this morning. The weather is really bad so he may be taking care of things outside. I'm sure he will be in to see me as soon as he comes." She lifted a hand to cup her ear. "I hear a customer," Jazz said, knowing full well there wasn't anyone. "I will return as soon as I can." Jazz spun around and rushed into the store, then hurried into the kitchen and prepared a plate of food for the old man. She poured two cups of coffee then headed to the back of the store. Loud snoring came from the back.

Setting the tray down, she placed the two cups on a nearby table. "Sir," Jazz said, shaking the old man's shoulder. "Wake up and drink this hot coffee."

The older man grumbled, but he sat up and leaned against one of the counters. "Thank you, Missy. The coffee smells good."

"I made you some ham and eggs too." Lightning lit up the whole room, followed by a loud boom. Jazz jumped. "That was close."

The bell jangled so Jazz hurried to the front of the store. "Oh, Cole, it's you."

"Yes, it's me. Were you expecting someone else?"

"Of course not. I'm glad to see you. I have to admit your

mama and I were both worried about you."

Shaking the rain off his heavy slicker, he walked into the kitchen and hung it on a peg to drip dry. "I am soaking wet, and I need to go change clothes. The coffee and food smells wonderful."

"Do you want to visit with your mama while I fix you a cup and a tray of food?"

"No," he said softly, giving her a disgruntled look and disappeared behind the heavy green drape into his mama's room.

~

"Where in heaven's name have you been this morning? You are always here before that gal you hired. She shouldn't be in this store alone. That girl could steal us blind." Her eyes narrowed at his wet pants and boots.

"I'm fine, Mama. I had to ride out to the farm this morning and check on my animals. Earlier, the roof over my room starting leaking, and before I could get out of bed, buckets of water poured down on me. So, please forgive me, but I need to change out of these wet things. I'll be back, but please allow me time to eat and drink my first cup of coffee. Oh, I stopped by the carpenter's shop, and he will be over to repair the roof."

Cole backed out of the bedroom and rushed upstairs to his room. "That woman is going to be the death of me," he murmured. Looking at the wet bedcovers and soaked mattress, he stretched his back. He was aching from head to foot from lying on the hard floor after the roof leaked.

Cole quickly changed into dry clothes and rushed to the kitchen. He helped himself to a plate of food and poured himself a cup of hot coffee.

"Oh, Mister, I'm so glad that you're feeling better." Cole heard Jazz speaking to someone in the store. "But, you cannot go outside. I just got you good and dry."

Cole picked up his cup and peeked into the store. The old man who regularly sat on his front porch was standing by the counter in brand new clothes. His hair was combed, and he was almost unrecognizable.

"Sam, is that you?" Cole asked, as he sipped his brew.

The old man held his head down and said, "Yep, it's me. I'll pay you for these clothes when I find a job. This here woman made me take them."

"It all right. I'll pay for your new things. You needed them." Turning to Cole, Jazz smiled. "Cole, he was soaking wet and freezing. I forced him inside and dried him off."

"That's fine, Jazz. We'll speak about this later." Cole turned to the kitchen and finished his breakfast. He heard Sam thanking Jazz for the food. So, the girl had fed the old man, too.

As he placed his plate in the dry sink, he was thankful that his mama had not seen the old man. There wasn't a charitable bone in her body. She would have never let Sam in the store, much less given him a new set of clothes. Cole chuckled to himself as he thought about Jazz. She would most likely give everything in his store away. Cole walked to the back door and opened it a crack. The rain was still pouring as his trash-can lid floated by the backdoor.

Pushing the door closed, Jazz rushed into the kitchen and pushed past him slinging the door wide open and practically throwing herself over the porch railing. Jazz held her stomach and vomited. She stood straight and then bent over and retched again and again.

Cole immediately grabbed a wet rag and a glass of water. He hurried to Jazz's side. She took the cloth and wiped her mouth and eyes.

"I'm sorry. I don't know what came over me. Please leave me alone for a few minutes while I pull myself together," Jazz whispered to Cole.

Cole didn't know what he should do—go or stay. Jazz was as white as a sheet, and her petite body was shaking. It was chilly standing outside with the rain splashing upon the porch.

"Please, Cole. I need a few minutes alone."

"Sure, but I will be just inside the store if you need me."

~

Jazz stood as still as death as Cole's footsteps walked away from her. She used the wet cloth and wiped her mouth again, then held her face up to the rainy sky and took in a deep breath. The wind began blowing the rain onto her shoes, so she jumped back and hurried into the kitchen.

A mirror was hanging on the wall beside the back door. Jazz surveyed herself but didn't see any difference. What she knew for sure was she was carrying Joe's baby under her breast. *Oh, Joe.* Jazz placed both hands over her face. *After four years of marriage, we longed for a baby, or rather I did. Now that you're gone, God has blessed me with a little piece of our love to remember you by. Why did you have to ruin our lives, Joe?*

A rumble of voices came from behind the kitchen curtain. Jazz pinched her pale cheeks and walked slowly behind the counter.

Cole was wrapping a package for a lady customer who appeared damp from the rain. "I wouldn't have ever ventured out in this weather, if I hadn't needed this material. Some of the ladies in our sewing circle are making a few dolls and clothes to match for Christmas. Since it's bad outside and I can't do anything else, this is a fine day for sewing."

"Can anyone make dolls and blankets for the children? I am good with a needle, if I do say so myself." Jazz smiled at the lady as she touched some of the material.

"Of course. We would appreciate all the help we can get. Christmas is several months away, but there are only a few of us, so we have to start early. I will be busy during the evenings."

"Sam, will you carry these packages out to the lady's wagon?"

Sam nodded and picked up the packages. "Be pleased to

help."

After the two left the store, Cole grinned. "Now you have Sam working for us?"

"Not really," she said, "He's working for you." Jazz went through the heavy drape into Mrs. James' bedroom.

Chapter 7

Later in the day, Jazz asked Mrs. James if she would like to sit by the large window in the storefront. "You will be out of the way of customers, but you can look outside and watch people walking by."

"Have you lost your mind? Do you think I want people to see me like this? I'm sick and I don't want to have to talk with those clucking hens who come in and shop. You just go about your business and leave me alone." Mrs. James turned over on her bed and faced the wall.

"I am going to work on the window's display this afternoon, and I thought you might want to help me decide what should go in it." Receiving no answer, Jazz left her and walked to the picture window.

"Cole, I want to remove some of the things in the window and put in a few items that might appeal to all the customers. Is that all right with you?"

"The storm hasn't let up, and we aren't overrun with customers. I don't see any reason why you can't make the window look nicer. Most of those old tools have been on display since before my pa died." He laughed and motioned for Sam. "Come on. You can help me store some of the shoes and boots up high on the shelves." Sam smiled broadly, seemingly glad to be able to serve in some small way.

Jazz removed some of the smaller tools and other objects that had dust caked on them. Cole was right. Some of the items had been in the window forever. Jazz chose a shiny dark blue material and smoothed it over the bottom shelf. She chose a lovely hat, a scarf that matched, and soft white gloves with a small button. On the other side, she laid a man's derby and brown leather gloves. On the opposite side of the window, she placed a small handmade, wooden horse, a carved handgun, and a blow gun for boys. There's wasn't anything to display for a little girl. Jazz made a mental note to make a doll or two to sell.

On another shelf, she arranged several small hand tools, a large hunting knife with a scabbard, and a gold watch chain.

Jazz stood back and was pondering about the gold watch chain when a customer rushed through the door, causing the doorbell to jangle loud enough to wake the dead.

Jazz turned around and looked into the face of a handsome young man. "Please, sir, step away from the door. That bell won't stop ringing as long as you are holding it open."

"Oh, I'm sorry," he said. "It sure is a nasty day, but as I was passing by on the way to the boardinghouse, I saw that gold chain. My father's birthday is tomorrow, and he'd enjoy wearing that on his Sunday vest. How much is it?"

"I just put it in the window. Let me go ask the owner of the store." Jazz rushed to Cole and asked him the price of the gold watch chain. He said it was seven dollars since it was coated with real gold. "That thing has been in the store for years." He laughed and walked with her to the front of the store.

"Hello," Cole said and offered his hand to the new customer. "My name is Cole James. I believe this is the first time you have been in my store. And you chose a beautiful day." Both men laughed.

As I just told your lovely clerk, I was walking past and noticed the chain in the display window. I want to purchase it for my father."

"We have had this chain in the store for a long time, so I will sell it to you for five dollars. It is coated with real gold. How does that sound?"

"I'll take it."

"Let me wrap it for you, since it is a birthday present." Jazz placed the chain in the box she'd removed it from and neatly wrapped it in brown paper. She chose a red ribbon, tied it around the box, and made a bow. Hopefully Cole didn't care that she used a two-cent piece of ribbon to make the box look nice.

"How's that?" Jazz asked as she handed it to the man.

"Perfect, just like you," he said as he inclined his face closer to hers before he noticed the black ribbon on her right arm. "I'm sorry, Miss. I meant no disrespect. Good day."

Cole's eyes narrowed as he watched the young man hurry away. A look crossed his face she didn't recognize. Irritation? Jealousy?

"Well, Mister Boss man, what do you think about your new window display?" Before Cole answered, she said, "It's so funny. I was thinking that I needed to remove the watch chain."

Cole smiled down at Jazz. "I believe we have one more just like it. Why don't you put it in the window?" He grinned and said, "To answer your question, I love the display. Hopefully we can sell some of the hats we have in the storeroom."

"We need a shelf to display them and a mirror nearby. Ladies love to try on hats before they buy them. I would want to if I was going to purchase one."

"How do you know so much about how to display items?"

"Oh, I lived in big cities with stores with fancy things. My mother liked flashy things so she shopped a lot, and I tagged along."

~

The doorbell rang as a slim, young man came into the store. Cole hurried to the front.

"I'd have been here sooner, but it has just stopped raining.

Carried my ladder around the side of the building already. We may need some long roofing tacks and another hammer. My handle is trying to break," he said, as he stopped in his tracks and looked Jazz up and down. "Hello, ma'am," he said, rocking back and forth on his heels. "You must be new to town. I'm Hank Johnson, the town's carpenter."

"I've been here about a week. Nice to make your acquaintance, Mr. Johnson, but gentlemen, you must excuse me. I have work to do."

~

Hank cranked his neck around as Jazz walked into Mrs. James' bedroom. "Man, that's one pretty gal. Is she single, Cole?"

"Didn't you see that black ribbon on her right arm? She a widow and she's in mourning. Leave her alone," Cole growled.

"She won't be in mourning forever," Hank said, as he whistled a little ditty. He went out the back door through the kitchen.

Cole waved at Sam. "Come and help me carry my mattress down the stairs. The rain soaked it last night. Hopefully, it will dry out in a day or two. If not, I will have to order myself another one."

'Do you think that fellow will need some help on the roof?' Sam asked.

"I'll take him some of the supplies that he'll need. And forget it, I'm not going to let you climb on that rickety old ladder. You'd think Hank being a carpenter would take the time and build himself a stronger one."

"Youngsters don't always think." Sam walked up the stairs ahead of Cole.

~

Good afternoon, Mrs. James. Did you have a nice rest after

lunch? Have you changed your mind about sitting in the store by the window?" Jazz walked around the room and straightened the covers on the bed.

"Don't you ever let a person answer one question before you ask another? You're nothing but a chatterbox."

"Would you like a snack with your afternoon tea?"

"No, I don't want to sit in the store, and no, I can't sleep with all that pounding on the roof, and yes, I want a sandwich with my tea."

"I'll be right back. Can you manage the water closet by yourself?" When Mrs. James didn't answer, Jazz exited the room and left her and came upon the men.

"Cole, Sam, I am preparing a snack for Mrs. James. Would you both like to take a break and eat something?"

"Sounds good to me and Sam too, right?" Cole glanced at Sam and gave him a smile.

After everyone enjoyed ham and cheese sandwiches and a piece of spice cake, Jazz placed some stew meat on the stove and chopped vegetables. She would prepare a stew and hot cornbread for supper before she left for the day.

Chapter 8

Today seemed like the longest day in Jazz's life. First thing in the morning, she discovered she was going to have a baby. Joe's baby. She had prayed many times during their marriage that she was with child, only to be disappointed.

But today was a day she would always remember. The morning sickness was terrible but glorious at the same time. She counted on her fingers how long it had been since her last monthly time. Nearly three months. So she would have a baby come this spring. A baby this spring! How many months would she be able to work? But once Mrs. James learned that she was going to have a baby, would she allow her to continue working at the store?

After she washed her face and combed her hair, she walked slowly down the stairs to the kitchen. Mrs. Browning and Georgia already had the food on the table for the evening meal. She was happy she could just sit and enjoy this wonderful food because she was ravenous.

Jazz took a seat and smiled shyly at the other boarders. Everyone began passing the bowls of food around the table. Georgia bent low next to Jazz's ear and said she'd missed her today. Jazz smiled and took a piece of cornbread from the tray that Georgia set in the center of the table.

After dinner was over, Jazz began helping to clear the table.

Mrs. Browning posted hands on her hips. "Now, Jazz, you've had a long day. Georgia can clean the kitchen."

"I know but I like to help. Please don't fret over me." Jazz carried a load of plates into the warm kitchen when she noticed Lily leaning up against the wall with a flushed face.

"Hello, Lily. How are you tonight?"

"I'm tired, but Mama won't let me lie down."

"Now, Lily, you know you're getting too big for me to carry you home. Please be quiet." Georgia shook her head and sighed.

"You need a wagon to pull her home, Georgia. Have you thought about that?"

"Well, Miss Jazz, that's takes money I don't have. She's fine."

After the kitchen was clean and all the dishes washed and dried, Georgia picked up Lily and placed her sleepy head on her shoulder. Jazz opened the backdoor and watched her until she disappeared down the dark alley.

~

Early the next morning, Jazz was concerned when Georgia and Lily had not arrived to help with breakfast before she had to leave for work. She made a mental note to return to the boardinghouse and check on them.

After arriving at the store, she was surprised to see several ladies already shopping. Jazz raced into the kitchen, then removed her shawl and bonnet. She placed a long white apron over her dark dress and made sure her black ribbon was still in place on her sleeve. Hurrying over to the counter, she smiled at Cole. "Looks like a good day for business. Are these new customers?"

"I heard one say that the wagon train heading to California had to turn around and take a new trail. Something about a rockslide that blocked their pathway."

Jazz smiled and headed into the bedroom to check on Mrs. James when she heard a woman call her name, "Mrs. Whitmire, is that you?"

Jazz turned to give the voice a sweet smile, when she

recognized the hawk-faced woman from the wagon train that demanded that the wagon-train master put her off. "Yes?"

"I can't believe you are working in this decent store. I was sure you'd be in one of the local saloons since you're nothing but a slut."

"What's going on here?" Cole stepped between Jazz and the customer.

"It seems you don't know who you have working for you. This girl was put off the wagon train because she isn't nothing but a whore. Her husband was a murderer and bank robber before he got hung. Two of a kind—low lives, both of them."

Jazz step forward and stared in the woman's face. "Why do you hate me so much? I never did a thing to you."

The woman turned her shoulder on Jazz and looked out into the store.

"What is she talking about, Jazz?" Cole asked quietly.

"Who's calling somebody out here a whore or slut?" Mrs. James stood in the dark green curtain that divided her room from the store front.

"Mama, please go back in your room. I'm taking care of this."

"Yes, Mrs. James, let me help you back to bed," Jazz said as she used her apron to wipe her face clear of tears.

"No. Don't you dare touch me until we get to the bottom of this. Something is going on, and I want to know who these women are. Why are they calling someone nasty names?"

"My name is Mildred St. Martin, and these ladies are my friends. We are traveling on the wagon train heading to California. This here gal was traveling with us until she was banished and left here while we traveled on. She's nothing but a slut, and her husband was a murderer and bank robber who was caught and strung up by a posse."

"Lord almighty, Cole. You brought this woman to work in our store knowing that everyone in town knows her background?

How could you! And you allowed her to take care of me?" Mrs. James swayed. "I feel faint."

"Come on, Mama, let me help you back to bed."

"Not before you toss that gal out of *my* store. A girl without morals who had a murderer for a husband?" Mrs. James's face was a vivid red and her teeth bared like a wild animal as she spat nasty words about Jazz.

~

Cole had never seen his mama conduct herself in such a manner. She had a temper, but to act like a crazy person was totally out of character for her.

"Come on, ladies. Let's go somewhere else to purchase our things. I can't breathe the same air where this whore has been." The three busybodies left the store as the bell jangled over the door.

Mrs. James stormed back into her bedroom with Cole on her heels. When Cole couldn't make his mother believe the truth about Jazz, he rushed out in the store and glanced around for her. On the stove was a fresh pot of coffee. Jazz stood in the corner of the back porch staring at a small wheelbarrow.

"Jazz, what in the world happened in there? Did you know those women?"

"Know them? No. They were on the wagon train, but they never had anything to do with me. There was only one family that befriended me. I never knew why the other ladies wouldn't include me in the bonfires or let me wash clothes near them. The wagon master said the ladies were jealous of me for being pretty and having a handsome young husband."

"If that was their only reason, they are petty."

"I don't know why the people turned their backs on me. When Joe was with me, they were friendly enough. Whenever Joe left me for a few days at a time, I had this young boy drive my wagon for me. His family was nice to me."

Cole waited for Jazz to continue, but she tried to remove the small wheelbarrow from the corner of the porch. "May I borrow this until I can purchase a wagon? I have a friend who could use this to push her small child back and forth to work." Her hands were shaking so bad she could hardly remove the wheelbarrow from its isolated place.

"Yes, take whatever you need, but tell me why that woman called you those ugly names." Cole took her shoulders and made her face him.

"I really don't know." Jazz wiped the tears away with the back of her hand. "She claimed that I paraded in front of the menfolk on the train, but I never left my wagon area. When a man attacked me a few days before we arrived in town, she claimed that I had invited that awful man into my wagon. That was a lie. The man wanted me to give him the money that my husband had stolen from a bank." Jazz peeked a look at Cole. "Joe never gave me any money except the money that we had when we started our trip. It was in a can hidden in the wagon."

When Cole didn't say anything, Jazz glanced up at him. "I had no idea my husband of four years was a bank robber, much less a murderer. I told my attacker that Joe had not given me any money, so he decided to have some fun with me. Thankfully, the men on the wagon train returned from a hunting trip, and the man raced away into the dark woods."

Cole leaned up against the porch post and looked out over the yard. When he glanced back at Jazz, she had taken the wheelbarrow and walked back into the kitchen. She was removing her apron and pulling her shawl and bonnet down off the pegs.

"I will go now. I am so sorry that this happened. I was going to tell you about it myself when we knew each other better. Sorry to leave you to care for your mother. She isn't an easy person to care for, but she's sad."

Jazz turned to leave, but Cole took her arm. "Please, Jazz, let me talk with Mama. I don't want to lose you . . . I mean, I don't want you to leave."

Jazz removed his hand from her arm and walked out the front door. Cole rushed over to the front window and watched Jazz stride toward the boardinghouse carrying the small wheelbarrow.

"Cole, come in here. I need you," Mrs. James called.

Rage rushed through his veins, and he stormed behind the dark curtain into his mother's bedroom.

Chapter 9

Jazz stepped out on the boardwalk and lumbered toward the boardinghouse. She tried holding her head up and fought back tears so other people wouldn't notice that anything was wrong. It wouldn't be dark before everyone in town heard all the ugly gossip that the women were spewing about her.

Entering the backdoor of the boardinghouse, she knew that the gossip had already reached Mrs. Browning. She quickly set the wheelbarrow at the backdoor and shuffled into the kitchen.

"I can't believe you have the nerve to show up here. I have never been as disappointed in anyone as I am in you." Mrs. Browning slapped her dishtowel on the counter causing Jazz to nearly jump out of her skin.

"Mrs. Browning, aren't you going to allow me to say my piece? You don't even know those women, but I did think that you would at least ask me about why those women were saying those things about me."

"Why would they lie about you? What reason do they have to make everyone in town turn their backs on you?"

"I wish I could answer that question. Mrs. St. Martin never said a word to me on the wagon train. I had no idea she even knew my name until the night I was accosted by a stranger in my wagon while I was alone. The men were hunting, and the ladies were at the creek washing and bathing."

"That woman said that you invited that man into your wagon.

Why would she say that?"

Jazz shook her head and continued with her story. "I didn't know my husband was a bank robber or a murderer. The man came into my wagon demanding the money my husband had stolen. He left when he heard the men returning."

"You story sounds convincing, but you still have to leave. I cannot have a loose woman, whether true or not, living under my roof. So, pack your few things and get out . . . tonight."

Jazz felt like she was twelve all over again being tossed out of the house when Mama entertained. One night she was all alone because her mother had run away with a boat gambler and never looked back. After missing the first of the month's rent, the landlord made her vacate the only home she knew. She remembered being homeless and hungry.

Lifting her chin, Jazz circled around Mrs. Browning and went to her room. She had no idea where she would go tonight, but she remembered how worried she was about Lily. Jazz would try to find where Georgia lived and check on Lily's health. Maybe Georgia could help her find a safe place for her to live.

~

Jazz placed her few personal items and two carpetbags in the small wheelbarrow and headed down the alley that she'd watched Georgia take when she left the boardinghouse. Deep into the night, with little light coming from the shanties, Jazz's nerves were frazzled. She was beginning to shiver—whether from the cold or from the unknown in the darkness.

Suddenly, a door opened with light illuminating the front of the house. Jazz was sure the woman tossing water out of a tin bowl was Georgia.

"Georgia," Jazz's voice was barely a whisper, but the woman stepped into the light of the doorway and said, "Jazz, is that you, girl?"

"Yes, it's me." Jazz was trembling so hard that she frightened

Georgia. Quickly, she rubbed Jazz's shoulders and arms and, speaking softly, assured her friend that she was all right now.

"Come inside, child. What in the world are you doing in this part of town, especially at night?" Georgia glanced around.

When the last hiccupping sobs ceased, Jazz attempted to tell Georgia what had taken place at the store and then with Mrs. James.

"My goodness, child. I can't believe after all the work you've done for Mrs. Browning that she wouldn't believe you. I know she can be a hard woman, but you have been the best boarder she has ever had. She told me how blessed she was when you wanted to live at her place."

"Maybe so, but she didn't believe me enough to let me stay. She said that I couldn't live under her roof any longer and told me to leave. I really thought she would have believed me, so I packed and headed down the dark alley that I'd watched you take several times. I wanted to check on Lily before I found a place to sleep tonight."

"Lily does have a fever, but I put some cold packs on her face, and she finally went to sleep. I'm sure hoping she will be better in the morning."

"Good, me too. Look what I borrowed from Cole. He had this small wheelbarrow that wasn't being used, and he said I could let you use it to carry Lily back and forth to the boardinghouse."

"What a grand idea, but I can't use this. What if his mother discovered I had it? She'd have a hissy fit, for sure."

"How would she ever know that you have it? You arrive early in the morning and leave after dark with Lily. I didn't tell Cole what friend needed it, and he didn't care. Said for me to take it."

"Thank you so much. Lily will enjoy riding in it, and it will help my aching back. She is growing tall and heavy."

"Well, I'd best be going. May I leave a few things here, and after I get settled I will come back for them?"

"No. Now you're not going anywhere tonight. You'll stay right here with me, and you can sleep on my lumpy couch in front of the fireplace. It's too dangerous for you to be wandering around town looking for a place. It will be hard enough in daylight."

"I didn't come here to put you out; I wanted to make sure Lily was all right." Jazz looked around the clean room. "Okay, I will stay tonight, but I will be gone tomorrow. Don't want it to get back to Mrs. Browning that you're caring for me. She'd fire you in a minute."

"I know. She claims to be a Christian woman, but she sure has the devil on her shoulder a lot of times. She can be darn-right scary."

Chapter 10

The red rooster sat on the fence next to the little shanty as Jazz, Georgia, and Lily sat at the small kitchen table eating a bowl of hot hominy that her neighbor had given her for washing and ironing a set of clothes for him. The people who lived in Georgia's shanty town didn't have money, but they shared whatever they could for receiving help. This area looked dangerous to outsiders, but to the people who lived here, it wasn't.

Jazz dressed quickly and helped Georgia dress Lily. The little girl's fever had gone, and she was chatting like her old self, which pleased both ladies. Jazz assured Georgia that she would be gone in about an hour, but she would keep in contact with her.

~

Cole woke early and rode the three miles out to his farm. He was a simple man who loved the old farm and land that his papa had willed to him. As a young boy, he enjoyed working the land and caring for the farm animals.

His mama hated farm life, and she convinced Papa to buy Grover's Merchandise in town when Mr. Grover took ill and couldn't take care of the business. Papa often bragged he got the business for a steal, so he couldn't turn it down.

After several months of driving back and forth from the store, his mother arranged for the two rooms upstairs to be made into living quarters for them. Cole continued working the farm and was happy that he had made the land profitable. He helped in the store whenever his pa received a large shipment and needed assistance in stocking the items on the high shelves or stored in the outbuilding.

Life on the farm was all Cole ever wanted. While working in the store, he hated to have to listen to the ladies spout gossip about their neighbors and have to hear about everyone's financial problems. He enjoyed the simple life of helping his animals give birth to their newborns and walking down the rows of his cornfields.

When he was twenty-two, his papa was carrying some grain to the rear of the store and had a heart attack. He died instantly. His mother blamed Cole for not being there to do all the heavy work and made him feel so guilty that he had to neglect his farm and animals to please her.

After he closed the store each night and made sure his mother was secure for the evening upstairs in her apartment, he'd ride out to his farm. In the spring and summer, he still had plenty of daylight to work some of his land and care for the animals in the corral and barn. It was more difficult during the cold, snowy winter days even to drive out to the farm, but he managed as often as he could. Many nights he stayed out there until early morning and, after caring for the animals, he would ride back to open the store. Each time he received a lecture from his mother, but he soon learned to tune her out.

In no uncertain terms, he had told his mama that he was a grown man, and he would do what he needed to do to keep his farm. He even offered to hire another man to run the store for her, but she wouldn't have any of that. She'd rather lord it over his head that he was the cause of his father's death.

Cole didn't know what happiness was until Jazz had come in the store and began taking care of his mother, then helped to make the store more inviting and friendlier. All of his men customers enjoyed having Jazz help them, and she had made it easier to leave work and go to his farm. Now that she had left, the life of the store seemed dead, and he felt even lonelier than before. Even Sam had stopped sitting on the front porch.

Cole had never seen his mama in such a rage. Even after Jazz left and he'd gone into her room to speak with her about what had taken place with the strangers from the wagon train. He told her that he was going to hire a man to come and work a few days a week so he could work his farm. As usual, his mother lit into him about how he didn't love her, then reminded him this store was their livelihood, and without it they would be in the poorhouse soon.

No amount of talking with his mother convinced her that they would be fine. As far as he could tell, she was well enough to come out of her bedroom and run the store like before, so he summoned his nerves and said, "If you don't want to help, I will hire two people." With that comment, she exploded, but he left her standing alone in her room. She wasn't going to make him feel guilty anymore.

As he walked to the post office and the bank, he saw Sam sitting on the steps of the café. "Good morning, Sam. I wondered where you got off to. Do you have a place to live now, or are you sleeping in the alleyways like before?"

"Oh, Mr. James. You know that little gal who worked for you was the only nice person to me. Everybody shoos me away with their brooms if they see me."

Cole stood over the old man and thought how much he had enjoyed him being in the store helping him with small jobs. He felt somewhat responsible for him after Jazz had taken him in and made him feel important.

"Listen, Sam. Would you like to help me out?" Before Sam could answer, Cole said, "I need help at my farm."

"Really? I saw your place when your pa was alive. Sometimes I would drive a wagon of grain out there for him."

"Well, I am trying to work the store and my farm, and I really need help caring for my animals. About run myself ragged. I have a nice house on the farm. Over the years, before I had to help Mama in the store, I had great plans to make it even nicer. I'd hope to have a wife and family one day, but you have witnessed how my mother has depended on me since Pa died. But if you come and help me out, you'll have a warm room, plenty of food, and very little work. I hate leaving my animals all alone while I am here in town. You will have the run of the place."

"Really?" Sam said but frowned. "Your mama won't let me go anyway near her house."

"Wait a minute, Sam. The farm is mine. My mother never comes out and sees me, and even if she did, it wouldn't matter. The farm is mine and I'm the boss. She has no say, believe me."

"When do you want me to walk out there?" Sam said.

"After I close the store tonight, I will pick you up right here and drive you out there. I'll show you what I want you to do and where you can sleep. How's that?"

"If you are sure about your ma. She really scares me. Will I be by myself all the time?" Sam walked over to the porch.

"No. Now that Mama is better, I will be coming out most days and stay all night."

"Sure. I'm willing to give it a try." He smiled and sat down on the stoop. "I'll be right here waiting on you this afternoon."

~

Jazz looked into the window of the dress tailor's shop. She noticed a white-haired lady sitting in a chair near the front window. Jazz needed a job, and sewing was something she enjoyed doing. She prayed this shop may need some help.

As she entered the front door, a bell jangled. Jazz stopped and looked up at it when she heard the older lady say, "Good morning, Mrs. Whitmore." The older woman spoke without lifting her face from her sewing. "What can I do for you this morning?"

"How do you know who I am? I have never seen you in the

James' Dry-Goods store before." Her eyes took in the lovely shop.

"I'm Ruby Goodman. My shop is the first place the ladies like to gather to spread all the gossip in town, true or false. If these old walls could talk, many people would be in deep trouble."

"So, I guess you believe that I'm a bad person who should be run out of town."

"I didn't say I believed everything that comes out of the women's mouths, did I?" She lifted her eyes above her wire-rimmed glasses and smiled.

"Well, I might as well spit it out—I need a job first, and then I have to find myself a place to live. I enjoy working with a needle. This garment that I am wearing is my handiwork."

"Come closer, child, and let me look at the hem and seams on your dress. I can tell a lot about your piecework that way."

Jazz stood close to the older woman as she examined the inside of her skirt. "Very nice, my dear." Lowering the hem of her dress, Jazz stood till as the older woman pondered.

"You know I can't let any of the ladies know that I have hired you. Would you mind sitting in my backroom to work? I know that is not a very pleasant workspace, but the ladies can be vicious and turn on me if they know I'm helping you. But the truth of the matter is you will be helping me. I am so far behind I'm afraid I am going to lose their business anyway."

"When do you want me to start? I need to find a place to stay before dark this evening."

"You can stay here as part of your salary. I pay by the piecework that you do for me. There's a nice bed and water closet in the back. You can enter and leave from the back door. How does that sound to you?"

"Wonderful. I can start now, if you like."

"Let's have some tea and cookies, and I will give you a dress that needs hemming and new buttons down the front."

Jazz took a deep breath for the first time since entering the shop.

While they enjoyed tea, Ruby Goodman said she was a widow and had owned the tailor shop for many years. She seemed very pleasant. Maybe life here wouldn't be so bad once the gossip died down about her.

For several hours, Jazz worked as fast as her fingers would allow, and she completed the dress in a few hours, which pleased Mrs. Goodman. She gave Jazz a blouse and asked if she could embroider some small yellow and green flowers on the collar. This was the type of needlepoint Jazz enjoyed, so it wasn't long before she completed the task.

"Mercy, child. You are like a machine. I wish I had two of you." Ruby Goodman laughed. "The day's over. Put the closed sign on the door, but leave the door unlocked if you have to go out."

"I need to go collect my carpetbags, but I won't be long—I'll return before dark." Jazz hurried out the back door and sped through the alley. She glanced both ways before she stepped out on the boardwalk.

~

Every day seemed to grow into another one, but Mrs. Goodman treated her well. Jazz always had a pastry for breakfast and small sandwiches and tea for lunch. She was on her own for the dinner hour. Jazz walked to the café, sat in the far corner of the room, and ate her dinner alone. Though she hoped to catch a glimpse of Cole, he never came into the café while she was there. Several of the regular customers even smiled at her. Life was improving, but she missed Georgia and Lily.

Today, she sat next to the small window in the back, replacing the pearl buttons down the front of a white shirtwaist. Voices came from the front. She hurried and made sure the heavy dark curtain was closed tight before she sat back down. Ladies giggled and talked about Cole's mother. Apparently, the old woman was struggling to walk around in the store. "She staggers like a drunkard," one woman said and laughed.

"She likes her wine, I was told," another lady commented.

Jazz couldn't believe those ladies were discussing Cole's mother like she was a drunkard. She jerked on the material, and several buttons went flying across the floor.

"Goodness, what was that noise? Sounded like marbles hitting the floor." One of the ladies walked toward the back and found two pearl buttons on the floor. "What do you have back here, Mrs. Goodman?" The woman jerked back the curtain while Jazz stood holding the shirtwaist close to her chest. She took two steps back hoping not to be seen.

"Look, girls, Mrs. Goodman has the slut who worked for Cole hidden behind the curtain. It looks like the shirtwaist that you brought here a few days ago, Milly. Isn't that yours that she's hugging like a lifeline?"

"What are your doing letting that girl work on my things?" Milly roared.

"Ladies, Mrs. Whitmire is a fine seamstress and can do lovely handwork. I need her help with all my business."

"Well, you're going to have less business when we tell all the ladies who you have working here. Gather my few dresses I brought in last week, and I'll take them with me. Now, you have less work already." The lady stood with a sneer at Jazz's face.

Mrs. Goodman lifted her chin, strode to a rack, and stuffed a few dresses in a large bag. Then she opened the door and waved her hand as if she was directing a flock of chickens into their pen. "Good day, ladies."

"One of the women whipped around and said, "You're going to be sorry that this happened." Mrs. Goodman slammed the door in her face.

Chapter 11

Jazz slumped down in a straight chair. "I'm so sorry, Mrs. Goodman. I couldn't believe what I was hearing about Cole's mother. Guess I released my hold on the buttons, and they went flying. Felt like crying when I heard those vicious lies about her. Please believe me. Mrs. James is not a drinking woman, and if she is stumbling across the room, it's because she is weak from being bedridden for a long time. She's not a friendly woman, but she is not a bad person. I think she is just very sad."

"Oh, Jazz, I have been in this town for years. I know Mrs. James very well and like you, I don't believe she has taken to the bottle. Her husband was a nice man who would give the shirt off his back to anyone, but not that woman. However, they have a business to operate, and sometimes it takes a strong-willed person to say no."

"Mrs. Goodman, you have been very good to me, but for your sake I must leave. I have enjoyed my time with you, and I will always remember your kindness."

"Jazz, I have to ask you, are you with child?" Mrs. Goodman spoke so softly that Jazz barely heard her.

"How did you guess?"

She gave Jazz a sweet smile. "You have a glow about you."

"My husband and I wanted a baby for several years, and now that he has passed, God has given me a small piece of his love. It won't be easy for me, but I'll manage."

"Please know that you can come and visit with me anytime. I am going to miss you." Mrs. Goodman placed her frail arms around Jazz and hugged her.

"Let me gather my things and I will go out the back way. No sense in giving those women anymore to gossip about."

~

Before night fell, Jazz had already asked all the businesses on the main street for a job. The butcher smiled broadly until his wife gave him a look to rein him back. "Sorry, Miss, don't need any help at this time," he commented.

The café owner was thrilled to know that Jazz could cook and make bread, but he already had heard the gossip. He knew how the ladies had gotten her fired at the dry-goods store and the tailor shop. So he politely told her no.

Standing on the boardwalk, there was only one place she had not asked for work. God wouldn't approve, but sometimes a person had to do the devil's work in order to survive. She would pray every night for forgiveness if the saloon hired her.

Moving slowly, Jazz walked through the batwing doors. Since coming from the sunny outside, the room appeared dark, smoky, and smelly. The piano player immediately stopped pounding on the keys, the men at the poker tables stopped betting, and the loud-talking cowboys at the bar ceased their arguments.

Dressed in her only black dress with a white collar, Jazz eased up to the bartender. "Sir, may I speak to the owner?"

"Well, young lady, this establishment belongs to me so I guess that makes me the owner." He smiled, revealing one gold tooth in the very front of his mouth. "My friends call me Big Al, but you can call me Mr. Booth."

"Mr. Booth, may we speak privately?"

"Sure, pretty thing. Come into my back office." He waggled his eyebrows as he motioned for Jazz to follow him. Several of the men laughed. Was she making a mistake?

"Now, what can I do for you, Miss?" The man turned and leaned against a messy desk piled with business papers.

"My name is Jazz Whitmore. I am a new widow and I need a job. Before you say anything, I have never been in a saloon before, but I am not naïve, so I know what goes on in this place."

Jazz looked at the room this man called his office. Papers were tossed all over the desk, and the dust was an inch thick on the furniture. It was apparent that he didn't spend a lot of time in here.

"Like I said, I need a job. I only want to serve drinks and chat with the customers. People will think because I work here, I am one of your girls that pleases your customers in all ways. I don't care what they think. I will know the truth."

"Well, young lady. You're asking a whole lot. You are the prettiest thing that has come through my doors in years, and the men are going to be fighting to take you upstairs. How are you going to handle that?"

"I can handle myself. Also, I need a place to stay. Can I rent a room upstairs while I am working here?"

"I haven't agreed on anything yet." He leered at her, his gold tooth sparkling in the light. "How much pay are you asking? Some of the girls get paid by the drinks they sell the customers. Do you want to do that?"

"No, I want three dollars a night. I won't encourage the men to drink, but I know they will anyway." Jazz remembered hearing her mama speak to men with authority in her voice. Her mother never bowed down to a man, so Jazz wasn't going to give in to any demands that she didn't want to fulfill.

"Do you have a wardrobe that you can change into at night?"

"Sorry, I don't, but don't you have special dresses for your girls to wear? Always heard that saloon owners keep things for their ladies."

He laughed and looked Jazz up and down. "Was your ma a saloon gal?"

"No, she washed and ironed for the townspeople, but I'm

sorry to say she did entertain some of her customers in the evening. She left me when I was twelve and ran off with a card dealer. I learned to take care of myself, and I survived on my own until I married."

"Come with me upstairs, and I will introduce you to Thelma. She will fix you up with some clothes to wear. Three dollars a night is all you are going to get until I think you deserve more." Mr. Booth walked out of the backroom with Jazz on his heels. He led her up the staircase to room five. After a short introduction to Thelma, he slammed the door and went back downstairs.

Thelma stood up from her dresser, snuffed out her long cigarette, and circled Jazz. "So, you gonna be the new gal?"

"It appears that way. I need a place to sleep and some money to survive. I have never worked in a place like this."

"What happened to your folks?" Thelma asked.

"My pa died when I was a baby, and Mama washed and ironed during the day. At night, well, she earned extra money."

"Did you ever watch your ma entertain her customers?"

"No, she was a good mother, but she drank too much," Jazz said.

"Hey, I didn't mean to talk ugly about your ma, but I work here, like you, because I have to. I like to eat and wear nice clothes. When I get myself a nice poke, I'll be leaving on a stage out of this town."

"Sorry, I didn't mean to speak so ugly to you. I have had a hard life, but I learned how to take care of myself."

"Now I know where I saw you. You were working in the dry-goods store for that nice-looking Cole James. Why did you leave there?"

"It's a long story, and I'll tell you later, but could you help me dress my part for downstairs? I know what I should look like, but I have never put on one of those fancy dresses before."

"Sure, honey. Let's be friends and I will teach you the ropes."

"I told the owner that I am not going to work up here. I am only going to serve drinks and talk with the men." Taking a deep breath, Jazz spoke softly to Thelma. "You see, I'm pregnant, but no one else knows, so please don't give my secret away."

Thelma walked over to Jazz, shaking her head. "Honey, your secret is safe with me, but it won't be a secret long."

"Long enough for me to earn some money to move away from here."

Thelma smiled. "Maybe we can leave together," she said as she walked to the closet and pulled down a short black dress with a large, ruffled neckline. "I believe this will be perfect for you . . . for now."

Chapter 12

Cole was thrilled that Sam was willing to stay out on his farm to care for the house and watch over the fields and animals. There'd been many nights that Cole stayed at the farm until the sun was coming up, and then he had to work at the store all day. His mother couldn't understand how much he loved his little farm that he inherited from his pa. She hated country life, but he thrived on it.

After his mother forced Jazz to leave the store, he hired a middle-aged man, named Herman Laker. He was a pleasant enough man who seemed to tune his mother out whenever she started ranting and raving about some small thing. Several times Cole witnessed his mama scowling at Herman, but the man only nodded and then went about his business minding the store.

"Cole, I want you to fire that man and hire someone with some manners. That fool Herman never does a thing I tell him to do," Mrs. James would scream at the top of her lungs, but neither man did anything in response to her demands.

Cole worked hard in the store for several hours every morning making sure that his supplies had arrived, and his inventory matched what he had on paper. He instructed Herman how to stock the shelves. Also, he told Herman if he had a better solution as to where something should go, he had permission to change it to suit him. Cole didn't have time to stand over him all day. One watchdog in the store was enough.

Right after gobbling down a lunch of ham and cheese sandwiches and a hot cup of coffee, he left the store to pick up Sam to take him out to his farm. He drove up in front of the café porch where Sam was patiently waiting. Next to him was a brown paper bag with all his earthly goods in it.

"Golly, Mr. James, am I happy to see you. There was a big ruckus at one of the saloons, and someone said a gal was hurt. I saw a bunch of men carrying something, but they disappeared before I could tell where they were going and what they were toting. Sure was a lot of angry men. The sheriff came and broke them up, then they all went their separate ways."

Cole laughed at Sam and patted the bench seat for him to climb up.

"When you get back to town, you find out all about it." Sam climbed up on the seat next to Cole and looked around. "Mr. James, how is Mrs. James taking it that you hired a fellow to work in the store while you're off at your farm?"

"To be frank, Sam, she's as mad as a hornet, but I don't care. When she fired Jazz, the best worker we have ever had, that was too much for me to bear. I told Ma that very day she could come out of her room and start working in the store, like she used to do. Of course, she screamed that she wasn't well, and she wouldn't be able to manage without me." Cole snapped the reins over the two mules' back and they trotted faster to his farm. "Today is my first day away from the store, but I am sure Herman can handle the store and my mom. If not, he will not be there when I return home in the morning."

"Is that your farm? Man, it sure looks different from the last time I was out here several years ago."

Cole pointed at the pale blue cottage with several rose bushes blooming beside the porch. "Remember I said I have been working as much as possible on the place? I want a nice home for my wife and kids one day."

"I can't imagine many more improvements," Sam said as his

eyes darted in all directions at the lay of the land.

"Well, I really want to add onto the house. Maybe build a nice closed-in room with a lot of windows and another fireplace. Also I would like two bedrooms added onto the back with a water closet in between them."

"You will have a mansion if you ever put on those additions." Sam shook his head and smiled.

"I have ordered a lot of lumber, and I am going to hire a crew of men who are experts in construction to come out. For years I've saved money, and now I am ready to build my dream house."

"Do you think your mother will come out here and live with you?"

Cole laughed. "I really hope not, but I would never refuse her a home. My mother is not really sick, and she loves her store in town."

He stopped the horse in front of the barn, jumped down, and headed over to the corral to pat several horses that had raced over to the fence to see their master. "How are you boys doing?" Cole said as he held out an apple for each of the horses.

Sam joined him at the fence. "This here's a real nice place."

"All the supplies I have in the wagon will go into the kitchen. You can take them inside while I check on my chickens and piglets," he said.

~

Sam was in shock as he looked around the front room of the house. A wall of smooth stone covered one wall from the floor to the ceiling to make a warm fireplace. In front of the fireplace, two large oak rocking chairs stood positioned on a colorful woven rag rug. A big tan leather wingback chair sat in the corner next to a walnut round table, and a two-seater blue sofa sat in the center of the room. Two tables with china lamps sat on each end of the sofa.

Sam moved slowly through the room to the back of the house into a roomy kitchen where a large table sat in the center surrounded by eight chairs. "This is already a mansion," Sam said aloud to himself.

After several trips to the wagon, Sam brought all the supplies in and began putting the items in the proper cupboards.

Cole walked in. "Thanks, Sam. I love my animals and I always take time to rub down my horses and check on my smaller critters. Now that you are here, I won't be worried about them."

He turned to face his new boss. "Would you show me around and tell me what you expect me to do each day? I will make sure I do everything just like you want."

"Let's first cook something to eat, then I'll give you a tour of my farm and introduce you to the animals. You will also have your own room inside the house. I want you to make yourself at home here."

"Golly, Mr. James. I feel like I am in heaven already."

"Please Sam, call me Cole. My pa was Mr. James, and he isn't here."

"Sure thing, if that's what you want."

Chapter 13

Jazz eased down the staircase of the saloon as every eye was on her. She smiled at the men and walked over to the bar. Three men rushed to stand next to her. Jazz couldn't move, so she softly pushed the men out of her face. Adjusting the bodice of her tight-fitting black dress, she could hardly breathe, but Thelma said it had to be tight to look good. The men's breath smelled vile, like the hard whiskey they had been drinking. It was all Jazz could do not to gag.

As the piano tunes got louder, a man jerked Jazz's arm and pulled her away from the bar. He grabbed her around the waist so tightly he lifted her feet off the floor. Around and around he danced until Jazz grew dizzy.

"Please, I can't breathe. Put me down."

"You heard the little lady. It's my time to dance with her. Put her down before I have to hurt you," a big guy butted into Jazz's partner.

Suddenly Jazz was released from the man's arms, and when she opened her eyes, the room was spinning. She took a step to the nearest table, but she fell to the floor before she could stop herself. A loud, hurtful pain exploded in her head and total darkness came next.

When she came to, a man stood over her and slapped her face hard several times. She lay flat on her back until one of the saloon girls yelled, "I think she's dead. Help her, you fools!"

"Come on, men, grab her legs and arms and carry her over to the doc's office." Big Al, the boss, shook his head and swore. "That little gal didn't last one evening."

As the men lifted Jazz over their heads and carried her down the middle of the street giggling like little boys, Jazz felt blood dripping down the back of her head, soaking her hair. That's the last thing she remembered.

~

Doctor Don Richards heard a bunch of rowdies coming toward his office, so he stood and held the door open for them. To his surprise, a lovely young woman was placed none too gently on his examination table.

"Bring her back to life, doc. She's the prettiest little thing we have seen in years," a burly man smelling of whiskey said.

"You think she's dead?" the doctor asked.

"Well, she hit the floor, and we couldn't get her awake no matter how hard Billy slapped her face."

The men filed out as quickly as they had come. The doctor waved a hand in front of this nose and glanced at the woman and child sitting in the seat.

~

Georgia ran a hand over Lily's hot forehead. The doctor had given Lily some medicine, and he wanted Georgia to stay at his office until he was sure it was doing the child some good.

"My lands, doc, this here is Jazz Whitmore, "Georgia said, as she looked over the girl in the tight-fitting dress. "She can't breathe in that laced-up garb she's got on. Turn her over and let me cut the laces loose."

The doctor and Georgia soon had the corset cut off her. "She has a bad cut on the back of her head. It looks like I will have to cut her hair and stitch up her scalp," the doctor said.

Georgia walked over to Lily and pushed two chairs together. She draped her shawl over the chairs. "Doc, I'm going to lay Lily down while I help you with Miss Jazz. She's my friend, and I hope you can take care of her."

"Good, I can use some help with her. Take that rag off her body while I go to my room and find her one of my nightshirts to wear."

An hour later, Dr. Richards had stitched Jazz's head, but she still had not awakened. The doctor didn't act surprised at all that she was still unconscious. "Her head wound is pretty bad, but she's breathing well and her heart rate is sound. I'm not sure but I think I heard another heartbeat. Do you know if she is with child?"

"No, I don't. She might not even know, but I'm sure she will be happy."

Doctor Richards walked across the room and felt Lily's forehead. "Well, Georgia, it looks like the medicine I gave Lily is working. She is not feverish. I'll carry Mrs. Whitmore into my surgery room and let her sleep on my extra bed. I would like for you to stay and watch after her until I return. She doesn't need to be alone. If you want to stay the night, I will give you some blankets to make yourself a pallet until morning."

"Thanks, Doctor Richards," Georgia said, as he walked to his door.

"I have some rounds to make and then I will be back to take care of this lovely young woman."

After the doctor left and she was sure that Miss Jazz was sound asleep, she picked up Lily and placed her in the wheelbarrow. She headed down the alleyway to the back porch of the dry-goods store. The back door was open, and she saw many boxes of supplies on the steps. She hoped it was Mr. James coming back and forth into the store. Suddenly, Mr. James appeared and stopped near the back steps.

"Georgia, what in the world are you doing out here in the alley? Why didn't you come in the front door with your list of supplies for Mrs. Browning?"

"Sir, I had to see you, and I didn't want your mama to overhear me. I come to tell you that Miss Jazz needs your help. You see, she was working at the saloon, and she got hurt by some men. They carried her to the doctor's office while I was there with my baby, Lily. That old Big Al, the owner of the saloon, sent over her carpetbag and said Miss Jazz was finished at his place." Georgia looked over Cole's shoulder to make sure his mama didn't come outside and overhear their conversation. "Miss Jazz has no place to go. I can't take her home with me, because Mrs. Browning would fire me for sure if she got wind that I was caring for her. The doctor will allow her to stay with him, but I don't like the way he looks at Miss Jazz. He gives me a creepy feeling, so I felt I needed to come to you for help."

"I appreciate you coming for me, Georgia. How is your little girl?"

"She's better, but I need to get back to the boardinghouse before I lose my job."

"Is the doctor at the office with Jazz?"

"No, sir. She hasn't woken up since the men carried her in the office. They tossed her on the table like she was a slab of meat. After the doctor sewed up her head, he left me with her while he went to see some other sick folks. Jazz is all alone now, but I hurried right over here as soon as he left."

"I will put some blankets in my wagon and take her out to my farm. Sam is living out there now, and he can help take care of her while I am in town. Now don't fret about her anymore. I will take good care of her."

~

Cole watched Georgia walk down the alley pulling her baby in the wheelbarrow. He'd wondered several times why Jazz needed a wheelbarrow, and now he knew the answer to that puzzle. Hurrying inside the store, he motioned for Herman to come onto the back porch with him. After giving him instructions what to do with all the supplies, he scooped up several new blankets and a pillow and tossed them in the back of his flatbed wagon. Cole told the man that he wouldn't be back until the next day.

As quickly as he could, he drove his wagon to the back door of the doctor's office and entered. Jazz lay on a clean cot. She looked like an angel with her body positioned on her side. A large white bandage covered most of the back of her head.

Cole could tell that she was in a deep sleep. He lifted the thin white blanket to see how she was dressed. Someone had placed the top of a man's union suit on her body. He quickly dropped the blanket. Scooping her up in his arms, blanket and all, he carried her to his wagon. He laid her on the makeshift bed, making sure she was covered completely, then he drove out of town.

~

Sam was surprised to see Cole driving the flatbed wagon to the front door of the house. He had been standing at the corral feeding the new colt an apple. Hurrying to the wagon to help Cole bring in whatever he had in the wagon, he couldn't believe his eyes when he saw the sweet lady who had worked at the dry-goods store. Sam had not seen her since the day Cole's mother had made her leave.

"Mr. Cole, what in the world are you doing with this young lady? Why is she lying in the back of your wagon?"

Cole almost laughed but restrained himself from doing so. "Remember you telling me this afternoon about a ruckus at the saloon and the men carrying something over their heads down the street?" Cole looked down at Jazz as she continued to sleep. "Well, this little gal was what the men were toting. They carried her to the doctor's office and dumped her there. Thank goodness, Georgia, Mrs. Browning's maid, was in the office and she came and got me. Jazz lost her new position at the saloon, and she has no place to stay. I brought her here hoping you wouldn't mind helping me care for her."

"Shoot fire, man. You know I'll do whatever I can for this nice girl. She took me into your store and saved my life. I was freezing and starved when she made me come inside."

Chapter 14

"Please, Mama, please turn around and come back for me. I need you, Mama. Please don't leave me in this awful place alone."

"Wake up, Jazz. Wake up. You're safe now." Cole gently shook Jazz's shoulder.

Twisting and turning, Jazz continued to beg and plead with her mother, so Cole took her into his arms and sat on the side of the bed. "Wake up, baby. You're safe, and I won't let anyone hurt you."

Jazz's eyes eased open and finally met his eyes. A weak smile appeared.

"What happened? Tell me what you were dreaming? What scared you so bad that you were screaming for your mama?" Cole rocked her slowly back and forth like a parent would do a new baby.

She placed her face upon his chest and shut her eyes again. "I forgot. . . I forgot I was a grown woman. In my dream, I was a little girl again."

"You had a bad childhood?" In all the time she had worked in his store, she'd never spoke about her past.

"Yes, but I don't want to talk about it," she whispered. "My head hurts and it's painful to keep my eyes open." Cole took the corner of the blanket and rubbed it across her cheeks to dry her face.

"Hush, sweetie," he whispered. "The pain will ease in a few minutes. The powder I gave you will help you to sleep."

She smiled again. "Your voice is gentle. Why did you rescue me? Were you at the saloon? What happened?"

Standing, he placed her back in the center of the bed, covered her with the blankets, and lay down beside her. He leaned on his elbows and kissed each of her eyes. "Go to sleep. Things will look better tomorrow."

Her eyes closed but the smile remained.

~

Later, as Doctor Richards headed back to his office, he drove past a field of yellow and black-eyed flowers. He remembered his mother calling them Black-eyed Susans. They reminded him of sunflowers with their bright yellow petals and black centers. The doctor slowed his horse to a stop and walked to the edge of the road while taking out his pocketknife. He cut more than two dozen long stems and carried them to his carriage. Opening his black bag, he took out a long piece of string and wrapped it around the flower stems to hold them together. "Nice," he said aloud to no one in particular.

After driving his horse and carriage to the livery stable, he walked to his office. He could hardly contain his excitement in knowing that a beautiful young lady was in his office waiting for his care. It had been a long time since he had taken a fancy to any woman, but he was attracted to Mrs. Whitmore almost immediately.

After entering his office, he had to light a lantern. He never dreamed that his office would be dark and empty. Where was Georgia? Hadn't she said she'd stay and take care his lovely patient?

He went into the back room where he had moved Mrs. Whitmore and stopped at the door. The lady was gone with all the bedcovers. Someone has carried her away.

As fast as he could, he grabbed his hat and coat on and rushed out the front door. He stormed over to the boardinghouse and pounded on the front door.

Mrs. Browning pulled the door open. "Good evening, Doctor Richards."

"Good evening to you, Mrs. Browning. Is your maid, Georgia, working for you now?"

"Well, yes she is. Why?"

"I need to speak with her immediately. Is she in your kitchen?"

"Follow me and I will take you to her. What's this all about?"

Georgia was washing dishes as she hummed a sweet song to her daughter, Lily, who sat in a small wheelbarrow.

"Georgia," Mrs. Browning spoke sharply. "The doctor would like to speak with you."

Georgia's eyes grew wide, and she leaned against a chair as the doctor entered the kitchen.

He demanded to know where Mrs. Whitmore was. "Why did you leave my office today and leave Mrs. Whitmore alone? I asked you to stay with her while I made my rounds. Now, she is not in my office, and I know she didn't just up and leave by herself."

"I had to come to work. You said Lily was just fine."

"I know I said she was doing well, but I requested that you stay and help me with Mrs. Whitmore. Now she's disappeared, and I know you helped her leave my office."

"No sir, I didn't do that." Her lips clamped together.

Mrs. Browning pushed forward. "Doctor Richards, I have given Georgia strict instructions about helping that woman whom everyone calls a slut and worse names. I told her if she helped that girl in any way, I would fire her." She huffed like a general in the Army.

He frowned at the general. "I know good and well that this woman helped my patient, and she knows where she is right this minute." He turned to Georgia and took a step forward. "Now tell me what you know about Mrs. Whitmore."

"The man at the store is taking care of her, ain't he, Mama?" Lily yelled and grabbed her mother around her knees. "Tell him, Mama, so he will go away."

Surprised, all three of them peered down at Lily. They had not even noticed her in the room. "Hush, child." Georgia patted her daughter on the back. "Get back in the wheelbarrow and be quiet."

"So, you went to the dry-goods store and spoke to Cole about Mrs. Whitmore." Turning to the doctor, Mrs. Browning continued, "She worked for him until those ladies returned on the wagon train and stirred up trouble for her."

"Mrs. Whitmore is staying at the dry-goods store with Cole and his mama?" The doctor quizzed Mrs. Browning.

"I doubt that," Mrs. Browning spoke. "Mrs. James fired Mrs. Whitmore, and I am sure she would never take her into their living quarters. You need to go see Mr. James."

The doctor didn't even thank Mrs. Browning or even acknowledge Georgia as he turned and flew out of the boardinghouse.

~

"Well, well, well, Georgia. When you finish with the kitchen tonight, don't return in the morning. You are fired. I don't believe we have anything more to discuss. I will keep your pay this week for the inconvenience you have caused me." She turned on her heel and stormed out.

Georgia laid the plate down on the table that she had been holding during the altercation between herself, the doctor, and Mrs. Browning. She lumbered over to the small closet and retrieved her bag and placed it in Lily's lap. "Come on, honey, we are leaving this place for good." Georgia surveyed the messy kitchen and smiled. "The old bat thinks I'm going to finish cleaning this room when she is going to keep my wages? Well, she can think again when she comes in the morning to cook for her boarders." Georgia gave a small laugh and pushed Lily out the back door for the last time.

Chapter 15

The next morning, the old rooster crowed and announced the beginning of a new day. Sam was outside checking on the animals inside the barn, while Cole stood over Jazz's bed. He gazed down at the lovely woman, her hair spread out on her pillow. Her breathing was normal. Cole's heart was filled with emotion. He wasn't sure if it was love, but he knew he cared deeply for this girl.

Cole had to keep her presence in his home a secret for a while. He had told Sam not to mention to anyone that she was staying at his farm; he would choose whom he would tell when he was ready.

For now, though, he might have to stop by the doctor to ask him to come and check on Jazz, but he would certainly be present when he checked on her. Cole said a silent prayer that she would awake soon, and her headache would be gone. Hopefully, the sleeping powder he'd given her had done its job.

After adjusting her covers, he walked into the kitchen to warm his cup of coffee. He looked out the kitchen window and watched Sam walk over to the corral and toss hay for his four horses. The old man rubbed his new colt's nose and gave him a carrot. Hearing a noise coming from the bedroom, Cole placed his cup on the table and rushed to the door of the room where Jazz slept.

Jazz was attempting to sit up on the side of the bed. Her long blond hair was hanging half over her face. She had one hand on her hair and the other on her bandage.

"Good morning," Cole called to her.

Jazz immediately reached for the covers and pulled the blanket up to cover her chest. "Good morning," she replied softly.

"How do you feel this morning? Does your head still hurt as bad as it did last night?"

"I need to have a few minutes of privacy. Where is the water closet?" Jazz didn't look into Cole's face. She pulled the blanket tight around her.

Walking over to the bed, he reached for her right arm. "Here, let me guide you to the closet. Do you think you can stand alone, or should I be your lady's maid and assist you?"

Barely above a whisper, Jazz said, "I'm sure I can manage if you assist me to the door. But look the other way. What am I wearing?"

"The top of a union suit. Do you feel dizzy?" Cole asked as he led Jazz across the room. He tried to appear as if he didn't notice her barely covered chest and her slim white legs.

"Please, I'll be fine," she mumbled as she closed the door in his face.

~

The smell of bacon made Jazz's stomach growl. She couldn't remember the last time she had eaten. Jazz had left Georgia's shortly after breakfast and went in search of a job. After Big Al took her upstairs, she spent hours with Thelma dressing for her debut as a saloon gal. Once downstairs, she tried to sip a glass of whiskey at the request of one of the customers, but her throat was on fire and she nearly choked to death before swallowing the awful liquid.

A knock at the door and Cole's voice pulled her back to the present. "Sam and I have breakfast cooked. Would you like a tray in your room, or can you come to the table?"

Jazz opened the door and gave him a weak smile. "I would like to sit up for a while, so I will join you both at the table." Jazz had discovered her carpetbag and was wearing a cotton, calico dress over the white underwear she had on earlier.

Cole gently took her arm and escorted her to the kitchen table where Sam stood waiting.

"Oh, Miss, it's so good to see you again. I'm sorry to hear that you are hurt, but with Cole's good food and all this wonderful fresh air, you'll be just like new in a few days."

"Thank you, Sam. I wondered what happen to you after you left the store. I'm pleased that you are here with Cole."

Cole placed a plate of bacon and scrambled eggs with dark toast in front of her. "Sorry, I don't have any jam, but I'll bring some from the store this afternoon. I want to check your bandage before I leave this morning. I'm afraid I will have to leave you two alone today while I work in the store, but I'll return as soon as I lock up."

"Now don't you fret about Miss Jazz. I'll take good care of her. Do you think the doctor needs to check her head again?"

Cole frowned and didn't answer right away. "After I check her stitches, I will decide whether he should come out here."

~

Cole stood in the alleyway in the back of his store. He was rolling a barrel out of the way of the steps when he looked toward the street and saw Georgia with her daughter watching him.

"Good morning, Georgia. How are you doing?"

"To be honest with you, Mr. Cole, I ain't doing so well. Mrs. Browning fired me last night, and I have been looking for work."

"How in the world is she going to get along without you? I understand you practically run that boardinghouse."

"Doctor Richards came storming in the boardinghouse last night demanding to know where Miss Jazz was. When he arrived back at his office, I wasn't there, and Miss Jazz was gone. He went into a rage. When he told Mrs. Browning that he had expected me to stay with her and I didn't, she fired me for helping Miss Jazz because she had instructed me not to help her."

"I am so sorry, Georgia." Cole peered over his shoulder to make sure no one was listening to their conversation. "How would you like to stay at my farm for a while? Jazz could use a lady to help her with her personal needs while she is recovering. Sam can only do so much, and she's embarrassed when I help her."

"How long?" She asked. "If I leave my house very long, the landlord will rent it to someone else. I'm going to be behind on my rent since Mrs. Browning kept my last week's wages."

"I could use a housekeeper and someone to wash my clothes. You and Lily can live on my farm as long as you want. Never thought I needed help until Sam moved in with me. And you and Lily will have your own bedroom in my house."

"Oh, Mr. Cole," Georgia couldn't hold in her tears any longer. They flowed down her cheeks. "You sure are an answer to my prayers. How soon do you want me to come to your farm? It will take me awhile to walk, but I will be there as quick as lightning."

"You go and pack up your belongings. I have a delivery out past my farm, so I will take the load instead of hiring Herman to do it. Then, I will drop you and Lily off at my house. Sam is there and he will help you settle in."

A few hours later, Cole had the wagon loaded and ready to leave the store. His mother appeared, hands posted on her waist. "Why do you have to make this delivery? Why did you hire that lazy, no-good Herman? Let him take it. You have all these boxes to go through." His mother waved her hand at the boxes sitting everywhere on the back porch and steps.

"I need to go to Mr. Cotton's farm and talk with him about another large order he is going to need. Herman can't do that. Go back inside and take care of the customers. Don't fret over what I do or don't do." Cole jumped on the wagon and slapped the mules' reins, but he needed to get away before he said something he'd regret.

Cole drove his loaded wagon slowly, looking for Georgia's small house. As his mules clomped down the dusty road toward the area where he was sure Georgia lived, he saw her and Lily standing on the leaning porch. A giant of a man peeked out from the backside of the house, then jumped back so Cole couldn't see him. Mother and daughter rushed down the two steps and waited for Cole to stop and pick them up.

Lily stood up in the back of Cole's wagon. She was smiling and pointing at all the flowers beside the road. It was obvious she was over her illness, and the fresh air was good for her breathing.

Cole drove into his yard and helped the small child to the ground. "Where's Miss Jazz?" she yelled, then raced into the house. Georgia rolled her eyes and waved for him to follow her. Cole entered the house and headed to Jazz's bedroom and knocked.

"Come in," she said. "How in the world did you get out here?" Jazz said to the little girl who'd thrown herself across Jazz's chest. She smiled at Cole in the doorway.

"Mr. Cole brung us! Mama is here, too."

She sat up on her elbows. "Oh my, where is she?"

"She coming in with that old man."

~

"Lily," Georgia called out as she glanced around the nice farmhouse. She was in awe of the lovely room with a stone fireplace.

"Here I am, Mama." Lily hurried to the opened doorway of Jazz's room. "Miss Jazz is in here."

Jazz shuffled into the living room. "Oh, Georgia, it is so good to see you. I can't believe you and Lily came way out here in the middle of the day. Whatever will Mrs. Browning think?"

Georgia hugged Jazz real tight and smiled. "Mrs. Browning

fired me, but Mr. Cole asked me to come here and take care of you. That old bat did me a favor." She took her hankie out of her apron and wiped her mouth. "Mr. Cole said I could be his housekeeper and take care of you." Georgia looked around and whispered to Jazz, "Mr. Cole sure has a nice place here."

"Yes, he does. So far, I haven't had a chance to look around since he brought me out here yesterday, but I sure am glad you are here with me. I worried about you and Lily while I was working at Mrs. Goodman's shop and wanted to come see you, but I was afraid of Mrs. Browning finding out so I stayed away."

~

Cole came into the house carrying several large bags of supplies. "Well, you two ladies will have plenty of time to visit," he said smiling. "Georgia, you want to put some of these food items away and see what you can whip up for us to eat? I'm starving."

"Yes, sir, Mr. Cole. How about a few sandwiches now, and I will cook a proper dinner this evening?"

"Sounds wonderful. There's plenty of ham and tomatoes you can slice. Sam and I are big eaters, so make a lot."

Cole hurried over to Jazz. "How are you feeling this morning?"

"I'm still a little dizzy, but all in all, I am feeling better."

"Why don't you sit in one of the rockers, and that way you can watch Georgia cook." He took her arm and led her toward the rocking chairs. Then he joined Georgia. "You and Lily can have the back bedroom. It has two small beds and a dresser. Sam will get you settled, and I'll be out taking care of the animals."

Chapter 16

Cole was knee-deep in inventory as he and Herman carried boxes to be placed on the shelves in the store. With the holidays not too far away, he had ordered many extra items to sell.

The bell jangled and Dr. Richards entered. He stood a head taller than Cole's mother who sat by the window. "Where's your son?" he practically growled at Mrs. James.

"Here I am, Doc. What can I do for you?" Cole joined him near the door.

"You know good and well why I'm here. Don't play silly questions and answers with me."

"Will you please keep your voice down," Mrs. James whispered loudly. "We have customers in here."

"Step out on the back porch with me, and we can talk privately." Cole turned and walked outside. He held the back porch door open and motioned for Herman to go back inside. "Help Mama with the customers, please. I won't be long, and we can go back to stocking the shelves."

The doctor's eyes glowered at Cole. "Where in the blazes have you taken the young lady? I've looked everywhere and asked everyone. No one has seen her since she was carried to my office yesterday afternoon."

"Why did you leave her alone in your office?"

His eyes narrowed. "So, you do know where she is."

"I asked you a simple question," Cole replied, trying to hold back his anger.

"I had patients to see, and I had to do surgery on Mr. Tanker's leg while I was at his home. It took several hours. And I didn't leave her alone. I instructed Georgia to stay with Mrs. Whitmore until I returned, but she didn't obey my orders."

"Now, you listen to me, Doctor Richards. Jazz is staying at my farm until she recovers from her head wound. Georgia is Mrs. Whitmore's friend, and I have hired her to be my housekeeper and take care of your patient. Thanks to you, Mrs. Browning fired Georgia and kept her hard-earned wages."

The doctor whirled around and pointed his long, narrow finger at Cole. "You can't keep that young woman at your place. It isn't decent."

"So, she can stay in your office alone with you until she recovers? I don't think so. At least at my place, she has a nursemaid to care for her. Besides, I also have a hired hand working at my place, so neither of the ladies are left unattended."

"Georgia is not a proper chaperone. The townspeople won't stand for her living with you. I will be coming to your place and rescue Mrs. Whitmore. We will be married as soon as I can make proper arrangements with the minister."

Cole folded his arms across his chest. "Over my dead body. Jazz is still in mourning for her husband, and she'll never agree to marry an old coot like you."

"She won't have much choice in a few weeks' times. For your information when I examined her, I heard two heart beats. She is with child, and the people of this town will never believe the child is her dead husband's."

Attempting to keep a solemn look on his face, Cole remembered Jazz being sick several times early in the morning after she began working for him. He quickly calculated how far he thought she might be, and if he was correct, she would have a child in the early spring.

Snapping back to what the doctor was saying, he couldn't

contain his tongue any longer. "Yes, the same women who caused my mother to fire her with their nasty rumors. The same women who caused her to be dismissed at Ruby Goodman's shop. Which left her with no job, then Big Al tossed her out of his saloon after one of his drunken customers harmed her. Those so-called women lied about her, and when Mrs. Browning heard the lies, she made her leave her boardinghouse in the middle of the night, knowing full-well she had no place to go. These so called God-fearing women make me sick. There's not a kinder woman in this town than Jazz. The women on that wagon train came into this town spewing lies about her because of what her husband had done. They should be ashamed of themselves. And that includes my own mother."

The doctor paused while he lit up a pipe. "What you say may be true, but nothing has changed. I am going to marry Mrs. Whitmore, and you will not stand in my way. Your mother will never allow you to marry her yourself."

"Who's getting married?" Mrs. James stepped out onto the porch and stood studying both men. Almost immediately, both men spoke at the same time. "I am."

"Cole, what do you mean? Who are you marrying?"

"Mrs. Whitmore, if she will have me."

"She won't have him, Mrs. James, because she will be marrying me. Good day." Doctor Richards leaped off the porch and strode down the alley until he was out of sight.

"What in the world just happened here? Cole, you can't marry that little hussy. I heard that she is working for Big Al as a dance-hall gal in his saloon."

"No, Mama, Jazz is living at my farm. She got hurt by one of Big Al's customers, and the doctor stitched her head up. Now he thinks he's going to be her knight in shining armor and marry her because of all the bad rumors going around."

"How can he marry her if you are?" her face reflected contempt.

"I said, he thinks he's going to marry her. I don't want to hear a word from you about it. I'm a grown man, and I am going to marry her as soon as she recovers. She took a blow to the head, and she is having a bad time of it." Cole rolled his sleeves down and went inside to retrieve his coat and hat. "Herman can finish putting these boxes away. I am leaving and I will be back in the morning. Go take a pill and lie down. You being ill today is not going to stop me from doing what I want to do." He strode away in a huff.

Chapter 17

Jazz sat in front of the fireplace while Georgia sat across from her. Lily was lying on the floor flipping pages of a book that she had looked at so many times tape held the pages together. "Georgia, I'm so pleased that you are here with me. I can't believe that I actually had the nerve to work in that saloon. A lady named Thelma dressed me in that short dress that you removed from me. She pulled the corset so tight I could hardly breathe, and once that man was trying to make me drink and dance with him, I stumbled backward and fell to the floor hitting my head on a table leg or something. When I woke up, I was dressed in, well, you know, how I looked. As I lay there, I was already planning on taking the last of my savings and catching the stagecoach out of town as far as my money would take me. I needed to make a new start somewhere where no one knows me."

Georgia grinned at her as she folded some clothes. "I am so pleased that Lily and I were in the doctor's office. She had a high fever, but he gave her something and said for me to stay there and let her sleep. Before you were carried into his office, he had just told me that Lily was fine, and her fever was so much lower."

Her eyes widened. "You were there when the men carried me into the doctor's office?"

"Yes. They carried you over their heads and tossed you on his stretcher like you were a slab of meat. One of the men yelled to the doctor not to let you die because they wanted you back at the saloon."

"Maybe that is why my sides and back hurt so bad."

"I wouldn't doubt it," Georgia said laughing. "After your head was stitched up, the doctor examined you from one end to the other. I sure didn't like the time he took, and he kinda gave me the creeps the way he ran his hands all over you." The very thought made her shiver.

"Thanks goodness, I was asleep."

"Later he had to leave and go see some other patients, but he told me to stay with you until he returned. He said he wouldn't be long, but I had to get back to Mrs. Browning's and help with the rooms and cooking dinner."

"You said that Mrs. Browning fired you? What happened to cause her to let you go?" She couldn't believe the wickedness of some people.

"That crazy doctor. He came home and found you and me gone from his office, so he stormed over to the boardinghouse demanding to know where you were. I told him that I didn't know, and after he left, Mrs. Browning fired me for helping you at the doctor's office. I should be glad that he did that because I would still be working for her."

Jazz smiled. "I am sure you will be happy living here. I haven't seen too much of the place, but the house is nice. While I worked for Cole at his store, he was kind, but his mama was a tyrant. She's a sad person."

Georgia felt her forehead. "How are you feeling now? Are you still dizzy when you stand? Would you like to sit at the kitchen table while I make dumplings to go in a pot of chicken and broth?"

"Oh yes, I would like to watch you make them. I enjoyed cooking, but there was very little I could cook over an open fire. Joe never complained about what I prepared. There's only so many ways you can cook soup or stews."

~

Lily ran to the front window and screamed, "Mr. James is home. Now we can eat."

"Child, you come and wash up and take your seat at the table. I'm sure Sam and Mr. James will be coming in ready to eat."

Jazz heard the commotion in the kitchen, so she ran her fingers through her blond curls and plaited them to one side. She smoothed the covers over her lap and pinched her cheeks to put more color in her face. Trying to look relaxed, she waited for Cole to come and see her.

~

Cole entered the house and declared, "Gosh, something sure smells good. Lily, have you been cooking?"

Lily giggled and said, "No, sir, Mama did it, and I'm starved."

"Me too," he replied as he removed his boots, coat, and hat. Sam followed and did the same as he entered the room.

"Go ahead and dip me a big plate of whatever smells so good while I check on Jazz. I won't be but a minute," Cole said as he walked toward Jazz's bedroom. He stopped and knocked on her door.

"Come in," he heard her call. Entering the room, Cole walked slowly across the room and stopped at the edge of her bed. "You're looking chipper. How do you feel today?"

"Better, thank you. Do you think that I could sit at the supper table tonight?"

"Yes, that would be wonderful. Let me get your robe."

Jazz sat up on the bed, then stood while Cole helped her. He noticed it was almost a rag, but he would replace it soon.

The men ate heartily, then requested seconds. The dumplings were a hit, so much that both men refused a piece of apple pie. "I will have my pie later," Sam said, rubbing his belly.

Cole was tossing hay to the cow and his two mules when he stopped, leaning upon the pitchfork and staring into space.

Sam must have noticed. "You have something on your mind, boss? I don't know if I can help, but I will listen."

Cole grinned at Sam. "I do have something that I need to talk to Jazz about. Doctor Richards said that he is coming out here to get her and claimed that she will marry him."

"Ha. That ain't never going to happen. Mrs. Whitmore is still mourning her lost husband. Besides, no young woman wants to saddle herself with an old goat."

"Hope you're right. I'm going to talk with her tonight. Maybe even convince her to marry me." He stood the pitchfork up against the wall and strode toward the house.

"Now that's what I call a love match," Sam said loud enough for him hear.

~

Tapping on Jazz's bedroom door, he walked slowly over to her bed and asked if he could pull up a chair. He needed to talk with her.

"Please, Cole, sit with me. How is your mama doing? Is she working in the store? And how is she getting along with the new man?"

Cole smiled. "You are something else. Always thinking about other people instead of yourself. But to answer your questions, she is working a little, and she would like for Herman to drop dead. I left her this afternoon madder than a hornet, but I couldn't care less."

"Why was she so mad? Because you came to the farm?"

"Well, she overheard Doctor Richards and myself having a heated conversation on the back porch." He sat silent for a minute.

"Go on, tell me what your conversation was about."

"It was about you. The doctor has been looking for you all over town, and finally he came to question me. When I told him you were here at my farm, he went a little crazy. He claimed that you couldn't live out here with me and Sam. He said that Georgia wasn't a proper chaperone for you, and he is going to come and get you and . . . "

"And what?" Her eyebrows raised.

"And marry you. He intends to take you straight to the minister and wed you so he can save your reputation."

"Marry me?" Jazz screamed loud enough for Georgia, Sam, and Lily to hear.

"I told him that you weren't marrying anyone because you are still in mourning for your husband, but he went on to say that the women in town wouldn't allow you to live here on my farm."

"What can the 'ladies' do to keep me from staying here?"

"They will shun you if you go to town, not sell you anything or allow you sit in church with them. Those old bats can make your life miserable."

"I told Georgia that as soon as I get well, I am going to take my savings and travel to another town as far as my money will take me."

"Jazz, I don't want you to leave. This is a nice town, and my farm is going to be one of the nicest in the state of Texas. I know I have a lot more work to do, but I am working every day to make it better. I want to share my home with you."

Jazz held her face in her hands and cried softly.

Cole slid off the chair and kneeled beside the bed. He took her hands away from her face and gently wiped away a tear. "Marry me, Jazz. Let me protect you."

~

Oh, my goodness. How could she marry this wonderful man while mourning for Joe? Marriage was complicated, not something two strangers decided to do without a good reason. Being jobless, homeless, and destitute were certainly good reasons, but what about her love for Joe? Cole really didn't need a wife. A housekeeper could do everything for him until he found the woman of his dreams.

Yes, Cole would be good to her; she knew that by the way he treated her while she worked in his store. Maybe in time, her broken heart would mend, and she could fall in love with this wonderful man who wanted to take her into his home and give her protection.

Thinking about the doctor wanting her to marry him almost made her ill. He was old enough to be her father, and the thought of him examining her body while she slept nearly made her sick. Yes, she would leave the country before she submitted to the doctor's demand to marry her.

She looked into Cole's sweet face. If she had to marry, God had chosen a wonderful man, but she couldn't deceive him. She had to tell him the truth that might keep him from making this rash decision. "There's something you don't know about me."

"I know everything I need to know." He covered her mouth with a deep kiss that would have made her knees buckle if she was standing. The kiss was long and passionate, and when he pulled back, she could barely remember what she had to tell him.

After catching her breath, she had to tell him, and find out what kind of man Cole was. Jazz swung her legs from under the covers and sat up on the side of the bed. She clenched her fists and braced her bare feet on the floor, mentally preparing herself for his objection of her.

"No, Cole. This doesn't just involve you and me. You must know—" she hesitated and took a deep breath. "I'm with child." Now that it was out, she rushed to explain. "Joe and I always wanted children, and for some reason God never granted us one. Until now. I didn't know for sure until recently."

Reaching for her hands, Cole had a hard time responding, due to emotion clogging his throat. He swallowed hard, taking a second to control the shaking of his hands. Cole recalled the doctor saying he had heard two heartbeats while examining her.

"Jazz, your child will be my child. I will love it with all my heart and all the children that will follow. I have always wanted a big family."

Large tears spilled down Jazz's cheeks. "Oh, Cole, I loved Joe with all my heart. I don't know if I will ever forget him." She rubbed her stomach. "I don't want to disappoint you in any way, but I'm afraid my reputation may hurt your business after the townspeople find out that you have married me. I wish I could make the ladies know that I am not after their husbands, and I've always tried to be nice to everyone."

"Time will take care of all your worries. My mother will accept you, or she'll be sorry. I will threaten to sell my part of the store, and she wouldn't want that to happen." Cole slipped back into the chair and hung his head. Jazz had been haunting his thoughts ever since he carried her to his farm. He waited for her to speak, still starstruck from the kiss they had just shared.

"How long do I have to consider your proposal?" Jazz asked, as she noticed that Cole's hair was thick, dark brown, and fell across his collar. His shoulders were broad and his arms were muscular. He looked more like a cowboy than a store clerk.

"You can take a day or two, but I want you to know I respect that you're still mourning your husband. I will wait to claim my husband's rights until you tell me that you're ready to be my wife. Still, I expect to share your bed. There's no reason why everyone should know that this isn't a real marriage, even Georgia." He waited for her to object but was surprised when she didn't.

She patted the mattress and peered at Cole with a shy smile. "You know this bed might be crowded when I start gaining weight."

Chapter 18

Before returning to the farm the next afternoon, Cole stopped in Ruby Goodman's dress shop and requested she make Jazz three day dresses with an empire waist. He didn't tell her Jazz was expecting, but that she needed dresses that would flow over her waist. He requested shifts that were made the same way and pantaloons with drawstrings at the waist.

"I'd appreciate it, Ruby, if you come in the store tomorrow and pick out materials, notions, and anything else you need to make these items. The dresses are needed as soon as you can make them. Later, I may ask you to come out to the farm and take her measurements for future outfits. I know Jazz can sew, but she's in real need of clothes. I will pay you extra for a rush job."

She waved him off. "I will gladly start on the dresses as soon as I choose the material. This will be our secret. I enjoyed Jazz working for me. She does lovely handwork, and she was a pleasant young lady to have in my shop."

"Thank you so much. I am sure this is just the start of your services."

After arriving home, Cole had a surprise for the girls. He had waited for his mom to retire upstairs before he cut yards of white muslin and brought home five different bolts of cloth for Jazz and Georgia to choose from. He knew the ladies needed new dresses, so he chose thread, needles, boning, and anything he thought they might need.

Jazz was thrilled to see all the items. She quickly told Georgia to choose several prints for new dresses and some that Lily would like. With the white muslin, she would make pinafores, gowns, and pantaloons for Lily. Cole had cut yards enough to make shifts and pantaloons for all three of them.

"I want you to take your time and continue to get plenty of rest," Cole said as he poured himself a cup of coffee. A loud voice bellowed from outside.

Cole walked to the front door to see Doctor Richard's carriage parked in front of the barn. "Mr. James is in the house," Sam said as he dusted off his hands. Then he spotted his boss standing on the front porch.

"There you are, Cole. I told you I was coming after Mrs. Whitmore yesterday, but I had to take a bullet out of a stranger. So, I'm here now and ready to take her away from this godforsaken place. No city gal wants to live this far from town."

Cole stood on the edge of his front porch and looked down on his roses that were in bloom. How sad they would look in a few weeks, especially if the doctor had his way. He swallowed hard, gritted his teeth, and motioned for the doctor to come forward. "You may come inside to speak with Jazz, but wait here until she is made presentable for company," Cole said, then went back inside the house.

Jazz and Georgia stood at the kitchen table looking over all the materials and goods when Cole came in the room. "Jazz, Doctor Richards has come to see you and take you back to town with him."

~

"I'm not going anywhere with that man," she said firmly. Jazz rushed to the window and pulled back the curtain to peek at the man who thought she was going to leave with him. The doctor was pacing back and forth. He kicked at the baby goat who had wandered over to him and attempted to sniff his pant leg.

"Jazz, you will have to tell him, but I will be here with you. Georgia, please take Lily and go into your room, and let us handle this in private."

"Yes, sir, I don't want to see him anyways." She reached for Lily, and they disappeared down the hallway to their bedroom.

"Are you ready to see him?" Cole asked Jazz.

"Let him in so I can send him on his way. Georgia and I have dresses to make." She smiled at Cole as she touched a piece of the lovely material.

Cole opened the door and told Doctor Richards to come in. He stepped inside the main room and removed his hat. "Good day to you, Mrs. Whitmore. I'm pleased to see you looking well." He walked within two feet of Jazz and attempted to take her hand. She quickly slid her hand behind her back and gave him a sweet smile.

"Thank you, Doctor Richards. Yes, I am almost my old self, thanks to the good care that I have received."

"May I speak with you privately, my dear?" The doctor glanced at Cole and frowned.

"That's not necessary. What you have to talk about can be said in front of Cole."

The doctor's face turned red, and he pulled on his collar. "Well, I wanted to speak with you about your future. I am here to offer marriage and take you home with me. As you know I have a fine practice, and I can give you everything your heart may desire."

"Why would you want to marry me? I only met you three days ago, and as you know my reputation is in shreds. No one in town will have anything to do with me."

"After you marry me, people will forget about your reputation with other men while on the wagon train and you being married to a bank robber and murderer. They won't even remember that you worked as a dance-hall gal. You will be renewed after you become Mrs. Richards."

"Will you, Doctor Richards, forget all those things about me?

Are you willing to take on a young woman who is called a slut and a whore?"

"No one will dare call you those awful names after you become my wife."

"Doctor Richards, you must know that I am still in mourning for my bank-robber husband. A man I lived with for four years and I loved with all my heart. Don't you understand I can't marry and just forget about him because I stood in front of a stranger, and he read some words for me to repeat?"

"I will make you forget all about him as soon as we are wed."

"So, I just learned that you aren't just a healer of people, but you're a miracle worker, too."

Doctor Richards looked stunned and was at a loss for words.

Jazz continued. "Thank you so much for your offer of marriage and to be my savior, but I'm afraid that I have already accepted an offer—something similar, maybe not as grand, but an offer nevertheless."

"What are you talking about? Another offer of marriage?"

Cole stepped in front of Jazz and crossed his arms. He looked as large as a lumberjack. "Yes, Jazz has accepted my offer of marriage. We will be married tomorrow by the parson. Now if that is all you have come out to ask Jazz, I believe you've said your piece."

Stepping close enough to Jazz, he glared at her. "You can't marry this man. His mother won't allow it," Doctor Richards raised his voice loud enough for Sam to hear him in the barn.

"My mama has no say over what I do or don't do. I am my own man, and she knows it. Now, I am not asking you to leave; I am telling you to." Cole reached out and grabbed the doctor's arm and led him to the door. He snatched up the doctor's hat and rammed it into his stomach. "Have a good ride back to town." Cole pushed him out onto the porch and slammed the front door. He leaned against the door and stared at Jazz. "So, you have agreed to be my wife?"

Nodding, she gave him a grin. "I need to get busy. It looks like I have to prepare something nice to wear," she said.

Chapter 19

Standing in the vestibule of the little white church in Yellowstone, Jazz felt the last moments of her freedom slipping away. For once in her life, she prayed, *please . . . let me be brave.*

With her first marriage, she could hardly contain herself before she was able to say *I do* and be tied to Joe for the rest of her life. She loved her young man with all her heart. But, that marriage was different.

An hour later, she headed to Cole's carriage with well wishes from the parson and his lovely wife. She closed her eyes and relived Cole standing at the altar waiting for his pregnant bride. She could still feel the pounding in her heart and the weight of the Bible as she laid her hand upon it. Cole stood tall, handsome, and gracious as he repeated the words, "I, Cole Patrick James, take thee, Jazmyne Morris Whitmore, to be my lawful wedded wife." He slid a gold band onto her finger.

Thankfully appearing calm, she was able to pledge the same to this man in a soft voice. She blushed bright red, not able to look into Cole's eyes because she didn't have a ring to offer her groom.

After the parson blessed the wedded couple, he said, "I believe it's customary for the groom to kiss his bride."

"Yes," Cole said, as his fingers moved around the tight bones of her jaw and lifted her face to his. His kiss met her lips in a soft, delicate kiss as she looked into his eyes. He smiled and gave her another sweet kiss. "You are so beautiful, and I am thankful that you have agreed to marry me. I will always remember this day," Cole said.

"I promise to be a wife that you will always be proud of."

"Come, Mrs. James, let's go home." Cole slapped the reins over the mules' backs and, in less than an hour, they arrived back to the farm for a celebration dinner with Sam, Georgia, and Lily.

~

After the dinner and a large slice of the wedding cake, Cole and Sam left the girls to clean the kitchen while they did the late evening chores. Sam took down a jug of rye and held it toward Cole to share a drink with him.

"When I took this job, I never dreamed I would be working for a fine married man. Shoot, I never thought I would ever see that young lady again. You know, Cole, that sweet gal was the only person who ever noticed me or dared to speak to me. She immediately took me under her angel wings and carried me into your store. I figured your mama would toss me out on my butt, but that little gal gave me my health back."

"She is an angel for sure," Cole said. He took a big drink from the jug and shook his head. "Man, that stuff is powerful."

"I'm so happy for you, Mr. Cole. I know she will make you a good wife once she gets over her dead husband. You know it was hard on her to learn that the man she loved was a bad person. She told me how much she loved him."

Cole turned up the jug again and took a longer drink. His head was feeling light, and things were turning a little fuzzy, but he was beginning to relax. "I'm a lucky man, Sam, but you know I have a bride inside my house, probably getting ready for bed right now. You know I promised her that I wouldn't make any demands on her until she told me that she wants me. Unfortunately, we have a ghost in our bed."

"A ghost," Sam slurred his words. "Is your house haunted?"

"The ghost of my new bride's late husband named Joe." The

jug was nearly empty, but Cole drained it and tossed it over on a pile of trash.

Sam quickly pulled the cork out of another jug and passed it to Cole. He burped and grinned at Sam. The warmth of corn liquor was sizzling through his body. As the evening wore on, the liquor flowed more generously between himself and Sam.

"Well, I'd better go inside to my new bride."

"You bet. Make that young ghost move over," Sam said as he leaned back against the stall post and saluted his boss as he staggered out of the barn.

Cole nearly stumbled as he made his way to the porch and grabbed a post to steady himself. He must have had more of the rotgut than he thought.

~

Jazz was aroused from sleep by someone careening around in the room. She wondered where Cole had gone after dinner. He'd said he had chores to take care of in the barn. "Cole," she called softly, "is that you? Are you all right?"

With the starlight shining in from the window, she was surprised to see her new husband swaying from side to side as he walked toward the bed. This was a side of him she never thought to consider. In all the time she'd worked with him, she never knew him to take a drink. Now he stood at the foot of their bed inebriated.

He lurched toward her, reeking of whiskey. She recoiled from him and huddled under the covers, never taking her eyes from him.

"My new bride, with your full breasts and round butt, you tempt a man even in your sleep." His arm swept across the night table and broke the new glass lamp that he had just placed there. The sound of shattered glass suddenly made Jazz afraid.

He leaned toward her and looked at her face, his head moving from side to side. "You may be my widow bride, but I'll take you when and where my heart desires. And I'll toss your young ghost out of my bed." He placed both hands over his face and rubbed his forehead and chin as to rub away some of his sleepiness. Then staggering to one side of the bed, he fell onto it in an alcoholic stupor.

Jazz watched him for a minute, expecting him to rise again and continue with his crazy threats. "Cole?" she whispered.

He did not move. His eyes remained shut, and she noticed he had a silly grin on his face. She picked up one of his hands, and it fell back onto the bed limp. He was out cold.

Slipping out of bed, she removed Cole's boots. This was one long-legged man and she needed help getting him in bed. She eased over to the bedroom door and called to Sam. He didn't come so she walked to the kitchen. Georgia was standing at the dry sink.

"Do you need help with your new bridegroom?" she said.

"Afraid so. I never dreamed Cole drank hard liquor, much less that he would pass out on our wedding night." She smiled at Georgia and sighed. "Let's roll him into the middle of the bed, and if you don't mind, I will sleep with you." After covering him with a blanket, she placed his hat on the wall peg while Georgia swept the remains of the glass lamp off the floor.

~

Early in the morning, the oil lantern flickering in the gentle breeze woke him up. Cole stumbled to the water closet and relieved himself. He dunked his face in some cold water, then shuffled back to the bed. For the first time, he noticed it was empty. Where was Jazz?

Sitting on the side of the bed, he remembered drinking from a jug that he had brought from the store to use for something on the farm. He nearly gagged from the smell of his own breath, and his head felt like he had been hit by a train. Cole rolled back in the bed and went back to sleep.

Chapter 20

As the rooster crowed, Jazz awakened abruptly. The bed sagged down on one side. Drugged from sleep, she opened her eyes and saw Cole sitting on the bed, shirtless, holding his head in his hands. She sat up and stared at Cole's back. She wanted to touch him, but she was afraid what he might think. How did she end up back in this room? He must have come and carried her.

Cole spoke to her without looking over his shoulder. "Jazz, all I can say is I'm sorry for acting like a big jerk last night. Please tell me that I didn't harm you in any way."

A chilling breeze blew through the open window over the bed. She pulled the cover up over her shoulders. "No, Cole, you didn't harm me. You did break the pretty lamp that you just brought from the store."

"Don't know what got into me. I never drink, and I can assure you it will be a long time before I do it again."

Watching Cole sitting on the side of the bed, a strange stirring came over her. She rolled off the other side of the bed, trying to keep her eyes off his near-naked body. Cole eased off the bed and left the room.

She watched Cole leave. Was this to be her destiny? To be married to a wonderful man and to refuse his attentions? She had loved Joe with all her heart. Surely, she couldn't replace his love for another man whom she had only known for a month. Maybe, in time, she would be able to accept Cole's affections.

~

The door opened, and she stood by the bed wearing only her new shift and corset. Cole leaned against the door frame for several seconds staring at her. A tightness settled in his chest. This lovely woman was his wife, and she belonged to him now. Would he be able to keep his promise and not rush her? He wanted her to come to him.

"I must apologize, sweetheart, but we can't waltz around each other all the time. This is my room, too. I will try to knock before entering again."

Cole looked long and hard at Jazz as she pulled the day dress over her head. "Why are you wearing that corset?" Before she could answer, he commented, "Remove that straitjacket, and let the baby breathe. I don't want to see you wearing that thing again until our baby is born." He spun around and strode out of the room, forgetting why he had entered. Stopping at the door, he smiled. A feeling of contentment swept over him, catching him by surprise. Matters of the heart were damn confusing, he thought.

~

It was after breakfast, and everyone had gone to do their work. Jazz grew restless in the house, so she told Georgia that she needed some fresh air. She laid the garment she was hemming in the sewing basket. Placing a shawl over her shoulders, she walked outside and witnessed Sam leading a pony in circles in the corral.

Jazz hurried over and stood at the corral fence, listening to Sam speaking softly to the white and brown pinto. He was the prettiest pony she had ever seen.

Lily was already positioned on a fence post watching and covering her mouth, so as not to disturb the process.

"Good morning, Lily. Do you like the horses?" Jazz asked as

she moved close to her.

"Yes, ma'am. They're my favorite. I do like the pigs, but I get muddy whenever I'm too close to them. Mama don't like me to get mud on my shoes, but they're so cute."

"You know what I think this farm needs?"

"What . . . ?" Lily raised her eyes and looked all around. "There's all kinds of animals here."

"I think we need a puppy," she said. "When I was little like you, I always wanted a puppy for my very own, but my mama wouldn't let me have one." She remembered that Joe had said he would buy her one when they reached California, but he didn't want one while they were traveling.

"Oh, Miss Jazz, I would love a puppy. Do you think Mr. James will let you have one?"

"I believe he will. I will ask him tonight if he can find a mama dog that is ready to find a home for her new babies. Maybe we can get two."

"Can I go and tell Mama that we might get one or two?" Jazz laughed as she watched Lily jump off the post and run toward the house.

"Tell her that Sam and I will be in for lunch in a little while."

Lily raced into the house, and Jazz could hear her telling Georgia the puppy news. She laughed and it felt good. Reaching for the black ribbon on her sleeve, she pushed it up toward her shoulder and decided it was high time to tour the farm. As she rounded the barn, she noticed the pen of little piglets. They were so darn cute but smelled to high heaven. "Whew," she thought as she covered her nose.

Sam came up behind her and laughed. "They do smell bad, but they are so cute and playful."

"They need a bath. We could fill the tub with water and dip them in it. That would help."

'Sure, but they'll just roll in that stinking mud all over again."

"We need to clean their pit. Fresh hay in the bottom will help to keep them cleaner. They can roll around in the hay then."

"We can give it a try. I'll tell you what I'll do. I will catch the little buggers and put them in the barn while I clean out their playpen."

She smiled at his suggestion. "I'll help you to do it. Let's go in for lunch and then we'll start afterwards."

"Now, Miss Jazz, you don't have any business getting dirty. I can do it myself. Cole ain't gonna like you working."

"Now, you listen to me, Sam. It's my idea that we make the pigs smell better, and besides, this is my home now. I want to help Cole farm the land and do whatever I can to help. Now, don't you fret over me."

~

Later in the day, Sam, Jazz, and Lily were all wet and muddy, but they didn't seem to notice. They placed each piglet into the tub of clean water and watched them squeal and kick their little legs. Jazz dipped the little ones in the water and passed them over to Lily so she could rub them dry. After each one was clean, Sam carried them to the clean, hay-filled pen. The sow sniffed each one from head to toe before she allowed them to lie down.

After all ten piglets were clean and placed in their pen, the trio pointed and laughed at each other. "Now we look worse than those pigs," Lily said. "Mama will make me take a bath before supper."

"We're going to have to clean our bodies too, little miss," Sam said.

Jazz was raking the extra hay into the pen when Cole rode into the yard. He walked his horse to the barn and stopped in his tracks. "What in the world have you been up to, Mrs. James? You look like you have been wallowing in the pigpen."

Jazz and Sam laughed out loud. "You are nearly right," replied Sam.

"We washed the pigs, Mr. James. They smell so good," Lily proclaimed.

"You washed the pigs? Did I hear her right, Jazz?" Cole walked closer to the pig pen. "Mercy, they are clean, and it doesn't smell bad out here either."

"Now, Cole, I told Miss Jazz that she didn't need to do this. I told her that I could do it by myself, but she wouldn't hear of it." Sam winced as if he were expecting a lecture.

"Jazz, I am glad to see you are feeling well enough to be outside, but you still need to be taking it easy." He walked closer to her and turned up his nose. "You three need to take hot baths yourselves. The pigs smell better than you three."

~

The fall storm had come from nowhere. The rain cascaded on the windows in heavy torrents while lightning sizzled and cracked all around the farm. Jazz slipped down into the triangle tub and blew on the bubbles. She dribbled water from the sponge across her face and knees. Breathing a sigh of relief, she leaned her head back against the rim and closed her eyes almost drifting off into sleep in the warm bed of water.

Just then a chill came over her body making her feel that she wasn't alone. Opening her eyes, she peeked at Cole standing in front of the fire. Maintaining an outward show of calm, she was irritated that he had invaded her privacy. Tired and sore, she had a dull ache in her back. Her apprehension grew as she ran her fingers through her hair.

"Cole, I can't believe you came into my room when you knew I was bathing. This is something that I love and look forward to. While traveling, I was only able to take a bath when the train stopped near a river or creek. I never was able to enjoy anything like this. Please leave and allow me a little bit of pleasure." Chewing on her lip, she waited for him to say something.

His eyebrow lifted, as he turned to face the warm fire.

Finally, he walked over to the nightstand and tucked a large ledger under his arm. He smiled and headed to the door. Hesitating a moment, he winked at his bride. "I'll leave you, but with your hair piled on your head, you are the loveliest thing I've seen in a long time. Oh, by the way, remember, this is my room, too."

Chapter 21

As Cole was ready to leave town, Mrs. Goodman waved at him to stop. "I have the new dresses ready for your bride. Would you like to take them to her?"

"Why don't you come out to the farm with me and have supper with us. The girls always cook plenty, and I know Jazz would enjoy your visit. I will have my hired man bring you home afterwards."

"Oh my, I would like to go with you very much. Let me go inside and gather the dresses." As she turned to leave the wagon, she asked again, "Are you sure it will be all right?"

"More than all right. Jazz will be thrilled to see you." Cole smiled at the dressmaker as he jumped down to help her in the wagon and load the packages.

~

Lily was like the town crier when she heard someone coming in the yard. She was the first to let them know Cole had returned from the store, but tonight she had a bigger announcement. "Mr. James is home, and he has a lady with him."

Jazz froze in place as she laid a plate on the table. Surely, Cole's mama hadn't come here with him, or had she? Glancing at Georgia, she continued to set the table as they both waited for Cole and his guest to come up on the porch. Lily stood behind her and they stopped setting the table to listen to Sam as he greeted the lady.

The front door opened, and Cole led Rudy Goodman into the living room. "Jazz, I have a surprise visitor for dinner."

Jazz inched into the living room, then the biggest smile came over her face. "Oh my, how wonderful to see you, Mrs. Goodman." She hugged her and reached for her hands. "I have missed you and our talks."

"Me too. I worried about you until I heard the rumor that you married the most sought-after bachelor in Yellowstone."

"I didn't know Cole was having to fight off all the ladies in town. While working in the store, I did notice a lot of young girls liked hanging around, but it didn't cross my mind that they were vying for his attention."

"Now, you know, my dear. I had to order new ribbons every week." He winked at Georgia and said, "Now that I have been snatched up and removed from the marriage market, maybe the other young men will have a fighting chance." He smiled and waggled his eyebrows.

"Snatched up?" Jazz shook her head and smiled. "Well, you just remember that, and all will be well at home."

Georgia and Mrs. Goodman laughed at their banter. Cole grinned, seemingly relieved to share good-humored teasing with his new bride.

"Something sure smells good. I hope you don't mind that I have come uninvited to supper. I have a few dresses for you that your new husband ordered, and I flagged him down to bring them home to you. He insisted that I come and visit."

"You are always welcome, and the clothes are an added surprise. I had no idea you were making dresses for me," Jazz said, as she laid her hand across her heart.

"Come, let's eat and then you can view the new things that I had Mrs. Goodman make for you." Cole led Mrs. Goodman over to the table and pulled out a chair for her.

"Jazz, you sit, and I will help Georgia serve the food."

"No sir, you sit down with your guest and Sam will help me. I've a large tureen of hot soup and a big cake of cornbread to start with." Sam carried the bowl and set it in the middle of the table while Georgia sliced the cornbread.

After Mrs. Goodman and Jazz were seated, Jazz noticed Cole peering into the kitchen where Georgia, Lily, and Sam were preparing to sit in the kitchen. "Georgia, I am sure Mrs. Goodman doesn't want us to change the way we share our meals. Please bring your bowls and silverware back to this table." Cole turned and smiled at Mrs. Goodman. "Everyone who lives here and works for me shares my table."

When no one voiced an objection, Cole said grace. Lily said amen louder than the others, which brought a laugh.

Mrs. Goodman spoke to the little girl. "How old are you, Miss Lily?"

"I'm almost four. My birthday is coming soon, and I want a dolly that looks like me."

"Lily, it isn't polite to tell people what you want for a present," Georgia scolded.

"How am I going to get what I want if I don't tell folks?"

"Now, Georgia, I think our Lily makes perfectly good sense. Let's all enjoy this delicious meal." Cole patted Lily's hand and ladled soup in her bowl.

After the table was cleared, Jazz and Mrs. Goodman took her new clothes in the bedroom for a fitting. "I can't believe Cole chose the patterns and suggested that you make shifts and other personal items."

"He picked out a few pieces and instructed me how to make them. Cole was so funny describing how high he wanted your waist to be so the materials would flow. You are a lucky young woman to be married to Cole. I have known him and his parents ever since I arrived in Yellowstone on a wagon train back in 1860. They were a nice family, at first, then over the years, Mrs. James started treating people different."

"How do you mean, treating people different? I know she didn't appreciate the help I gave her, but she was feeling bad and took it out on me. Cole was angry and upset most of the time that I worked there."

"After Mr. James died, she became angry. I believed she blamed God for taking her husband and leaving her all alone. When she finally convinced Cole to move back to the store, she began acting like her old self again." The seamstress shook her head and continued. "She was happier, but she seemed to sap the life out of Cole. He loved this place and only wanted to live out here and work the land."

Jazz smiled. "He has told me how much he loves it here, and I can understand how he feels. I never had a home when I was growing up. My mama worked as a laundress and rented an old cabin. After she left me for a man, the landlord put me out on the street. Usually, I worked in cafes and slept on a wobbly old cot, if I was lucky. I bounced from job to job, town to town, until I met Joe, my husband."

"Bless your heart, child. You never spoke of your childhood while you were working for me."

"I was happily married to Joe. He treated me good, and he and I had big plans to settle in California. Joe was going to build me a fine home and we wanted many children. But, the good Lord had different plans for us both."

"Same with me," replied Mrs. Goodman. "I always wanted a successful seamstress shop with several ladies working for me, but that never happened. I would like to give up sewing full-time, but there hasn't been another opportunity where I could work and support myself." Mrs. Goodman turned Jazz around and admired her handiwork. "Lovely dress. It looks so good on you, and no one would guess you're with child."

"How did you know?" Jazz asked. She laid her hands on her stomach and peered at the dressmaker.

"Child, not many young ladies wear high-waistline dresses.

When Cole was instructing me as to how he wanted the dresses to be, I knew why he wanted your things to be made like this."

"It was so kind of him to order these things. I love them all and the personal items, too," she said as she fingered the white shifts. "I don't want Cole to be embarrassed to be seen in public with me. It won't be long before everyone will know that I'm with child."

"Honey, that man loves you so much. He would never be ashamed of you, but I want to warn you." Mrs. Goodman picked up her bags and purse. "Please don't allow his mother to come between you two. You know she will try, mark my words."

After a long goodbye, Sam drove Mrs. Goodman to her shop. Jazz and Georgia went back inside the house while Cole walked to the barn. "Come, Georgia, and see all my dresses and other things that Cole had made for me. I feel like I have died and gone to heaven. Never have I had so many nice things at one time."

Chapter 22

A large man walked down the dirt road searching for the first farm about three or four miles from town. He had stayed on Georgia's front porch until the new tenants moved into her old house. The man of the house ran him off, but he had no place to go. After questioning around town about Georgia's whereabouts, he finally heard that she was working for the storekeeper on his farm.

After walking about three miles out of town, the man noticed smoke coming from the edge of a wheat field. Shading his eyes with his hand, he watched a man on horseback fanning a large stick of fire, then drag it across the edge of the field. "Hey, man, what are you doing?" he called to the stranger as he ran toward the field.

Before he knew what had hit him, a sting grazed his head, but he kept running toward the fire and the man on horseback. Too late, he realized the man on horseback was racing away.

The old man stood, removed his shirt, and tried putting out the flames. He stomped the fire until he was satisfied the flames were out.

Suddenly, dizziness overtook him, he fell down on one knee, and swiped at the blood running down his cheek. Sitting on the ground until he could catch his breath, he lay down on a patch of grass near the road.

The big man didn't remember how long he had been asleep

when he awoke to find the proprietor of the dry goods store shaking him. "Hey big guy, are you all right? It looks like you have been shot in the head. Let me help you up and take you to my place."

Everything was doubling up in front of him. "Georgia, I am looking for Georgia. Do you know her? She was my neighbor."

"Yes, she works for me on my farm. Let's put you in my wagon, and Georgia will take care of you." As Cole was helping the man into his wagon, he said, "Where's that smoke coming from? And what happened to your shirt? It looks like it's been burned to pieces."

~

Lily came running onto the porch screaming for Sam and Miss Jazz to come. "Mama Pig is lying on her side, and she's bleeding. Hurry!"

Sam raced out the front door with Jazz on his heels. Both rounded the barn and Jazz noticed the wheat field was on fire. Dark smoke was filling the air. "Sam, grab some wet rags, and let's save the wheat field. Hurry, Lily, go get your mama." Jazz hurried to the well and dropped the bucket down in it. After hearing a splash, she pulled it up and dipped rags into the water. She grabbed the bucket and rushed to the section of wheat that was burning. "Thank the Lord, it rained last night," she yelled to Sam as he took the bucket of water out of her hands. Jazz slammed the wet rags down on the fire and smothered the flames.

Georgia came running with another full bucket of water, and Sam tossed it over the wheat, soaking it until the flames were put out.

Dirty and wet, their faces covered with soot, the three looked at each other, proud of the job that they had done to save the wheat. "Who set this field on fire, Sam?"

"Why do you think it was deliberately set?"

"Well, none of the animals would have done this, right?"

"Of course not. Let's go check on the sow," Sam said, as he glanced at the girls.

Lily was squatting down beside the dead sow. She had been shot in the head, and several of the piglets were crawling all over her belly. "Gather the piglets, Lily, and put them in the barn. I'm going to cover the sow until Cole has a good look at her. He is going to be upset to learn that someone set the wheat field on fire and killed his prize sow." Sam dragged a tarp over the pig and anchored a few big boards to hold it down.

"Lily, do you think if Cole brings us a few baby bottles, you can help me feed the piglets? A couple of them can drink out of the trough already, but a few still need help."

"Oh, Miss Jazz, I will be a good mama to those little babies. I will help." Lily scooted closer to her mother.

"Come, Miss Jazz, You need a good bath and a long rest. You must remember that you have to take care of yourself. Now come along and I will heat some water. We all smell like smoke, for sure."

~

Cole drove his wagon to the side of the barn and sat for a long moment. Dark smoke was billowing in the air. The wheat on the east side had been on fire, just like the west side of his farm. He went to the back to help the black man up.

Sam rushed out of the barn and saw the man lying in the back of the flatbed wagon. "Golly, Cole, where did you pick this fellow up? The big guy looks like he has been shot."

"Found him beside the road. He must have fought the wheat fire about two miles from here. The wheat was on fire here, too."

"Yep, but me and the girls fought the flames and brought them under control." Standing with his hands tucked under his armpits, he appeared a little proud of himself.

"Jazz, too?" Before Sam answered, Cole said, "I hope Jazz didn't harm herself."

"I have to admit, we were all tired but happy we saved the field. You know, I couldn't have stopped your new wife from helping. That young woman loves this farm of yours." Sam's face beamed.

Cole grinned. He was pleased to hear Jazz loved his farm. Maybe, she would learn to love him too. "This man is looking for Georgia. Run in the house and bring her out so she can help me with him."

Georgia came out of the house with Lily on her skirt tail. "Mercy, Mr. Cole, this is Ugly, my friend and protector. He slept on my front porch and made sure no one ever bothered Lily and me."

Cole peered over Georgia's shoulder, shaking his head as to why Georgia called this stranger, Ugly. He glanced at the house and asked, "Where's Jazz?"

"She's bathing and I told her to lie down and rest. We had to fight the wheat field fire, and something else has happened. She was pretty upset."

Sam lifted a hand to hush Gerogia, but it was too late. "Boss, I'll fill you in a few minutes."

Cole nodded, then turned to the woman. "What would we do without you, Georgia? This guy needs tending to. Someone shot him in the head. I don't think it's serious though. Just a graze."

After Sam and Cole carried the man into the house, Georgia had the men place Ugly on her bed. She asked Sam to bring her two buckets of water. "Place one bucket on the stove fire and bring the other one into my room."

Cole left when Georgia had the situation under control and knocked on his bedroom door. Receiving no answer, he cracked the door and saw Jazz sound asleep. She lay on her back with her lovely blond hair spread over the pillow. Her mouth was open, and she was breathing softly. He hoped she had not harmed their baby. *Their* baby. Yes, the child she carried in her womb was his child now. Grinning, he pulled the door closed and motioned for Sam to walk outside with him.

As they walked to the barn, Sam explained how Lily had found the sow dead and all the little piglets climbing over her body. "So sad," he said.

Cole looked down at his prize sow. He couldn't believe that he had paid good money for her, and now she was dead. "Sam, do you have any idea who would want to kill her? I can't believe anyone would want to burn my wheat field, but to shoot my prize sow? A man can't get much lower than that."

Sam stuffed his hands in his pockets. "I hate to say what I've been thinking all afternoon. Don't want you to get angry at me."

"Tell me your thoughts. They can't be any worse than mine."

"Well, your mama wants you to move back to town. Maybe she asked someone to burn your wheat field because she knows how much you're depending on it to feed your animals this winter."

He frowned. "What about my sow?"

"I can't believe she told someone to do that. She's got a mean streak, but I don't think she would want to kill an innocent animal."

"You and I are thinking the same way. Whoever she hired must have known that my sow was the best producer of pigs in the county."

Sam sighed. "Yes, and with your sow gone, theirs would be more in demand."

"Correct, now I am going to have to buy another one soon. The girls can feed the little piglets until they can drink on their own, but I need another sow to give me more babies. Pigs will be in great demand come this spring."

Cole stood looking off into the sunset. Maybe the big guy in the house saw who shot him. It's possible he came upon a stranger burning the field. He might be able to identify the person, he thought. "Come on, Sam. Let's go in the house and speak with that giant I brought home."

"That guy is the biggest son-of-a-gun I ever did see," Sam shook his head as he followed Cole from the barn.

Chapter 23

"Good morning, Georgia, how's your friend doing?" Cole asked as she poured him a fresh cup of coffee.

"He had nightmares, and I was so afraid he was going to disturb you and Jazz. Ugly must have been mistreated pretty badly after I moved. He kept begging for the boys to stop hitting him. Some of those young'uns in my old neighborhood are big and can be downright mean."

"So, am I to understand that he came looking for you because you made sure he was fed and he could sleep on your porch without being pestered by the neighbors?"

"Yes, sir. It wasn't all one-sided. He did protect me and Lily. If some man came crawling around the house, he ran them off. Just his size scared the woolly out of most of them."

"Yes, I can see that." Cole chuckled and wiped his mouth.

"Mr. Cole, do you think you have it in your heart to let him stay out here with us? He follows instructions real well, and he could be a help to Sam with the planting and harvesting. Ugly's a gentle man . . . I have left Lily at home when she was sleeping, and he watched after her real good."

Cole could see the possibilities. A man of his size would be a great help on the farm. Good protection when Cole was at the store. "Sam, do you think you and the big guy could help me close in the back of the barn and make a room for him? I have an extra potbelly stove at the store that I could bring out, and there's more lumber at the yard that belongs to me."

"Sure thing. If you have time this morning, show me what you would like, and I can start on it after I finish the morning chores." Sam smiled and dug into the plate of hot cakes that Georgia had set in front of him.

~

After breakfast and giving instructions on the back of the barn, Cole climbed up on the bench of his flatbed wagon. "I'll bring out more supplies to help with the room this afternoon."

Suddenly, a shot rang out, and Cole fell forward in the wagon. "Cole, Cole, oh my goodness," Sam yelled, leaped upon the wheel of the wagon, and lifted Cole's body into a sitting position. Blood was flowing down his right cheek, but he was coming   around.
Jazz and Georgia raced outside, while Ugly came out of the barn. The man pushed past the ladies and climbed onto the back of the wagon and stepped to the front bench where Cole was leaning. "Here, Sam, you get down, and I will lift Mr. James down to you."

"Please be careful," cried Jazz.

Georgia was pacing from the front of the wagon to the back when the two men carried Cole inside the house to his bedroom.

"Heat some water and bring me some clean rags, Georgia." Jazz had pulled the covers back on the bed and was removing her husband's boots. "I don't believe he was shot anywhere else, do you, Sam?" Jazz said.

"I didn't see any blood or holes in his shirt. Whoever was shooting at him nearly blew his head off his shoulders," Sam said, regretting his remark as soon as it flew out of his mouth.

~

When a wet rag was rubbed across his cheek, Cole tried to sit up. "What happened?" he quizzed Jazz, grabbing his head and moaning.

"It seems like someone tried to kill you. They came pretty darn close to doing it, too."

"I'm fine." He moaned as he attempted to sit up on the side of the bed. Dizziness and the shooting pain forced him to remain in bed.

"Did anyone see who might have shot at me? Sam, did you?" Cole muttered. "I remember talking to you, and then I felt like a brick had hit me. Whoever it was had to be a pretty good shot."

"Cole, please settle down and let me care for your wound. The right side of your face is already swelling, and I am sure you're going to have a black eye."

Pain shot through his head the minute Jazz touched his bloody face. He lay back down and closed his eyes, then fell into a deep sleep as she placed an ointment on the slash under his right eye.

~

"Sam, ride into town and tell Mrs. James that Cole will not be coming into work today. Tell her he is feeling under the weather. Don't tell her that he was shot. No sense in getting her all worked up."

"I will get a list of supplies that we need from Georgia, and I'll go to the lumberyard and buy the materials that Cole said he would bring home today. Might as well make it a productive trip, if I have to ride into town."

"Please don't mention anything about what happened here this morning. If Cole wants to report it to the sheriff, he will do it after he's up and around."

"The big guy is outside, so you don't need to be afraid with him guarding the place. I'll be back as soon as I can," Sam pointed his finger toward the barn. "I will leave him Cole's rifle."

After Sam left the room, she covered Cole with a quilt. She tiptoed out of the bedroom, leaving the door opened a little ways so she could hear him if he called or tried to get out of bed.

"Georgia, call your friend in and let's feed him and Lily some breakfast. "

"Thank goodness," Lily said. "I thought you had forgotten all about me."

"Oh you, hush your mouth. You know we're caring for Mr. Cole," Georgia scolded her little daughter. Then she went to the porch and called her friend. "Ugly, come inside and have breakfast."

"Georgia, shame on you," Jazz whispered. "I can't believe you called your friend ugly."

"That's all right, ma'am. Ugly is my name." The big guy twisted his hat around and around in front of his large frame. "Sorry, I don't have a shirt."

"Let me get one of Cole's. It may be a little small, but it will cover part of your chest." After giving the man the shirt, she asked again. "What did your folks call you?

"Ugly, my name."

"Well, I never," whispered Jazz. "You don't have any other name?"

"Pa called me Ugly from the time I can remember. I never knew another name."

Jazz walked over to the stove and picked up the coffeepot. She shook her head in disgust. "Well, I can tell you now that I'll never call you by that name. I believe you need another name, and I am going to think on it."

"Can she do that?" Ugly looked at Georgia.

"Miss Jazz can do whatever she wants, and if she wants you to have a different name, then that's what she'll do."

A big smile spread across Jazz's face. "Sir, I believe I have the perfect name for you. Georgia tells me that you were her protector when she lived in that neighborhood. Come and sit down at the table, and I will tell you what I am thinking." Jazz watched the tall man shuffle over to the table and sit down. He pulled on the white union-suit shirt that stretched over his large frame.

"Georgia told me she was never afraid at night with you close by. There's a story in the Good Book, 1 Samuel something, I believe. It's about a young boy named David. He was filled with faith and passion for his people, and he was very brave." She glanced at the man and smiled. "Yes, I am going to call you David from this day forward. What do you think of the name David?"

"My mama talked about her God all the time and said that I was to believe in him, and I would never have to fear Pa. I tried to believe, but as a little boy, it was hard to believe in a man I couldn't see. You see, I was scared to death of my pa. He was a mean man who beat me all the time. Mama tried to take care of me, mostly by praying over my bloody, bruised body, but her God never answered her prayers."

"Oh, Ugly, I mean David, you never told me any of that. I'm so sorry you were mistreated as a child." Georgia blinked back tears.

Lily jumped up from the table and hugged her friend's knees. "I hate your pa!"

The man patted Lily on the back and said that his pa couldn't hurt him anymore. "Now you get back in your chair and eat."

Ugly sat for a few minutes and then looked at both of the girls. "I like the name David. He sounds like a good man." He grinned at Georgia and then turned to Jazz. "Thank you. I will only answer to my new name from now on."

Chapter 24

"The weather is going to be bad in a little while," Sam said to Herman, the store clerk. "I need for you to hurry with my order, if you don't mind."

"Mr. James hasn't come into the store this morning. Have you seen him?" Herman asked, while looking over his shoulder for Mrs. James.

"Tell Mrs. James that Cole will not be in today. He's a little under the weather."

"What do you mean—Cole's under the weather? What's wrong with him? My boy is never sick." Mrs. James stood in the doorway of her downstairs bedroom.

"I was given this list and instructed to tell you that he wouldn't be here today. Nothing else," Sam said as he spun to avoid the old bat as quickly as he could. The old woman hated the sight of him, and he didn't like her company either.

"Tell my son if he isn't here tomorrow, I will be making a trip to his farm to check on him." Mrs. James turned and disappeared into the store's kitchen.

"I'll be back shortly. I've some lumber to pick up at the lumberyard. I want to return to the farm before the storm hits." Sam placed his hat on his head and held the door for several ladies to enter the store.

~

David rushed out of the barn and helped move the flatbed wagon inside before the bottom fell out. Lightning flashed and thunder rumbled while the men stood in the doorway of the barn. The big guy had moved the piglets, the goat, and two milk cows. He placed the goat inside his cage and gave the two cows extra hay and locked them in their assigned stalls. He figured he and Sam would begin working on his new room at the back of the barn, but he wanted the animals inside out of the storm.

Sam signaled to him. "Let's hurry inside and eat lunch. Afterwards we can start sawing the lumber and start laying the floor for the room."

"The room is going to have a wood floor?" David asked. "I ain't never slept in a room without a dirt floor."

"I can assure you Cole does everything first class on his farm. He will want a floor, two nice windows, a potbelly stove, and a locked door. You'll share the room with supplies, but you'll have plenty of space for a big bed, and hooks on the wall for your clothes."

'Windows and a warming stove. I'll feel like I'm in a fancy hotel." David's smile was as wide as his face.

"I brought out the windows and the potbelly stove today. They are covered on the wagon. We'll bring them in after lunch." Sam beamed.

~

Cole awakened to the sound of laughter. It was a strange, unfamiliar sound coming from Jazz and Georgia. He touched the bandage that covered his cheek. The movement made the soreness in his cheek hurt something awful. It felt large, and so did the side of his face. He reached for his shaving mirror that lay on the side table to catch a glimpse of himself.

Damn it, he looked awful, he thought. He moaned as he attempted to swing his long legs off the bed. Suddenly, he felt clammy and nauseated, but he had to reach the water closet before he embarrassed himself. Shuffling, he stumbled to the wall. Cole glanced down and saw that he was practically naked. Well, this was just great.

As he leaned against the wall, waiting for the dizziness to vanish, he wondered why someone had shot him. Whoever did certainly wanted him dead. The idea that someone wanted to kill him was a puzzle. He didn't have any idea who had a grudge against him, unless it was the town doctor, but to kill him? No, that wasn't possible. Somebody must have a concealed hatred for him, but who?

Jazz hurried into the room and posted her hands on her hips. "Well, my hard-headed husband, you could have called to me. I was sitting at the kitchen table having coffee."

"Yes, I heard you laughing. I didn't want to bother you." He noticed the black ribbon on her upper right arm. It seemed to always be there.

"You are my husband, and you've been hurt. Hold on to me, and I will lead you. Do you need my help inside?"

"No, thank you. I can manage the rest of the way."

"I'll be here when you are ready to come out."

~

Jazz waited patiently for Cole to complete his task in the closet. She straightened his bedcovers and felt that his pillow was damp. Hurrying to the pantry, she grabbed a fresh pillowcase and placed it on the pillow. She reached for his robe that was hanging on a hook by the window. Hearing him moving around, she waited at the closet for him to open the door. Cole moaned but walked a little steadier as he stood before her.

"I need to lie down. Will you please bring a bucket to sit by my bed? I'm a little nauseous."

"Should I send for the doctor? I'm sure he would have some medicine for you, and he could check your cheek."

"No, please, don't send for anyone. You and Georgia have

done a fine job on my face. My stomach will be fine after I have rested."

"Sam went into town this morning to pick up some supplies and lumber. I told him not to mention what had happen to anyone. He told your mama that you wouldn't be into work today, and she said that if you didn't show up tomorrow, she was going to come out here."

"I don't want her out here. I'll send her a note that I have a bad cold, and if she comes here she could catch it. She hates colds." Cole grinned, remembering how she made his pa care for him when he was a small child with fever and chills.

"Sam can ride in early tomorrow morning. He needs to pick up some clothes for David."

"Who in the world is David?" Cole asked, hoping that the girls had not taken in another man or child.

"David is Ugly' s new name. I refuse to call him by that name, so I gave him another. I chose David from the Bible. Believe it or not, he is happy with the name. What do you think? No one should be called Ugly."

"You are something else," Cole commented to Jazz as she helped him back to the bed. Holding her hand, he lay down and smiled. "I like the name David. Is he the boy in the Bible who hit the giant using a slingshot?"

"Yes," Jazz said. "I guess you went to church and learned all about God and all the people in the Good Book."

"I went every Sunday whether I wanted to go or not," he mumbled. "My parents had to be seen in church, or they would have to answer to all their customers." He closed his eyes and fell asleep as he continued to hold her hand.

Jazz stood looking down at the man she had married. He was a good man who was raised in the church with the teachings of Jesus.

Jazz had learned from others that she was a child of God. Learning about Jesus brought harmony to her life. She'd listened to her elders where she worked and learned to trust in Jesus. The sun would rise and set daily, and she would never be alone. "Please God, guide me to be a good wife for this Christian man. I have deep feelings for him," she prayed softly.

Chapter 25

Climbing the backstairs to his room, Herman opened the door and peeked around the corner of the hallway to make sure it was clear. He rushed into his room and locked the door, then leaned up against the door frame and took a deep breath. Rushing over to the window, Herman looked down over the street. He pushed the curtain back and saw Sam driving a flatbed wagon down the street toward the lumberyard.

Herman quickly cleaned his gun and stroked the shiny nickeled rifle finish while pointing it toward the window. It was a fine rifle that had cost him fourteen dollars, and it was worth every penny. He needed this gun to help with his future. Herman had no future until he came to Yellowstone. Hearing men out in the hall, he abruptly put it back in the box and slid it under the bed.

Grabbing his hat and dress coat, he hurried down the stairs, dashed out the front door, and headed to the dry-goods store. Upon entering the store from the back, he saw Mrs. James looking out the front display window. "Good morning, Mrs. James," Herman said as he moved closer than necessary to her back, breathing gently on her neck.

"Good morning to you, Herman," replied Mrs. James, a flush creeping over her skin.

"Can I make you some coffee?" he said, inching even closer, his hands lingering near the cash register. He knew what he had to do real soon and this time, he wouldn't miss his target.

"I've already made it," she stammered. "Go and pour yourself some, and let's get busy. I hope Cole will be here this morning."

~

The doorbell jangled and Sam came in. His eyes widened at how cozy Mrs. James and Herman seemed as they stood close together. He did a double take. What was he witnessing? "Mrs. James, Cole will not be here this morning because he has a real bad cold and is running a fever. He said for you not to worry about him and please don't ride out to the farm. Cole doesn't want you to catch it."

"Thank you for coming in to tell me. Let my son know that I am concerned about him, but I understand. Do you have a list of supplies to take back to the farm?"

"Yes," he said, taking it out of his pocket and giving it to Herman. "I need several pairs of overalls, three long-sleeved shirts, and three pairs of long white union suits as large as you have." Sam followed Herman to the back of the store where the men's things were stored.

"Who are these clothes for?" Herman asked, as he pulled the overalls off the table.

"Cole hired a giant of a man to help harvest the last of the wheat."

Herman glanced at Sam and handed him the other items. "Do you need anything else for the hired help?" Herman said sarcastically.

"Socks. Five pairs of heavy wool ones," Sam said, cocking his head while raising his eyebrows. The sarcasm was not lost on him.

Herman piled the socks on the other clothes, then hurried to the front of the store while Sam followed with his arms loaded down.

Mrs. James peered up from her place behind the counter.

"Your kitchen supplies are ready. I will put these things on Cole's list. He would want me to do this so he can reorder everything when he returns to the store." Mrs. James' lips pinched together, daring Sam to say anything against what she was doing.

"I know he appreciates how hard you work," Sam responded and walked out the door. He glanced over his shoulder. Herman and Mrs. James had something going on between them.

~

After arriving back to the farm, Sam learned that Cole had been up and ate a hearty breakfast, but he was still dizzy. The bullet had grazed his cheek and caused him to have dizzy spells and headaches. Sleep seemed to help.

David was ecstatic with his new clothes and the girls couldn't get over how different he looked in his new overalls. He strutted around in the living room and smiled. "I ain't never had anything so nice. I will take good care of them, and I'll sure pay Mr. James back for buying them for me."

Jazz smiled and looked David over from his head to his new socks. "Next trip, you'll have to go into town, so Cole can fit you with new boots."

"Oh no, ma'am. He done gave me enough," David said.

"We'll discuss that later." Jazz headed into the bedroom to check on her husband.

"Come on, David, now that you have modeled your new duds, we need to unload the lumber and start building that room of yours."

Sam and David cut the four by fours and butted them together to make a frame for the floor of the barn. After nailing them together, they cut the lumber into planks and covered the floor completely. Even with the cold weather outside, sweat covered both men. Sam had David walk on the floor and even jump up and down. It was strong and sturdy. The men smiled at each other and shook hands for a job well done.

The granite wall needed a coat of gray paint, so Sam covered the new floor with an old sheet and went inside the house to ask Lily if she wanted to help paint.

There were no words to describe her excitement. Georgia covered Lily's clothes with Cole's old shirt and wrapped her feet in two old flour bags. She placed a rag over her black curls and smiled. "Now you're ready," Georgia said. "Don't paint the men."

"Mercy, I had no idea you were going to have to get all dressed up to paint," Sam said laughing.

Georgia cooked beef stew for supper and baked a cornbread cake. Jazz made a dried-apple pie for dessert.

~

Cole awakened to the smell of cinnamon. His stomach rumbled. Jazz had set a small bell beside his bed for him to ring if he needed her. He decided it was time to sit up, so he rang the bell.

"It's so good that you can follow orders. See, I am here to assist you, and you didn't have to fall on your face."

Cole smiled at Jazz, but he couldn't help but noticing the black ribbon on her arm, which symbolized the wall between them. One day, he hoped she would remove it.

Jazz eased down on the bed beside him. "How are you feeling?" she asked.

Cole placed his hand on Jazz's stomach. "How's this little fellow doing?"

Jazz didn't jump up or attempt to evade his touch. She placed her hand over his and said, "Fine. I felt it move this morning. It was like a flutter."

"That's wonderful. I would love to feel it . . . sometimes."

"Cole, I feel so bad that I have caused a split between you and your mama. Can't image how she is going to feel about me when she learns I'm with child." Sighing, Jazz said, "You've been disgraced in town for marrying a loose woman who was married to a bank robber and murderer. I don't want my baby to be a

138

disgrace."

Squeezing her hand, he said, "We, you and I, both know the truth, and that's all that matters. Do you think we should tell everyone about the baby?"

"Georgia already knows the baby can't be yours. She guessed a while ago when I was sick and sleeping over at her place."

"Everybody who is important in my life will be happy for us," he said.

She sighed again. "I feel that I should leave after my baby arrives. My leaving won't give your mama even a moment's pause, but she'll be thrilled to have her son back."

He sat up and winced. "Now you listen to me and hear me good. You will not be leaving here. Understand me, Jazz. You are my wife now and forever, and your baby will carry my name."

The two sat quietly and contemplated their future. "You know lying is a sin, and we seem to be getting a lot of practice." Jazz gave Cole a cocky grin.

Chapter 26

After three long days of resting, Cole's headaches and dizziness disappeared. He rode into town to work at the store, waving at several of his friends and customers as he rode into the livery.

"Morning, Mel, will you give my poor horse a good rubdown and extra feed? The weather is sure nasty, and I will be at the store most of the day."

"Sure thing. I heard that you've been under the weather. What happened to your face?"

"I fell while working in the barn, and the rake flew up and hit me in the cheek," Cole said, the lie coming easy as he answered the liveryman. Mel would retell this story to all the men that hung around the warm stable.

Cole circled to the back of the store and went onto the porch. His eyes surveyed the mess. Boxes were stacked unevenly on top of each other, and canned-good boxes were opened with several cans missing. How could things have gotten so out of hand in just a few days?

Walking in the door, he saw Herman standing so close to his mom a person would think that they were an intimate couple. Coughing, Cole approached the counter. His mother and Herman moved apart, and his mama smiled broadly.

"Oh, Cole, it's so good to see you. Have you completely recovered from your cold? It seems you still have a cough."

Cole gave Herman a hard stare and said," Yes, I am better, thank you." He noticed Herman didn't leave to give them privacy.

"Herman, the back porch inventory is a mess. Please go outside and put the boxes in order. I will be out in a while to assist you. I've never seen such a mess."

"Now, dear, Herman has been busy in the store and the weather has been too cold to work out there."

"Nevertheless, he can put on a jacket and do his job." He glared at Herman who quickly grabbed his heavy coat, slamming the back door as he exited.

"Would you like a cup of hot coffee before you get busy?" Mrs. James asked.

"No, but I want to know what's going on between you and my hired man. I saw how he was trying to cuddle up to you."

Her eyes narrowed. "You'd better watch your mouth. I am not interested in our hired man, as you called him. Why, I never."

"Mama, I don't care if you take a new man. You're a grown woman, but he'd better know that he will never get his hands on this store."

"So, you think he's only after me for the store?" She turned red and nearly screamed her words.

"One thing I know for sure, it's certainly not your sweet disposition. You are a mean-tempered woman who makes everyone miserable with your complaints. I work as hard as I can for you in this store, but it's never enough. Now I have a new wife and a few hired hands who do a good job in helping me."

Cole decided to speak his mind, since he'd already started. "All you think about is yourself. When Pa was down and sick, you made his life miserable. You didn't feel sorry for him; you actually blamed him for taking ill and making you unhappy. Well, it's time you take responsibility for yourself. If you want to play tootsies with that man—" Cole turned his head to look over his shoulder, "you go ahead, but you'd better tell him what I said about this store."

Placing her hand over her heart, she shook her head. "What has that hussy done to my sweet son? Before you married that girl, you never missed work and you were kind to me. Now you're a tyrant who claims that I'm playing fast and loose with my hired man."

"My wife has only made me open my eyes to really see my mother for the first time. She was helpful in the store and very kind to you, but you treated her so bad, and because of your actions, she couldn't get a job in this town. The saloon was her last choice and look what happened to her."

Cole turned to walk away but stopped, "Jazz is a kind, hardworking girl. I'm proud that she agreed to marry me." He glared hard at his mother. "I am warning you now, when she comes in this store, you had better be on your best behavior toward her." Cole whipped around and strode outside to give Herman further instructions.

"Mr. James, your mother has been very concerned over your health. I wanted to go to your farm and check on you for her, but the weather was too bad. I'm glad you're better," Herman said.

Cole only glared at the man and tapped his notebook. "Let's move all those canned goods toward the door. It looks like a good many can be placed on the shelves. Do you know if some cloth dolls came in any of these boxes? We need to put them in the store window so the mothers can purchase them for their children."

"I'm not sure, but I will look in the bigger ones," Herman replied through gritted teeth.

Once order had returned, and the inventory was completed, Cole found the box of dolls and carried it into the front window. "Mama, please place these baby dolls in the display window. There's another box that has some toys for little boys. You know how to make everything look nice. I need to go talk with the sheriff, but I'll be back soon to close up for the day. Looks like snow, and I need to get home."

~

"Are you sure this person was trying to kill you?" The sheriff asked, his eyebrows furrowing into a straight line.

"Yes, I'm sure. Another few inches and I wouldn't be here telling you about it. A bullet grazed my cheek, and I was laid up for a few days. The day before, my wheat fields were set on fire. My hired man and wife were able to stop the blaze near my barn, and another man put the fire out in the outer field. My hired man was walking to the farm when he saw the arsonist dragging a burning bush near the edge of the wheat. When he realized what was happening, he took off his shirt and smothered the flames."

"So, you're saying that someone is trying to destroy your farm and kill you?" The old sheriff stood and walked around his desk. "This is so hard to believe. I've known you all your life, and never have I heard a bad word spoken against you."

"Believe me, I have racked my mind as to who would have a grudge against me or would want something I have. The doctor and I had a disagreement about who was going to marry my wife, but he's no killer." Suddenly a thought came to his mind. Herman might want him out of the way so he could marry his mother and get his hands on the store. Surely, that weasel wasn't a cold-blooded killer, was he?

"All I can do now is listen out for any gossip about you. I'll go into the saloon tonight and question Big Al. If something is going down, he might have heard. I'll keep you informed, but if you think of someone, you let me know." The sheriff walked Cole to the front door. "Watch your back."

After leaving the sheriff's office, Cole drove his wagon back to the store and pulled it close to the back steps, then jumped down and unlatched the door. The sacks he had picked up at the train depot were heavy, but he didn't want to ask that weasel Herman to help. He squatted down and lifted the bulky bags on his knees, then foisted them onto the porch.

Cole would keep his eye on Herman. His suspicion was growing every day. The fury inside his gut made him work faster. In just a couple of minutes, he'd stacked the boxes and grain on the porch. Someday soon, he swore to himself, he would catch Herman, and when he did, he would break his scrawny neck and run him out of the county if he was still standing.

Chapter 27

Sunday morning was a beautiful, bright, and sunny day with just enough chill in the air to make all the animals playful. Cole stood at the corral, watching the colts kick up their heels and the goat run around in circles. He patted his stomach as he entered the kitchen to a wonderful aroma of fried ham and hot biscuits. "Good morning, ladies, "he said to his lovely wife and Georgia.

"Am I a lady too, Mr. Cole?" Lily asked as she slid into her chair at the kitchen table.

"You certainly are one of them, Miss Lily, and a mighty pretty one, too. How would you like to go to church this fine morning?"

"Can we, Mama, can we? I'd love to go and sing. Us young'uns clap our hands, too."

"Well, I would like to attend services, but I am afraid our church is too far for us to reach on foot." Georgia smiled at her little girl.

"Jazz and I can drop you off at your church. We'll pass right by it on our way into town." Cole looked at Jazz as she stood frozen in place at the stove.

"Cole, may I speak to you in the bedroom?" Jazz bit down on her lower lip.

Cole turned to Georgia. "All of you begin eating while Jazz and I have a little talk. Georgia, would you please butter me a couple of those hot biscuits?"

"Yes sir, I sure will. Come and sit, Sam and David."

Jazz waited until Cole had entered the bedroom before she closed the door. "Cole, I'm not sure I'm ready to go into town, much less to church. What will the townspeople think?"

"I don't know what they will think, nor do I really care. We are a family now, and I have always gone to church. The people in Yellowstone will accept you or they won't, but they will not say anything rude to you, I can promise you that." He took her hands, pulled her close, and kissed her hair, then moved down to her throat.

Slowly wiggling out of his hold, she looked at him with determined eyes. "If you're sure you're ready to test the waters with your new wife, then I will put on a brave face and go with you." She spun around and opened the door. "Georgia, let's finish breakfast and put something on for lunch. It looks like we're all going to church this morning," Jazz said with a lot more enthusiasm in her tone, but he could read the tone beneath her words.

"Not me. I'm staying right here. Those folks in town don't like me. I'll stay home and guard the place in case we have another intruder," Sam said, as he spooned jam inside his buttered biscuit.

Cole nodded. "That is a good idea. You sure you don't mind staying home all alone?"

"I won't be alone. I have all my animal friends to keep me company and busy, too."

"Maybe sometimes you can come to church with Mama and me. I would like for you to hear me sing." Lily smiled at Sam. "I'm really good."

"And loud. Sometimes I have to cover her mouth," Georgia said.

Everyone laughed and ate a hearty breakfast. As soon as the dishes were washed, Georgia began preparation for a beef stew, while Jazz rolled out pie dough and made two apple pies to go into the oven.

~

Georgia placed the stew on the stove to cook while she and Lily dressed for church. She plaited Lily's black hair into four pigtails and tied ribbons at the end of each to match her floral-print dress. Sam said she was as pretty as a pup, which made her giggle.

"When do you think we might get a puppy for the farm? I sure would like to have one." Lily twisted as her mother worked on her hair.

"I tell you what, Miss Lily, I will start asking my customers if they have a mama dog with a batch of puppies to give away this week," Cole said.

"This farm could use a dog to alert us to strangers. Besides, I have always wanted a puppy, but my mama would never allow me to have one," Jazz added.

"Let's all be ready to leave in thirty minutes. We don't want to be late," Cole said as he entered the bedroom.

As Cole closed the door, Jazz eased over to Georgia and whispered, "I'm not looking forward to this morning, Georgia. Cole's mother will be there and some other ladies who don't care for me. I hope no one will embarrass Cole."

"Think of it as one giant step into the community as a married woman. Cole will be right beside you." Georgia patted her shoulder and hurried into her bedroom to dress.

~

Reverend Harrington stood on the front porch and welcomed everyone. "Good morning, Mr. and Mrs. James. I was praying that you would come, and here you are. The service will begin in a few minutes so go inside and take a seat."

Dressed in black widow weeds, as Cole described her dress, Jazz was still a beautiful woman any man would be proud to have sitting beside him. A small black veil covered her blond curls. Her cheeks were rosy, but tears clouded her beautiful eyes. Cole patted her hand and looped it through his arm, pulling her closer than was proper in church. He didn't care.

~

When it was time to sing a hymn, Jazz's voice rose like a songbird. People surrounding them in the pew turned to see who had the beautiful voice. Several men smiled and nodded while the women punched their husbands to face the front. Though the entire church service, Jazz managed to maintain a straight back and an impassive expression, but inside she was so angry at those spiteful ladies who were staring at her she didn't hear a word of the preaching. Jazz glanced numerous times at Cole who met her eyes with a sweet smile.

When the service was over, her insides were in a boiling rage, and she could barely offer a word to anyone. Cole whispered to her that he was going to get the wagon and would meet her out front. As she stood and began to step into the aisle, one of the ladies who had come into the dress shop blocked her exit.

"You have your nerve coming into this church. You're nothing but a slut who was married to a bank robber and murderer. Just because you managed to snatch the most eligible bachelor in town doesn't change what you are."

Reverend Harrington moved between them. "Mrs. Meriwether, please step aside and allow Mrs. James to go and meet her husband. I'm surprised at the words you said to this lovely young woman. I believe your husband will have something to say about the vile, vicious words that you were spewing to another in God's house." His eyes dared the woman to say another word.

"How dare you threaten me. My husband pays your salary, so you'd better be careful how you talk to me. You just wait until I tell him how you took up for that woman and embarrassed me." She whirled around, bumped into several people standing in the aisle, and rushed out the front doors of the church.

"Go on home, folks, and pray for some of our members that

they will soon have love for each other," the pastor said to the onlookers. Jazz watched as everyone filed down the aisle and out to their waiting horses and buggies.

"Thank you so much, Reverend Harrington. I am so sorry that Mrs. Meriwether hates me so much. As far as I know, I have never done anything to her. I told Cole that people were not ready for me to come." She had more to say, but she restrained herself for Cole's sake.

"Mrs. James, you did nothing but come to worship in God's house. Please don't apologize. We must pray for people like her. I am sure her husband will have a lot to say about her actions."

As he started walking up the aisle, she stopped him. "Please don't make trouble because of me. She doesn't need any more reason to dislike me."

"All right. I won't be the one to tell him, but I am sure this little scene will be told and retold among the townspeople. He will hear it, and if he comes to me, I will explain that you had nothing to do with her behavior." The pastor walked her to the door.

"Jazz, what happened? I have been waiting for you," Cole said, a worried expression covering his handsome face.

"It's my fault, Mr. James. I was talking to your wife." Reverend Harrington escorted her down the porch steps.

Once the couple was on their way to pick up Georgia, David, and Lily, Cole said, "Guess what?" Before Jazz answered, he continued. "I talked to Mr. White, and he said that his dog has ten puppies. He wants to find them a good home. I told him I would take a girl and boy pup. Might as well get one for you and one for Lily. How does that sound?"

"Oh, Cole. Are they weaned from the mother? When can we bring them home?" The thought of a new puppy made her feel calm once again.

"Hold on there. One question at a time," he responded, laughing. "We are going to pick up the others and stop at the Whites' farm on the way home. The puppies are pulling the mama down, so he wants us to come for them today. You and Lily can have the pick of the litter."

"What a surprise for Lily. She'll be so happy." Jazz moved closer to Cole, and he looked pleased that just maybe she was relaxing around him like a wife should. "Jazz, I have to go out of town Tuesday. I was going to tell you, but I kept forgetting. There is a display show, or some call it a convention, in Dallas for businesspeople, mostly store owners. I go every year, and this helps me to keep up with the latest gadgets. There are tools and utensils that help make farm work and housework easier. I would love for you to go with me maybe next year, if . . . well, maybe next year."

"How long will you be gone?" Jazz asked as she looked at Cole.

"Maybe a week at the most. I will be traveling on the train. It will make many stops, but it's better than the stage."

"After the puppies are settled, I'll pack your clothes for the trip. I want you to have everything you need in good repair."

"I appreciate that. Thank you," Cole said, as he pulled the horse to a stop. The girls and David were waiting at the edge of the churchyard. He waited while David helped Georgia and Lily into the wagon.

Chapter 28

The house seemed so empty, knowing Cole wouldn't be coming home for a while. While he was gone, Jazz wanted to make his home more inviting and comfortable. She added crocheted doilies on the two tables and the dresser and placed a vase of the last wildflowers of the season in the center of the dining room table. Then she made a heavy tick to lay over their mattress to make it more comfortable and covered it with a piece of solid blue material. The following day she gathered all his dirty laundry, and she and Georgia washed and ironed all his shirts and pants that he worked in at the store.

Sometime later, the two ladies and Lily took an accounting of all the scrap material that they had. With Christmas coming, Jazz wanted to make some cloth dolls for the women's group in town. "Georgia, I want to make a little family of dolls for Lily without her knowledge. She plays so much by herself she needs little friends. What do you think?"

"You are so sweet. She will love all of them. Let's tell her the dolls are for other poor children."

"She can help pick out the dresses, pants, and shirts for the dolls. Let's ride into town tomorrow and purchase everything we need to make a whole bunch of small rag dolls. We don't need to tell Mrs. James, and after we complete them, we can let Cole take them to the church. I know the reverend's wife will give them to the needy children."

Once the girls were back from town, Jazz collapsed on the soft grey couch and sighed. "That was an experience for sure. I am so happy that Herman was the only person in the store, and he didn't seem interested in what we were going to do with all the small pieces of materials, buttons, black and yellow yarn, and embroidery thread."

"I will make some sandwiches to go with the leftover soup for supper. Sam and David won't mind as long as it's enough." She laughed as she watched Lily stretch out in front of the fire.

Jazz took a candle from the mantel and touched it to the orange flames twitching in the fireplace. She walked over to the linen closet and gathered a fresh towel, bath cloth, and scented soap. After the water was warmed, she stepped into the tub. The water felt heavenly running down between her heavy breasts.

Her teeth held the corner of the washcloth as she lifted her hair and pinned it on top of her head. The bath was wonderful. She took her time because she wasn't worried about Cole entering the room. Jazz ran her hand down over her stomach and patted it. Her baby was growing so fast and she was getting bigger each day.

A soft knock on the door, and Georgia peeked in. "Here, let me help you out of the tub."

She hesitated and then stood, allowing Georgia to wrap her in the big soft towel. "You are a jewel, my friend. My bath was lovely, but it is getting harder to climb in and out of the tub. Right now my life is a mess. I don't want to be a burden to anyone, especially to Cole. I am hoping that once this child arrives," she said as she patted her belly, "that I will be able to get a job and take care of my child."

"Now, Miss Jazz, Mr. Cole goin' to be caring for both of you. He ain't never goin' let you go anywhere. That man is head over heels in love with you."

"Oh, Georgia, you know how we came to be together. He didn't feel like he had any choice but to marry me. Cole all but said that he would do anything to keep that nasty doctor's hands off me."

"Now, Miss Jazz. Mr. Cole could have done several different things, but he chose you. No one could have made him marry you if he hadn't wanted to do it."

"The closer the time comes to have my baby will tell how he really feels about me. I'm going to be as big as a barrel soon, and he's going to wonder what he was thinking when he decided to marry me."

"You ain't never goin' to make me believe that nonsense."

~

After a few days of missing Cole, Jazz needed to get out of the house for a while. She hurried to the barn and took the two puppies out of their small cage. The puppies cuddled in her lap and licked each other. Lily had named her girl pup, Rosie, and she named her boy dog, Pip. Both of the puppies were adorable. As Jazz held them in her lap, she heard a wagon coming into the yard. She quickly placed the puppies back in their cage and wiped her hands on the front of her apron.

An unkempt man was riding a horse beside the wagon while another large Black man sat in front holding the reins. The man yelled at the wagon full of Black men to keep still and remain quiet or they would be sorry.

Sam appeared from the back of the barn, but seeing the wagon, he motioned for David to stay in his new room in the barn.

"What can we do for you?" Sam asked the man who remained on his fine-looking stallion.

"I need to water my horse and these mules that are pulling my wagon. If you have any food to spare for me, I would appreciate it, too," the man said.

"You can water your animals over by the bar. How many men do you have in need of food?" Sam walked closer to the wagon and saw that the men were chained together with irons on their wrists. "Why are these men in chains? Are you the law?" Sam asked.

"We're his prisoners, but we ain't his slaves," A young man yelled. "He stole us off Master Wainwright's plantation where we worked as freed men."

"Shut your mouth, you fool. You'll be sorry once we get to the auction block in Dallas." The man leapt down off his horse and hit the young man with a short whip.

Sam reached inside the barn door and grabbed his rifle. "Man, you'd best not hit another person while you are here on my property. I don't tolerate that kind of behavior on man or beast."

"Sorry, fellow. I just lost my temper. Some of these men are liars, and they love making trouble for me. Now how about giving me something to eat?"

"Why don't you allow your men to get down and sit in my barn, out of the cold? You can go in the house with me, and my cook will prepare some bread and cheese for your bounty. That's the best we can do on short notice."

The man growled at the driver of the wagon, "Luther, you all stand and file into the barn. Sit in a circle and keep your mouths shut. Remember, I have eyes in the back of my head, and the first one of you steps out of line will die a quick death." He grinned through yellowed teeth at Sam and leered at Jazz as she led him into the living room. He hurried over to the fireplace and held out his hands in front of himself. "This is a nice place. I sure can use some grub."

"Have a seat in the rocker while I prepare you some hot soup and coffee." Jazz felt unsettled having this terrible man in her house. She needed to help those poor men who were chained. Tears clouded her eyes, so she looked away from the man so he didn't see her eyes turning red.

Jazz recognized the man as being a Yankee carpetbagger who stole the freed men who wandered the countryside searching for jobs. This evil man sitting in her rocker seemed to have stolen the wagon full of men out of the fields of a plantation. The owner probably had no idea where his hired hands had gone off to.

She was not going to allow those men to go another mile with this mean old man. With a shaky hand, she reached into the cabinet and took down the laudanum and laced a cup of coffee with a double dose. This amount of medicine would put him into a deep sleep, if it didn't kill him. Sam and David could set the men free while the man was unconscious for hours. Pulling Georgia aside, she whispered the plan and told her to tell Sam to get busy unfastening the men's chains.

Jazz called the man to come and sit at the table. "Please be careful with the coffee. It's very hot. I hope you like vegetable soup and cornbread."

"Lady, this is a feast," the man said as he looked Jazz and Georgia up and down.

~

Georgia carried four loaves of fresh bread and a large block of cheese outside. She carried her knife and set the items down on Cole's table in the barn.

After slicing the bread, David passed each man a big helping. Sam passed a bucket of fresh water, and each shared the dipper. The men thanked him.

David watched the door while Sam told the men he was going to use the large wire cutters and break the chains that held them together. The men appeared thrilled to learn that they would be free, as long as they didn't get caught by the man who held them prisoner

One of them warned Sam, "Sir, if that man comes out and catches you trying to free us, he will kill you and a couple of us too. I never knew a meaner man."

Sam assured him that David was standing guard, and nothing was going to happen to them while they were on Miss Jazz's farm.

David and Sam worked and worked, but the chain was too heavy for the only tool that they could find in the barn. Suddenly,

Jazz came running from the house with the key in her hand. "Hurry, unlock the irons on their wrists and then the chains. I put sleeping medicine in that crazy ole fool's food, and he's sleeping like a baby in front of the fireplace. You'll have to hurry and get as far from here as possible."

In just a few minutes, all the men were free and ready to leave the barn. Suddenly, David stopped them. He told them the old man was staggering off the front porch.

"I need to pee," he said loud enough for everyone in the barn to hear.

The footsteps stopped and the old man fell face down in the front yard. Sam rushed to him and led him to the outhouse. He propped a board under the door handle and rushed back to the barn.

"Hurry, and God go with you," Jazz said, as she shook each man's hand as they filed out of the barn.

"Will you all be safe with that man? Remember, he's bad," one of the men said.

"Sam and David will take him to the sheriff. We'll be fine." The three stood in the barn doorway and watched as the men veered off to the side of the farm into the deep forest.

Sam shook his head. "You know, all three of us have had bad times in our lives, but we are fortunate to live on this farm and have Cole James as our protector. Please say a prayer of thanksgiving tonight and ask God to lead those men home to their loved ones."

~

Sam led the evil man's mules and wagon out of the barn. "Jazz, I am going to take the old man into town while he is still asleep. I'll chain him up like he did the men. Hope the sheriff will do the right thing and place him in jail, but he might not."

"As long as you have him chained, he can't chase the men he held as prisoners. Maybe they will have time to get far away from this place."

Sam drove the old man into town and went straight to the livery. "Hey, Mr. Carter. I have a wagon and four mules for you to take care of for this prisoner I have chained in the back. When he gets freed, if he can't pay you for all your trouble, then you just keep the wagon and mules. I 'm going to drive him to the sheriff's office, and then I'll bring this wagon and mules back to you. I am hoping the sheriff will keep him in jail."

"What did this fellow do?" Mr. Carter questioned as he looked in the bed of the wagon at the old man, who was snoring loudly.

"The carpetbagger stole a dozen freed men off the plantation field they were working on and planned to sell them at a slave auction."

"Slavery is over. Where has this fool been?" Mr. Carter asked.

"The old buzzard had the nerve to stop at Cole's farm and ask for food for himself. He got upset when Miss Jazz wanted to feed his wagonful of prisoners, but that didn't stop her. She invited the old man into the house and dished him a hot meal. While he was eating, she laced the man's coffee with a sleeping drug. While he lay cozy in front of the fireplace, David and me helped the men escape."

"God bless her heart. That old man is going to be spitting mad when he wakes up in jail." Carter laughed.

After thirty minutes, Sam was walking down the road back to the farm. He had forgotten to take a horse for himself. Pulling his heavy coat up around his neck and cussing under his breath for being so dumb, he looked up to see David towing a mule behind him.

When the giant reached him, he smiled broadly. "Miss James said you forgot to take a ride home. I told her we would hurry right back, so let's get moving."

Chapter 29

A couple of days after Cole returned from his trip to Dallas, he was busy at the store, mostly answering customers' questions about the situation that had taken place with the wagonful of prisoners. Of course, he was proud of Jazz, Sam, and David for rescuing the men from the hands of the Yankee carpetbagger. They all rejoiced when the traveling judge sentenced him to five years of hard labor.

With Christmas only a few days away, he was pleased that all the dolls Jazz and Georgia had made were sold. Every little girl who came in the store begged for one. The little cream-faced dolls with freckles and blond or brown yarn hair were big sellers. He'd have to ask the ladies to make more dolls for the display window.

He stocked all the shelves with the supplies he'd purchased while on the trip and was pleased that his mother had hired Lulu Merriweather, a sixteen-year-old girl, to help with the customers. Lulu was excited about earning extra money for her family. Her ability to wrap beautiful packages was a blessing for the men who purchased gifts, their purchases ready to be placed under their Christmas trees.

Cole picked out a navy winter coat for Georgia, a bright red coat for Lily, and a dark dress suit for Sam to wear to church. He selected a large, colorful poncho for David because there wasn't a coat in the store to fit him. While in Dallas, he had chosen a long black cape for Jazz with a warm fur hat and gloves to match. He hoped she would be pleased with his selection. Lulu wrapped all his gifts before he left the store.

He gathered several jars of pecan pieces Mrs. Jackson had brought in to sell. The ladies could make pecan pies for Christmas dinner dessert. He grabbed a handful of peppermint sticks, a bag of oranges, and a box of delicious red apples, then carried all his items to his wagon parked behind the store.

The clouds were hanging low, looking like it was going to snow. A white Christmas would be perfect this year. He wanted to hurry home and pick out a large Christmas tree. Sam and David could place it in a bucket of dirt and water it really well until they were ready to trim it.

"So, Cole, it looks like you aren't going to come and spend Christmas dinner with me. You have half the store already packed in your wagon." Cole's mother stood with her arms crossed and her face red.

"Mama, I will be very happy to pick you up and bring you out to my farm. Jazz would enjoy having you join us for dinner." Cole had not discussed the invitation over with the girls, but he was sure Jazz wouldn't object.

She was so surprised to have been invited to dinner that she hemmed and hawed. "Can I tell you tomorrow if I will join you?"

"That will be just fine. We can close the store at six on Christmas Eve and stay closed Christmas Day. I will have Sam or David come and pick you up in plenty of time for Christmas dinner. Then I will drive you home."

"We haven't ever closed that early, and we've always stayed open Christmas Day to help people who have forgotten something."

"This year will be different. I have already had Lulu print signs to place on the door and one behind the cash register. I have a life now, and I am going to celebrate this year with the ones I love." Cole turned and was placing the new items up on a shelf when Ruby from the tailor shop came in. "Hello, Mrs. Goodman. I was just thinking about you. What will you be doing Christmas Day? Do you already have plans?"

"The same thing I do every year. Sit in front of my picture window and watch the day go by." She sighed and smiled at Cole.

"Jazz and I are planning a big dinner, and we would love for you to come out and join us. I will be happy to send Sam out around three to pick you up, and he will bring you home afterward. Please say you'll come."

"Oh my, I don't know what to say."

"Say, yes, and we will see you on Christmas Day," Cole said.

"Yes, I must bring something, but right this moment I don't know what it will be. Oh, I am so happy that you invited me. Thank you from the bottom of my heart, and I will be ready."

~

Jazz and Georgia were busy baking pies and special breads for Christmas Eve and Christmas Day's dinner. While the desserts were baking, they were cocooned in their bedrooms completing their Christmas projects and wrapping the ones that were ready.

David and Sam were both busy in the barn. Hammering sounded from David's room. The smell of paint drifted into the house. A lot of laughter came from the barn.

At supper the day before Christmas Eve, everyone was very quiet. No one said a word about what they were doing. Lily was excited enough for all of them. "Do you think that old fat man will be able to find me since we've moved from town?"

Cole waited for Georgia or Sam to answer the child, but they didn't even look up from their supper plates. Finally, he said, "Lily, this old fat man who you are speaking of has special powers. He knows everything. Haven't you heard that he knows when girls and boys have been good or bad?"

Lily shook her head but didn't reply. Cole described the old man's powers. "Well, he knows where you have moved. I am sure that Old Saint Nick will be arriving very late Christmas Eve. But, you have to be asleep, or he won't leave anything if he knows you are awake and watching for him."

Everyone at the table stopped eating to watch the interaction between Cole and Lily, amused expressions on their faces. This was going to be a wonderful Christmas for all of them.

~

When Christmas Eve arrived, Cole pulled down the shade and locked the store's front door. He turned over the sign that read, "Closed until December 26th." He was pleased that he had taken a couple of hours off for lunch and had gone to the farm. With Sam's and David's help, the three of them carried in the lofty, fresh green Christmas tree. The girls were surprised and clapped their hands to see the tree was ready for them to decorate.

Lily danced all around the front room. She said that St. Nick would surely find her now that they had a beautiful tree all ready for him to place her presents under.

"The tree isn't ready yet, sweetheart," Jazz commented. "Once Cole arrives home, we will decorate it, but we can start making colorful paper chains and threading popcorn to place on the tree. We will place the candles on the tree last. Oh, what fun we're going to have this evening."

"Lily, you want to help me make special Christmas cookies to enjoy while we decorate tonight?" Georgia asked her little girl.

"Can I help decorate the cookies once they are taken out of the oven?" David asked.

"Oh, yes. I can help you with the afternoon chores so we will be ready when Mr. Cole arrives home," Lily said.

A few hours later, Lily rushed into the house and grabbed Georgia's hand. "Come, Mama, help me wash up, so I can help decorate cookies. I need to watch David. He might eat 'em all."

~

Cole drove to the barn and Sam helped him carry the

packages into the pantry until the Christmas tree was decorated. Laughing, both men hurried over to the kitchen table and grabbed a decorated cookie.

"Hey," Lily frowned. "Mama, you said David and I couldn't eat any of the cookies, and those two are gobbling them up."

"It's all right, child. You and David can each have one but only one." She laughed as she walked over to the stove and stirred the gravy.

"Look up, sweetheart," Cole said, grinning while holding a sprig of mistletoe.

Jazz whirled around and looked up and said, "What's that?"

"Mercy, girl, haven't you ever stood under mistletoe and been kissed by a special fellow?"

"No," she said as she dropped her chin.

"Well, look up at me," he said, waiting. When she did, he gave her a peck on her lovely pink lips. Everyone laughed and clapped.

"Merry Christmas, love." Cole smiled and helped himself to another cookie. He chuckled as Lily squealed.

Cole stood on one side of the tree and passed the paper chains and strings of popcorn to Sam. The two men circled and wound the strings up and down the tree limbs. Jazz held up the candles to be placed on the tree. They would light them after the Christmas dinner. David had cut out a wooden star and painted it white. He picked Lily up on his shoulders so she could place it on top.

Jazz wiped tears with her clean apron. "Why are you crying, Miss Jazz," Lily asked as she wrapped her little arms around her waist.

"This is the most beautiful tree in the whole world, and it belongs to us," she said, stooping down to look Lily in the face. "You know, this is my first tree."

~

Cole awakened to the sound of laughter. It was a wonderful sound which wasn't familiar to him. His parents never laughed. It was a pleasant noise, so he lay there and listened. He couldn't stop the big smile from spreading across his face.

Hurrying, he dressed as fast as he could and entered the kitchen, sniffing its sweet smells. Georgia and Jazz, still dressed in their night clothes, were taking honey buns from the oven. The large pot of coffee was sitting on the back of the stove with several cups lined up on the counter.

"Good morning, ladies," Cole called. "It looks like you got up really early. I hope you didn't scare off St. Nick."

"No, we didn't run into him, but he certainly did come. Lily is going to be one happy little girl," Jazz said, as she rubbed her big belly.

"I can't believe Lily is not up. Let's all have a cup of coffee and then wake her up. You two need to dress while I go and wake up Sam and David. I know they want to watch Lily as she unwraps her presents from them."

Everyone was surrounding the tree as Lily came plodding into the living room. Her eyes widened at everyone watching her. Suddenly, she spotted the presents under the tree. To everyone's shock, the child covered her face and started crying.

"Goodness, child, why are you crying?" Georgia hurried to her little girl and gathered her in her arms.

"I prayed and prayed that the old fat man would come, and he did. I haven't been all that good, and I was afraid he would just pass me by."

"Oh, Lily, you are a special little girl, and you have been such a big help to me and your mama. St. Nick and the good Lord know what a blessing you are to all of us. Cole, Sam, and David love you very much, too." Jazz wiped away Lily's tears. "Now, sit down on the floor, and your mama will give you a present."

Lily plopped down on the floor and reached for a small package. "This present is from Cole and Jazz." Cole looked surprised but smiled at Jazz. Lily carefully unwrapped the present. "Oh my, look, Mama. I have a mama doll and a little girl doll that looks just like me. Oh, Miss Jazz, thank you so much. They're beautiful."

"This next present is from me," Georgia said to Lily, and this time Lily tore off the wrap.

"Goodness, now my new babies have clothes to wear. They will be the prettiest little girls in church." Lily held the dresses up to the mama doll and then to the baby.

Sam stood. "This present is from us, me and David."

Lily stood because their present was big and heavy. "What in the world can this be?" she asked with big eyes. She ripped the brown paper away from the white doll cradle and covered her mouth. "You made this?" she asked David and Sam. "Now I know why you wouldn't let me come in your room out in the barn. Oh, thank you both. My babies can sleep beside me when they aren't in my bed." She rushed over and hugged both men.

Both men blushed and smiled. "It's a little heavy, so we'll carry it in your bedroom when you're ready," Sam said, glancing over at David.

"There's another present for Lily from Jazz and me. I bought it while I was in Dallas. It's the present next to the wall," Cole said to David.

The long box was beautifully wrapped. Lulu had done a good job and made a big bow to go in the center of the brown paper. "It is a pretty box. I hate to mess it up by ripping it open," Lily said.

"Well, I can just keep it and let it stay under the tree," Cole teased.

"No, I'll open it," she said giggling, as she tore the paper.

Once the box was open, Lily couldn't touch the lovely red coat. Tears filled her eyes.

"Oh, Lily," Cole said, as he slid out of his chair down on his knees. "I didn't want to make you cry. Please, sweet girl, let's take this coat out of the box, and you try it on for me." He winked at

Georgia, whose mouth stood agape.

Cole stood Lily onto her feet and lifted the lovely red coat from the box. He slid it on each arm and pulled it around her chest. It was a perfect fit with a little growing room.

Lily swayed back and forth and finally twirled completely around. "Oh, Mama, look how pretty I am."

"What do you say to Mr. Cole and Miss Jazz?" Georgia managed.

"Oh, thank you and thank you," Lily said to Cole and Jazz.

Georgia pulled Lily into her arms and hid her head. "Thank you to everyone. Lily loves all her presents."

After everyone smiled at Lily, Jazz said, "Before we open any more gifts, why don't we have some breakfast. I am starved."

After the dishes were washed, everyone gathered around the tree again. "Lily, why don't you pass everyone their gifts, since you have opened all of yours."

"I will be happy to do that. This big one is for Mama, ain't that right, Mr. Cole?"

Once the present was opened, Georgia's lips trembled. Mr. Cole had bought her a long, navy-blue coat. "I've never had a new coat, or even an old hand-me down coat that was this beautiful. Oh, Mr. Cole, this is too nice."

"You deserve a new coat to wear. I didn't know that I needed help on my farm until you and Lily came to live with me. I am so happy that you like it." He watched Georgia as she tried the coat over her thin body. It was perfect.

Lily passed another present to Georgia from Jazz. It was a pretty calico dress and a new white shift to wear beneath it. "Mercy, I am going to be the best dressed lady at church. Oh me, I shouldn't have said that. What will God think about me bragging on my looks?"

Everyone Laughed as Georgia's face flamed bright red. "Lily, pass that box over to Jazz." All eyes turned to the big box that Lily set down in front of Miss Jazz. "Do you want me to help you open it?" Lily asked since Jazz didn't have a lap anymore.

"Please, untie the ribbon, and we both can lift the top off the box." Jazz was thrilled with the long black cape. It was beautiful and very warm. "There's more in the box," Lily said.

Jazz lifted the pretty fur hat and immediately placed it on her head. A perfect fit. Lily handed her another wrapped package that was in the bottom of the package. It was a pair of black fur-lined gloves.

Jazz stood and wrapped the cape around her shoulders. Cole stood and immediately attached the three big buttons at her neck. He straightened her hat and helped her slip on the gloves. It was a perfect fit, and he was thrilled that he had purchased these gifts for her. He wanted to pull her into his arms and kiss her breathless, but instead, he pulled her close and kissed her on the forehead. Then he whispered, "Merry Christmas, my love."

"Oh, Cole, I love these things, but you shouldn't have spent so much money."

"You are my wife, and I only want the best for you. Besides, you need these things. And I wanted our first Christmas to be special for everyone who lives with me."

"There are more gifts to give out, Mr. Cole and Miss Jazz. Please tell me which present to give now," Lily said.

"Those two presents are from me to David and Sam. The heavy one is for David and the other is Sam's," Cole said as he took his chair to watch the men open their gifts.

Sam was thrilled with his new suit." Now I can get married or buried or both in a nice suit of clothes," he declared as everyone laughed.

David opened his box and pulled out the colorful poncho. He held it up as if to say, "What is this?"

Cole jumped up and took the heavy poncho from David and instructed him to stand. He pulled the poncho over David's head and pulled it down in the back. It was a perfect fit, just like all the other gifts.

"Oh, Mr. Cole, I ain't never had anything so grand. You sure this is for me? Do I have to give it back when I leave?"

"Are you planning on leaving?" Cole asked, as Jazz and Georgia froze in place.

"No sir, unless you run me off. I like it here."

"I have to admit you gave me a scare. I thought you were planning on leaving. We don't want you ever to leave us. This is your home now. If I give you something, it is yours to keep."

David's smile said it all for Cole.

"Lily, please pass out my gifts to the men," Jazz said.

Each man opened their gifts that held long, warm knitted scarfs to wrap around their necks while outside. Cole's gift was embroidered handkerchiefs and two large dark brown aprons with his name embroidered across the top in bright gold thread—*Cole James* and under his name, *Proprietor*—in bright gold letters. On the front of the apron were two deep pockets. Also in his package was a lovely navy-blue knitted scarf to wear under his leather jacket.

Jazz stood in front of Cole just as he had done for her. She wrapped the scarf around his neck and made a loop in it. "Merry Christmas, my husband. These few things will never compare to what you have given me." She stood on her tiptoes and kissed his cheek. Suddenly, they both felt the baby kick as he held her close. Both of them looked surprised and suddenly laughed. "It seems that the baby is trying to tell us something," Cole said with a big grin.

Chapter 30

Christmas morning was a dreary, cold day. The white clouds hung low and were moving slowly. Sam looked at the sky and saw a flock of geese flying low, a good sign that snow was in the near future. He hoped it would hold off today because he had to drive back and forth to town. Mrs. Goodman and Cole's mama were going to join them for Christmas dinner, and afterwards he would be taking them home.

Everyone was inside baking and cooking for the big dinner. Cole had gone to the butcher's shop and bought a twenty-pound dressed turkey and a whole ham. Georgia had baked several skillets of cornbread yesterday to make the stuffing. Several pecan, and two apple pies were cooling on the back counter in the kitchen. Snap beans with bacon, mashed potatoes. and giblet gravy, pickled eggs, corn on the cob, and collard greens would round out the dinner.

After a quick lunch of cold sandwiches and fresh fruit, Sam and David along with Cole made easy work of all the afternoon chores. Sam dressed as warm as possible and drove to town for the ladies.

His first stop was to pick up Mrs. Goodman who needed him to help her carry a hot Mexican dish and a small Christmas gift. She brought a lap robe that would be used to keep them warm. The next stop was in front of James' Dry-Goods Store. Sam jumped down to assist Mrs. James up on the front bench beside Mrs.

Goodman. Mrs. James was empty-handed except for a large shawl that she was going to use to wrap around her head as they traveled.

"I had no idea that you were invited to my son's farm for dinner," Mrs. James said, sarcastically.

"I don't know why not. I have been a friend of your son since he was knee high. And besides, Jazz is a friend of mine, too. A lovely girl."

"Cole never mentioned knowing you before except as one of our customers. Of course, his wife worked for you for a while."

"You know, Milly, we were friends once. At least while Mr. James was alive. We had some good times together. It's a shame you have grown into such a bitter old woman."

"Sam, turn this wagon around this instant. I will not be traveling with this woman one more second," Mrs. James demanded.

"I'm sorry, Mrs. James. We're almost to the farm. Cole is standing on the front porch." In a few minutes, Sam stopped the team of horses as Cole took the lead horse's rein.

~

"Welcome, ladies, and Merry Christmas to you both," he called up to the passengers.

Both ladies allowed him to help them down from the wagon. Mrs. Goodman took her gift while Sam hurried inside with the hot dish of food. Mrs. James' square jaw jutted out, and her lips were tightly closed in a thin line.

"What's wrong, Mama? Don't say nothing because it is all over your face," Cole asked.

"I didn't know that witch was coming to your dinner or I wouldn't be here now. Although I instructed Sam to turn the wagon around and take me home, he wouldn't. Hope you're satisfied that I'm here."

"I am pleased that you came. Please, don't spoil our dinner with a bad attitude. It is Christmas, and everyone is happy today.

Do try to be your pleasant self for me, if not for anyone else."

"For you, and Christmas. No one else, so don't ask." Mrs. James stepped on the porch as Cole opened the door for her to enter.

Dinner was a big success. The ladies had set two tables which was fine with Georgia. She and Lily sat at a table with David while the others sat together. After all the dishes were washed, Jazz offered coffee and pie, which everyone enjoyed.

While sitting in front of the fireplace with the candles lit on the tree, Mrs. Goodman handed Lily her gift. "Lily, I hope you will enjoy this small Christmas present from me. While I was here before, I noticed you liked to read."

Lily opened the present, which was a book made out of material. Each page had a padded, colorful animal with a place at the bottom to write the animal's name. It had twelve pages. "Thank you so much. May I look at it now while I rock my babies to sleep?"

"Of course, you may. What nice manners you have, child." Mrs. Goodman smiled at Georgia. "You are raising a fine little girl."

Jazz pushed to her feet and handed a gift to Mrs. Goodman and one to Mrs. James. Cole kept staring at her with wide eyes while the ladies waited patiently for the other one to open her gift. Mrs. Goodman opened her present first which contained several embroidered hankies with her initials.

Mrs. James held her package until Mrs. Goodman had opened her present. She opened her gift and seemed so surprised to see her name embroidered in gold letters—*Milly James* and under it, *Proprietor*. There were two light brown aprons with deep pockets.

"What a thoughtful gift, Cole. I am surprised you had time to have these made while in Dallas."

"I didn't purchase your gift. Jazz made the aprons and did the embroidery herself, just for you. You need to thank her."

So softly, the people in the room could hardly hear, Mrs. James said, "My child, this is such a surprise. I wasn't expecting anything. Thank you for thinking of me. I will wear these with pride."

Jazz walked over to Mrs. James and gave her a hug and said she was so happy that she'd come to dinner. Mrs. James half hugged her back and looked down at her gift.

"I hate to have to leave good company, but Sam might better take me and Ruby back home. The weather looks like snow might be coming soon," Mrs. James said.

Mrs. Goodman appeared pleased that Milly had called her Ruby instead of Mrs. Goodman.

Sam hitched the horses while Jazz prepared a plate of food for the two ladies to take home with them. After a lengthy goodbye, the house was quiet for the first time all day. David had gone to his room in the barn, Georgia and Lily had retired to their room to get dressed for bed, and Jazz continued to sit in a rocker in front of the fire.

Cole rushed over and stood in front of the fireplace warming his hands. "What a cold day!" he said with a broad smile at Jazz. "Thank you so much for thinking of my mother. She really loved her aprons as I do mine. I had no idea that you made her a Christmas gift."

"Well, Cole. She's your mama, and no matter how she feels about me, I know you love her. I didn't know if you had already given her something at the store or not, so I wanted to do something special for her anyway. I am glad it pleased you."

"You please me in every way." Giving her a big smile, he said, "Merry Christmas, love." He leaned down and gave her a peck on the lips. He was surprised that she didn't back away from him. "I hope Sam makes it home soon. The weather is terribly cold, and now the wind is blowing pretty hard. Why don't you go on to bed? I am going to wait until Sam returns before I retire."

Chapter 31

The next morning, Cole was the first one up, dressed and ready to head to the store. He put on a pot of coffee and went outside to hitch up his horse and wagon. The ground was covered with a light snow, and all the water troughs were frozen over with a thin layer of ice.

David rushed out of the barn and took a shovel and crushed the layer of ice from the troughs. Sam had not appeared, but maybe he was sleeping a little later since he had been late getting to bed.

David and Cole went inside the house and greeted Georgia who was already dressed and slicing bread while the bacon sizzled in the skillet.

"Just slice me a large piece of that pecan pie, and I will be on my way," Cole said to Georgia. "I need to get to the store early, since we were closed yesterday. We'll surely have customers waiting for me to open, and Mama will be biting at the bit if I'm not there this morning."

"Don't you want me to pack you a lunch? We sure have a lot of leftovers—ham, turkey, and the like," she commented.

"No thank you, but I will be happy to have some of those leftovers for supper tonight. Please let Jazz sleep as long as she wants to this morning. The baby is sure growing, and she tires more easily." He stuffed his mouth with the pie as he wrapped his new scarf around his neck. Grabbing his coffee, he shot out the door.

~

Several hours later, Sam still had not come out of his room for breakfast. Jazz and Georgia had decided to handwash a few personal items and hang them in the pantry to dry since the air was freezing cold outside.

"Georgia, I believe I'll check on Sam. It is not like him to sleep this long. I'll knock on his door." Jazz dried her cold hands on a towel and walked down the hall to Sam's bedroom.

After several knocks when he didn't respond, Jazz slowly opened the door and stepped inside. "Sam?" she called to him. Still no answer.

Jazz walked to the bed and saw Sam cuddled under his covers shivering. "Oh Sam, you're freezing," she said. I need to warm a couple of bricks to go under his covers, she thought. She stepped in the kitchen with Georgia. "Sam is burning up with a fever. He's caught a very bad cold, and at his age it could turn into pneumonia. We need to warm him up. His sheets are soaking wet from the fever, so we need to change them right away."

Georgia placed several bricks in the oven while she mixed up hot tea with honey. She dashed it was a splash of whiskey and gave it a good stir. Then she retrieved fresh linens and several more quilts.

Jazz had wakened Sam and removed his wet union shirt. Georgia immediately removed the wet linens and remade the bed. She jerked off the bottom of Sam's union suit and quickly covered him. "David can redress him later with fresh underthings. But for now we want to get him dry and warm."

"Sam, sit up and open your mouth. You need to drink this toddy that I've made you. It will warm your innards," Georgia demanded.

Sam obeyed and nearly gagged, but Georgia held his mouth closed and he swallowed. He shook his head and tried to talk, but nothing came out.

"Good boy. Now lie back down and try to rest."

As he lay down, he had a coughing spell. Georgia patted him on the back and said, "That's good. Cough that mucus up."

Finally, exhausted, Sam laid his head back on the fresh pillowcase and seemed to ease into sleep.

All day the girls took turns checking on Sam. Several times, Georgia forced hot tea and honey down his throat. The drink helped with his coughing, but his fever was still high.

"Do we need to send for the doctor?" Jazz asked Georgia. "I hate sending for him without asking Cole first."

"Why don't we send David to the store with a note to Cole? He may have something for a fever at the store, or maybe he can call on the doctor for a prescription." Jazz continued to wipe Sam's forehead with a cold cloth.

~

A few hours later, Cole drove up into the yard with Doctor Richards riding his horse beside him. David rushed to the doctor to take his horse's reins and led him to the barn. "Thanks, David, the doctor won't be here long, but give his animal some water." Cole jumped down and signaled for the doctor to walk ahead of him to the porch.

Cole opened the door and called to the girls. Lily spotted the doctor first. She raced into Sam's bedroom and hid behind Georgia.

The girls rushed into the living room to see the doctor standing next to Cole.

"I asked Doctor Richards to come and look at Sam. I told him that he has a very bad cold," Cole commented as he led the doctor into Sam's room.

Jazz and Cole stood beside Sam's bed as the doctor opened his black bag, placed a stethoscope around his neck, and listened to Sam's heart. "His heartbeat is very weak." He took a thermometer and placed it in his patient's mouth. After taking it out, his read, "104."

Sam began to cough. Jazz sat behind him and held his shoulders up so he could cough without struggling. His body began to shake.

"This man is very sick. I must bring down his fever, and there is one good way to do it quickly. We can carry him outside and lay him in the snow and pour buckets of cold water over his body until he stops shaking."

He jerked the cover from Sam's body. Jazz gasped at the doctor's actions. Finally, she screamed, "Stop! Are you crazy? You're not going to take Sam out of this warm bed. You want to kill him?"

Cole didn't know what to say. He was sure Jazz was correct. "Do you have another idea that might help him?"

"Of course." He reached into his black bag and pulled out a jar. "I can place leeches over his body, and they can suck the fever until it is gone."

Jazz witnessed the jar of creatures slithering around in the quart jar. "Where in blazes did you go to medicine school? You will not take those nasty things out of that jar and put them on Sam."

"Listen to me, your husband asked me to come out and help this old man. The only other thing left for me to do now is to bleed him. Bleeding is the last thing I like to do because it makes a body very weak."

"You said his heartbeat is already weak." Jazz shook her head and glanced over at Cole. "Doctor, Georgia and I will nurse Sam until he is well. Please pack your instruments and go back to your other patients, if you have any that are still alive. Thank you for coming out today. Cole, please see the doctor to the door."

Jazz stood at the bedroom door as Doctor Richards murmured that the old man was going to die if she wouldn't let him help. He stormed pass Jazz and hurried out the front door. Cole followed him as David brought his horse from the barn, and Cole gave the doctor a few dollars.

"I shouldn't take this, since I wasn't allowed to help the old man. Your wife is surely going to kill him. Good day."

Cole and David watched the doctor ride back toward town. "How is Sam, Mr. Cole?" David asked.

"Better for sure, since my wife wouldn't let the doctor touch him." Cole laughed and entered the house.

~

For several days and nights, Jazz and Georgia continued bathing Sam with alcohol baths to cool him. Feeding him chicken broth and hot tea toddies worked, and Sam's fever finally broke. He was weak, but he could sit in front of the fireplace where Lily treated him like he was her patient. She and her new family of dolls kept him company while Jazz and Georgia cooked, washed, and ironed.

Jazz needed to make her baby a quilt. Georgia helped cut squares from leftover dress materials. Sam helped by passing squares of material to Jazz as he sat with her. Every day he slowly became stronger.

As Jazz whipped pieces together, she sneezed and began coughing. Georgia jumped out of her rocker and placed a hand on Jazz's forehead. "Good Lord, child, you have a fever. Put that material down and let me help you into bed. You can't be too careful now that you're getting close to giving birth. I believe you caught a nasty cold from Sam." Then she winced when she realized how that must have come out.

"Oh my, I hope she don't get sick because of me. I'll just die if she becomes ill, like my wife and two children who died of malaria so many years ago," Sam said.

"Please, Sam, don't fret over me. I only feel tired—maybe a little warm, but I was sitting in front of the fireplace. I'm not sick enough to go to bed." Jazz continued sewing material together.

"Do you want me to call Cole in from the barn? He will carry you into that room and tuck you in bed himself." Georgia pointed at the couple's bedroom.

Jazz sighed and knew not to continue arguing with her friend. "I am only going to lie down for a while." Before she could finish complaining, she started coughing again. She had to admit her chest hurt, and she felt like she had something in her throat.

~

Lily barged into the barn, her doll tucked under her arm. Cole glanced up. "What is it, Lily?"

"Mama said you need to go see Miss Jazz. She's in the bedroom with Sam's cold." She shrugged and trailed a finger along the wooden rail.

Jazz was undressing when Cole barged into the bedroom. She gasped and pulled her robe to cover her, but the gap was enough for him to see the gentle swell of her breast. He needed to look away, but he couldn't. Cole wanted to run his fingers down her smooth skin and rip away the gown. Finally, he cleared his throat and said, "Georgia said that you caught Sam's cold. How do you feel?" He honestly didn't know how long he could stand staring at her without rushing over and taking her in his arms.

As Jazz slipped her gown all the way down over her large stomach, a coughing fit overcame her. She had to sit down on the bed and cover her mouth.

"Here, let me help you into bed."

As he reached for her, Georgia entered and handed him a glass of cold water. "Have her drink this before she stretches out on the bed."

He turned to Georgia. "Maybe you'd better make her a toddy with hot tea and honey only."

"Yes, sir. I will do it right away." She hurried into the kitchen.

"Sweetheart, how do you feel?" Cole was beside himself with concern for his wife and baby.

"I am a little achy and tired, but otherwise, I feel fine. I did start sneezing a while ago. But, I didn't start coughing until just a few minutes ago." Jazz smiled weakly.

"Between Georgia and myself, we'll give you great care and help you get back on your feet. You must do as we ask because you have our baby to think about too."

"*Our* baby?" Jazz smiled at Cole as she rubbed her hand across her belly.

"I told you before we married that your child will be mine. I already love this baby," he said as he rested his hand over hers on her stomach.

"I would like to take a short nap now." Jazz closed her eyes.

~

Several days passed before her fever broke and her appetite returned. Cole never left her side for long. The moment she was awake, he was there. The moment she turned over, coughing, he was there to assist her, beckoning her to cough up the mucus. She found smiling difficult at times, but when she did, he grinned back at her. How he could stay away from work, she didn't ask, but when she awakened to find Georgia at her bedside, she was a tad disappointed. Her heart skipped when she heard him in the next room. She was always impatient to see him. When had she started feeling this way about him?

Georgia brought in a plate of chicken and dumplings with a lot of hot broth. "Eat as much as you can," she instructed. "We need to build up your strength. That baby of yours has been moving around a good bit. I believe it is a boy."

"I do feel better. Wish I could have a good hot tub bath. Do you think I might be able to wash my hair?"

"Not for a day or two more. Don't want you to have a relapse and catch a chill," Georgia said. "I can help you change into a fresh nightgown and place a ribbon in your hair after I comb it for you. That should make you feel human again." Georgia laughed as left to serve Sam, David, and Lily lunch.

Jazz was back to herself but far behind in her preparations for her baby. Georgia helped her hem flannel for diapers, make small blankets, and take a drawer from the chest to pad and make a bed. Cole had assured them that the store had anything they might have forgotten.

~

Cole was working on the back porch of the store when he decided he needed to close in part of the side wall to help keep the supplies dry when it rained. He entered the store and stopped. Herman was holding his mother's hair back while he was kissing her neck.

Fury like he had never felt before flowed through his body. "I thought you two had more brains in your love-sick heads than to be standing in the middle of the store smooching like two lovesick kids."

Mama jumped away like she'd been caught. "How dare you speak to me like that? We aren't smooching. Herman was telling me a secret that he didn't want anyone else to hear."

"Really? Who were you expecting to hear your so-called secret, since there's no one else in the store?" Cole waved his hand around. "Herman, why don't you share your secret with me?" Cole smirked.

"It's not a secret one would share, Cole. Besides, it's none of your business," his mama snapped.

"Fine, but let me tell you both something. If I find you in each other's arms again, I will toss you, Herman, out on your butt.

and Mama, you will soon earn the name, 'hussy.' Take your pick."

"Well, I never!" Mama pushed past both men and hurried into her bedroom.

"Herman, if you want to continue to work in this store, you'd best keep your hands and lips to yourself. I came in here to ask you to go to the lumberyard and pick up some 2x4 boards, so we can close in the side of the porch. Choose about twenty boards and hurry back." Cole whipped around. Who did this man think he was?

~

Herman watched Cole walk outside. He tapped on Mrs. James bedroom door. When she answered, he said, "After Cole leaves to go home, I will return. We can finish our...discussion." Grinning, he let his fingers brush over her breasts.

Mrs. James grabbed his hand and giggled, blushing bright red.

Chapter 32

Herman watched from the window of the rooming house to make sure Cole had left town. He grinned to himself as he rubbed some sweet-smelling hair tonic through his dark wavy hair. Donning his brown jacket over his vest and clean shirt, he hurried down the back alley to the mercantile. He tapped lightly on her door. Milly James was waiting for him. She had removed her beige apron and placed it on the rack next to Cole's.

"Come in, Herman," Milly said, sniffing his tonic as he walked into the room. "We'll continue our morning conversation in my bedroom, if you don't mind. I don't want anyone to see us through the display window."

As she led the way into her bedroom, she closed the heavy curtain as Herman grabbed her from behind. He slid one hand up on her face and the other over her firm breast. "I have been waiting for that son of yours to leave for over an hour. Just the thought of touching your body has driven me nearly crazy," he said, swallowing a laugh.

"Now, Herman, I hope I haven't given you the wrong impression." She didn't attempt to move but pressed her body into his. It had been years since a man touched her in such an intimate way.

"Never, my dear woman. You are above reproach, and I wouldn't do anything that you didn't like." He released her so she could turn and face him. "It's just that I want us to be together out in the open. I want people to know that you're my woman."

"Oh, my goodness, Herman, are you asking me to marry you?"

Sucking in a deep breath, he stuttered, "Not right at this minute. I need you to buy your son's half of the store so we can run it together. He loves that old farm of his, and I'm sure if you offer him enough, he'd gladly accept. Why wouldn't he? He would be rid of the store and you."

"And me?" She looked total shocked. "Why . . . why Cole loves me. We may not always agree, but I believe with all my heart that he cares deeply for me. For gosh sakes, I'm his mother." She jerked out of his hold and muttered, "I can't believe you would even suggest that."

"Milly, my love, I didn't mean to hurt you, but surely you know how much he loves that little tart he married. Maybe one time he loved you, but that gal is going to have a baby. You can see that he doesn't have time for you anymore." He could tell that she was considering what he'd just said. "Hellfire, woman, he hates the sight of me because he knows I care for you. Cole doesn't want you to marry."

"Maybe he has a reason for disliking you." She held up her chin and looked him in the eye.

"What reason does he have?" Cole sure didn't know that it he who had set his wheat fields on fire.

"I don't know, but I will ask him—you can bet on that." Tilting her chin up, she said, "I can remarry or go to China if I like. I don't have to have my son's approval."

~

As Cole traveled to his farm, the fury inside him grew. The thought of that weasel, Herman, cozying up to his mother made his blood boil. The man was sneaky and a thief, too. He knew the disappearance of his inventory of ammunition was still unaccounted for. When he asked his mother if she had sold some, she shrugged and said she would've written any sale in the ledger.

Canned meat and fresh loaves of bread were missing, too. Cole wondered if the man was eating in his room to save money. What was Herman up to? Cole hadn't asked enough questions when he hired him, but now he was going to check on his background. He would ask the sheriff to question Mrs. Browning at the boardinghouse. That nosy woman knew everything about all her boarders.

When he arrived at the farm, David met him with a dismayed face. "Oh, Mr. Cole, I'm sure happy you're home. Miss Jazz is not feeling so good."

"Has she been very sick?" He climbed down from his wagon but didn't give David time to answer. "Take care of the supplies while I check on her."

With Christmas over and January and February passed, Cole was sure it was approaching Jazz's time to have her baby. Hurrying into the house, he saw Jazz moving slowly around in the front room. Lily was playing with her dolls at the dining room table, while Georgia was peeling potatoes in the kitchen. Everything looked normal, until he saw Jazz grab her stomach and bend over.

"Sweetheart, what's going on? David said that you have been feeling bad."

"Bless his heart. I have been having back pains, but it feels good to walk. Oh, my goodness," Jazz doubled over nearly to her knees. Water puddled at her feet.

"Georgia!" Cole yelled.

Georgia rushed from the kitchen. "Her time is near, Mr. Cole. You'd best ride over to Mildred's shanty and bring her here. She's my friend and she's a midwife."

"I'd better send for Doctor Richards." Cole wanted the best for his wife.

"No." Jazz doubled over in pain and practically screamed. "I would rather die than let that old fool touch me. Go, send Sam or

183

David after the midwife. Georgia has already made arrangements with her."

"But, Jazz, surely Doctor Richards has delivered many babies. I won't leave you alone with him. Of course, I wouldn't let him hurt you."

"Do you want him to cut me open to deliver the baby or put leeches on my back or bleed me? That man is crazy." Jazz wouldn't even look at Cole as Georgia began preparing their bed for the birthing.

"Please, Mr. Cole, send for Mildred. I promise you she knows what to do. She has delivered hundreds of babies, black and white."

Cole rushed out the front door and sent David on his way to pick up the midwife. Hurrying back in the house, he noticed Jazz was carrying the big tub into their bedroom, humming away.

"For gosh sakes, Jazz. Let me carry that thing. Please go and lie down." Cole practically yelled.

"Now, look what you have done. You have made Lily cry. I want to take a bath. If you want to help, go and heat some buckets of water."

"You're going to take a bath. Now?" Sweat was running down Cole's face.

"Yes. Are you going to help, or do I need to carry the water myself? Maybe you should go to the barn with Sam. I am sure he has a jug that you two can share."

Touché. She was probably remembering their wedding night. Cole could not believe the words coming from the sweet woman he knew. She sounded like an old fishwife. He hoped that she had forgiven him for his actions on their wedding night, but obviously she had not forgotten. Cole sighed and rushed out of the room. He grabbed two empty buckets and headed out to the well.

"Mr. Cole, I'll bring the water into the kitchen. You go on back to Miss Jazz," Sam said.

"I feel safer out here. My precious wife is not herself right now."

"Would you be if your body was going to be torn apart?" Sam shook his head and took the buckets from Cole.

"Guess you have a point. I've never been around a woman who was preparing to give birth. You're right, I'd better go back inside and try to calm her fears."

"Just go along with whatever she wants and don't question her."

Sam dropped the second bucket down the well.

"You sound like you have experience."

"My wife gave me two beautiful babies while she was alive. They all died from malaria years ago. I held her hand until the baby started coming. Nearly fainted. The ladies pushed me out of the room."

"David should be back soon with the midwife. Is there anything I can do now to help Jazz?"

"Just assure her that you are near. Georgia may need an oilcloth and old sheets to cover the bed. You could ask her." Sam grabbed the two buckets of water. Cole opened the door and helped place the water on the stove. He looked in on Jazz, who was still milling around the bedroom. "The water is heating, and it will be ready in a minute. Can I do anything more for you?" The bed was ready for the birthing. A small pan was on the nightstand, and baby clothes lay on a chair. A clean gown and robe were hanging on a peg next to the bed.

"It looks like Georgia has everything ready. David should be back soon with the midwife. Please, Sweetheart, know that I will be very near. I will stay with you and hold your hand if you want me to."

"Oh, Cole. You are so dear. Thank you for everything. Just knowing you are in the next room is a great comfort to me."

Cole couldn't believe the change of attitude Jazz had toward him.

David arrived with Mildred, the midwife. Jazz was

comfortable in her bed with Cole sitting beside her. Suddenly a muffled sound came from Jazz's lips. The pains had begun. Georgia asked Cole to step in the other room so Mildred could check her.

While he stood in the kitchen, Jazz moaned in pain and mumbled something, too deep for him to comprehend. He wished he had some knowledge of human birthing. His animals didn't make that much noise. Jazz's cries increased in strength. Once, he heard her call for Joe; his heart fell.

Between the pains, she seemed to lie quietly. Cole came in and sat beside the bed, watching as the contractions built and the pain increased. Someone had told her to scream if the pain became unbearable. With each cry of pain, he held his breath. Georgia ordered him out of the bedroom as she and Mildred prepared for the birth.

As he stood near the bedroom door, his thoughts were only of Jazz, the baby having no part in his thoughts. What seemed like hours passed before the wailing of the baby came. Cole felt his love for Jazz grow.

When he didn't hear Jazz's voice, his shoulders lurched and his head fell forward. "Please God, don't let me lose my love. Let her be all right."

Finally, the door opened, and Georgia stood with the baby wrapped in her arms. "Cole, you have a son."

Cole smiled down at the child. He was happy for Jazz. She had a son to remember Joe by, but this child would be his in every other way. He would love and protect him as if he were his own.

"Can I see her?' he asked, as the baby's gusty cry brought a sense of wonder to him. He sat down in a chair and held out his arms to take the baby.

"You can see Jazz in a while. Mildred is cleaning her up, and she has already fallen asleep." Georgia smiled down at Cole as he cuddled his son.

"Are they both all right?" He asked, even though he knew the baby had strong legs and all ten toes.

"Let me tell you something, Mr. Cole. Jazz is small, but she's tough. She bit through the piece of oak wood that I placed in her mouth. Now, don't worry. Mildred says they're as fit as a fiddle, both of them. Georgia looked down on Cole's face. "Mr. Cole, you're as pale as a porcelain bowl. Now she is not to lift anything other than the babe and keep to her bed for two weeks. Of course, I will be here to make sure she behaves herself, and I'm sure you will give her strict orders." Smiling, Georgia took the baby from Cole and went back into the bedroom.

It was late into the night when Sam took Mildred back to town. Cole had told her that he would make a bed for her, but she insisted that her young'uns would need her at first light.

David came out of his room in the barn and gave a small chuckle. "Mr. Cole, you look like you could have delivered that big healthy boy yourself."

"I guess it's not easy, seeing and hearing the one you love in so much pain, and you can't do anything to help but stand by and wait."

"I reckon that is the truth. Sure, glad it's over for that little lady."

"Me and you both."

Chapter 33

The next morning, when Jazz awakened, she felt as if she was in a foggy dream. She fell again into a heavy and deep sleep for long hours, only awakened when her son was brought to her to nurse. She only ate and drank when she was told to do so. The second day, as light filtered through the curtain, she awoke to the tiny, mewing sounds coming from the cradle. Cole had surprised her with the cradle a few weeks ago.

Looking around the room, she saw she was alone, except for her son who lay sleeping. The house was quiet as she listened for any sound coming from the other part of the house. Cole had not slept with her, so he must have slept on the couch or out in the barn.

She reached for the babe without leaving the bed. The boy was lying on his stomach trying to place his fist in his tiny mouth. Oh, you're so beautiful, she thought. He had dark black curls, just like his father, Joe. Sadness overflowed her body for a minute. She remembered how she and Joe had talked about having a baby, and now he would never see this beautiful bundle of joy.

Someone had asked her what she was going to name the baby. She had given names a lot of thought, but she never voiced any of them to Cole or Georgia. But now, the little one needed a name. Joe's real name was Jeffrey. She liked that, and he could be called Jeff. Cole's name was Coleman but his parents called him Cole. She liked the name Jeffrey Coleman James. Jazz was sure

Cole would like it too.

Suddenly, a sensation came over her as she cooed at the baby, remembering the man who claimed to love her. Cole, her husband, who had sat beside her for hours while she slept. She could still hear him praying for her.

A surge of doubt rushed into her thoughts. *Did she love Cole? But how could she?* Joe had only been gone for six months, and now she had just given birth to his child. She would never forget her first love. Joe was sweet and gentle with her, but he did want his way like a spoiled child. Cole wasn't anything like that, she thought. He wanted to give her everything and asked nothing in return. He was kind, generous to a fault, and protective. Both men expressed their love for her, but they were very different.

The first week brought a parade of people. Mrs. Goodman rented a buggy and brought several pies and some fresh baked rolls from the café. She had made a lovely baby blanket in soft green flannel. "Wasn't sure what color to make it, pink or blue, so I chose green," she said laughing.

~

Cole's mama asked to come home with Cole so she could see the babe. She brought several little dressing gowns and knitted booties. "Surely, you don't think to dress my son in a long gown?" he raised his eyebrows as he questioned his mother.

"All babies wear gowns at first. Later, I will buy him a complete cowboy suit, hat and boots. Will that satisfy you?" She actually smiled for the first time in a long time. Cole was pleased that she wanted to visit with Jazz.

Jazz was sitting up, wearing a new gown Cole had brought home from the store. Her hair was unbraided and flowing down her back. She flashed a radiant smile as Cole led Mrs. James into the room.

"My, you look like a picture of health. I am so happy that you are doing well. I brought you a small gift for the boy. If it's not to your liking, you can always exchange it for something else." Milly seemed a little nervous, since she had not been out to visit since Christmas.

"Oh, how kind of you, Mrs. James. I'm so pleased you came this evening. I'm sure Georgia will have dinner in a little while, and we would enjoy having you join us."

"I would like that. Thank you, but for now I'd like to see this boy." Mrs. James peered into the cradle as Jazz pulled back the new blanket.

"Mercy," Mrs. James chuckled. "Well, seeing this boy proves to me I was wrong." She chuckled and said, "I can tell this child isn't Cole's."

"What do you mean you were wrong?" Jazz asked, confused.

"When Cole married you, I figured he had already compromised you. What other reason would he have in marrying a loose woman?"

Cole couldn't believe what he had just heard come from her mouth. "Mama, you never change, do you? You are one mean-mouthed woman. I want you to know I married my wife because I fell in love with her from the first day she started working in our store. The first day I discovered that she had helped you back into your bed and cared for you until I arrived. Jazz has always been good to you, and you repay her with your insults?"

"But Cole, I know now that the child isn't yours. He's small and has a head of black curly hair. If he was your son, he wouldn't have anything but fuzz on his head, and he would have big hands and feet. Anyone half blind can tell this child looks nothing like you."

"So, this is the only reason you wanted to come out here? You wanted to see if the baby looked like me? Well, now you know." Cole opened the bedroom door and led her to the front room.

"I want you to know something, and you had better hear me good. Jazz is my wife, and her son is mine. I already love that baby as much as I would if he was from my own loins. Now, you can accept the baby as your grandson, or Sam will drive you back home. You will not be welcome in my home again. Do you understand?"

Mrs. James marched over to the door and stopped. "I guess Herman was right about you. He said that you didn't want me in your life anymore, and that you didn't love me." She hung her head and called to Sam, who was sitting at the kitchen table drinking a cup of coffee. "I'm ready to leave." She put on her coat and hat and stormed out onto the porch.

Cole followed her outside. "That weasel has been trying to come between us ever since he started working at the store. I hope you will think about what I said about my family. We want you to be in our lives, but you have to meet us halfway." He helped her onto the wagon. "I will see you in the morning." Cole stopped before returning inside the house and prayed, "God, please help us all."

~

Spring was approaching, and it seemed like most of the days were the same. Jazz enjoyed working in the summer garden that David and Sam had plowed for her, forming furrows in the soil and turned the soil up. She sowed all kind of seeds.

With little Jeff wrapped in warm blankets, she hoed and pulled weeds. With all the exercise in the garden, it wasn't long before she was back to her small size, but Cole fussed that she was eating like a bird.

Sam came out of the barn to help Jazz in the garden. The heat had intensified as he wiped his face with a clean handkerchief. He smiled down at the baby and nearly gasped. "Girl, what in the world. You have Jeffrey wrapped up like a mummy in this heat. It must be nearly eight-five degrees. You want to give him a heat rash?" He reached down and began unwrapping the blankets from his body.

191

"What are you doing? Won't he catch a chill?" Jazz tried to stand between Sam and her son.

"You kidding? Ain't nobody going to get a chill in this heat." He untied the knitted booties and freed the baby's feet. "Now he's gonna have room to move and grow." Sam handed Jeff to Jazz as he used the three blankets to make a soft pallet for her to lay the child down.

Jazz continued to hold her son tight. Sam reached over and gently took Jeffrey from her and laid him on the blankets. He sat down beside the boy and asked him if he was cooler. "Of course, you are."

The baby kicked his short legs and placed both fists in his mouth. The boy looked up at Jazz with the biggest blue eyes, and she laughed.

She eased to the ground and sat beside her baby. "How do you know so much about babies?" She peered at Sam as he held his finger out for the baby to try and grab.

"I had two babies once. A little boy and the prettiest little girl you ever seen. Big blue eyes and long blond hair. I lost my wife and children to malaria about twenty years ago. My world turned upside down, and I never felt I had anything to live for after that."

"Oh, Sam. I am so sorry." Jazz looked down at her baby. She didn't know what she would do if she ever lost this little one. Losing Joe was different. He had lived to become a man, but he made some wrong choices. Jeff would be different. Her son would always have her love and protection. "Sam." Jazz reached out and took Sam's hand. "Look at me." She waited until he raised his face to hers. "You have several reasons to live now. I love you like a papa that I never had. Cole couldn't do without your help, and Jeff needs a grandpa." A tear fell on her hand as Sam sat so still. "We love you, and you are family now. We want you with us always."

"I don't know what I did to deserve your devotion and kindness, but I sure am a happy man now."

David came out of the barn and laughed as he looked down at

the baby. "Now, that's the cutest critter I have ever seen. Look how much he has grown. Look, he is waving at me." Everyone laughed as Sam stood and helped Jazz off the ground.

"We'd better get busy with this hoeing before it's too hot. I hope this garden will produce enough fresh food that we might be able to supply the store with some vegetables," she said.

~

The afternoon sunlight dappled on the wooden buildings as the locals strolled down Main Street of Yellowstone. A few men and women meandered in and out of stores. Joe Whitmore realized that in a few minutes he and his partner would soon be spotted as strangers, and people would stop and stare. His emotions were still too raw to speak or acknowledge any of them.

He was sure he wouldn't be recognized because Joe Whitmore, a bank robber and murderer, was dead. Besides, he wouldn't get too close to anyone since he had been hanged. Thank goodness for his partner, Orem Murphy, who had saved his life.

His original plan was to travel as far away from Texas as he could and never think about the state again. But being broke and listening to his stomach growl night after night, he needed to find an easy target and refill his saddlebags with enough cash to help him settle in Mexico.

As he traveled toward the border, he remembered that the wagon train was going to stop in Yellowstone to pick up fresh water and supplies. The wagon master had said that Yellowstone was growing, the surrounding farms and ranches were plentiful, and the town businesses were successful. The bank had to have a lot of money in its safe. That thought was on his mind when he entered the town's barbershop where he needed a shave, a haircut, and a bath. He could hardly stand himself.

"Welcome, fellows. Do both of you want a haircut?" The barber asked the two unkempt cowboys.

"Yep, but after a trim of my beard and haircut, I would like a hot bath as well," Joe replied.

"That will be mighty fine. Let me tell my Chinese man to fill a barrel with hot water." The barber disappeared behind a curtain and returned in a few minutes. "All right, climb into my chair." After placing the cape around Joe's neck, he asked how much hair he wanted cut and how much trim he wanted off his beard. The barber must have noticed the deep scar on Joe's neck that he kept covered with a handkerchief, but the man made no comment.

Joe looked in the mirror and was satisfied with how his hair looked. He wore his hair long, but it was trimmed up to the lower part of his neck. His beard and mustache were trimmed close but still covered his face.

As his partner climbed in the chair, Joe walked behind the curtain and let the man help him climb into the barrel of steaming water. He sighed and slipped down until his shoulders were covered with the clean, hot water.

As he relaxed, he heard a man enter the barber shop. "Howdy, Bill. I'll be with you in a few minutes."

"Ain't in no hurry," he said. "Well, the trial is over and the judge gave that old man five years in prison. I bet he's sorry he ever stopped at Cole's farm."

"I figured all the men were over at the saloon where the trial was held. You know, I didn't know what crime the old man committed. I just returned from visiting my daughter in Louisiana. Had to take my wife to be with our daughter while she gave birth to her first baby. I didn't think I was ever going to get her on the train to return home. She cried most all the way back here."

"So, you haven't heard that the old fellow who works on Cole's farm brought in the man who was attempting to steal a dozen black men and sell them as slaves?"

"Are you talking about that old man who sat on the steps in front of the dry goods store? I wondered what happened to him."

"That's the fellow. Cole took him out to his farm and put him to work. He don't look like the same person. He's filled out and cleaned up right nice."

"Go on with your tale. When did all this happen? I haven't had any free time to leave the shop, and no one has come in with that kind of gossip."

"It ain't gossip. It's a fact. That man's trial is over, and the black men are free, thanks to Cole's brave little wife. The story goes that she let that old man in her house while the prisoners were chained and left in the barn. While she was feeding him, she doped him with a sleeping medicine, and soon he was out cold. Sam and Miss Jazz, you know that's her name, used the key and unlocked the chains and set the men free. Sam chained the old man and brought him in to the sheriff's office."

The barber laughed. "I did know that Cole married that pretty little blonde who worked for him awhile back. You know the doctor wanted to marry her first, but Cole wasn't about to let her get hitched to him. She does have an unusual name, Jazz. I have heard that she's still in mourning for her husband who got strung up for robbing a bank. Poor kid, but I have to say she is one lucky gal to get hitched up with Cole. He's a nice man and wealthy to boot."

Joe gasped. Jazz was here in Yellowstone? The love of his life? The only person who ever cared about him? He robbed banks to have enough money to build her a mansion when they reached California. Of course, things didn't go his way, but to find her again and learn that she was married was upsetting. *Married.* This was a hard pill to swallow. She would never be another's man wife, not as long as he had breath in his body. Jazz belonged to him.

~

Jazz was thrilled to hear Sam and David ride back into the yard. She stood on the front porch and waved them into the house.

"Let us put the animals up for the night, and we'll be right in. Tell Georgia that I could eat a horse," Sam yelled to Jazz.

Laughing, Jazz watched the two men ride over to the corral as she turned to enter the house. "The men are back, and they're hungry," Jazz said. "I think everything went well. Both of them are smiling."

With the wind blowing stronger than usual and the sky's clouds heavy and dark, the men jumped on the porch just as pellets of hard rain poured down. "I didn't know it was going to rain tonight, but I'm glad we made it back before we were caught in it," David said.

"Come in and shut the door. Go into the bedroom and close the windows. Lily, is your window closed?" Georgia called out.

"Yes, ma'am. Can we eat now?"

David scooped up Lily into his arms and held her over his head. "So, little gal, you're hungry too?"

"Yep, I could eat a bear." Everyone laughed as they took their seats at the table.

"So, Sam, how did the trial go?" Jazz asked.

"Believe it or not, the judge believed me. He didn't even question David. He sentenced that old man to five years in prison."

"The sheriff said he would send a telegram to Mr. Wainwright in Huntsville and tell him that his workers are on their way back to his plantation," David said.

"I hope we aren't the talk of the town. Cole might be upset to learn that we let those men stop at his farm. I have embarrassed him enough," Jazz murmured.

"Now, Miss Jazz, Cole will be happy we helped those men. He would have done the same thing. Don't start looking for trouble," Georgia said.

Once the dishes were washed and put away, the men hurried to the barn to care for the smaller animals. The girls pulled out their sewing and sat in front of the evening fire. Jazz had drawn faces on cream-colored material and embroidered blue eyes, cute dark pink noses, and rosy color lips.

After Lily was in bed, Jazz pulled out black material and,

using a piece of chalk, she drew a face. Then, she made lovely brown eyes, a nose, and light red lips. She included black eyelashes on the eyes to make the face special. Lily would love this doll.

After Jazz had embroidered several more cream faces and drew a few orange freckles across the little noses, she was ready to start stuffing the dolls. She yawned. "It's been a long day. A very different day, I must say, and I am exhausted. I'll finish the dolls tomorrow."

"I think we're all tired. You go on to bed, and I'll wait until Sam comes inside and locks up. Maybe, we can work on David's room tomorrow and have it already by the time Cole returns home."

"Yes, Cole will be pleased. I know he will have a lot of work waiting for him at the store, so we need to do as much as we can to help him here." Jazz stood and stretched her back. She went into the water closet, dressed in her long white gown, and went to sleep immediately.

Chapter 34

The old rooster crowed and announced the beginning of a cold but sunny day. Jazz sat on the side of the bed, yawned and stretched, and watched Jeffrey moving around in his bed. She smiled and patted him on his back. He had filled out and didn't look so small now that he was six months old.

Cole had proven to be the best papa in the world. When he arrived home from the store, the first thing he did was rush to the baby. Even if Jeff was asleep, he would scoop him into his arms and sway him back and forth on his hip. He kissed his little cheeks and cooed to him. Afterward, he would asked how her day was and if he could do anything for her. Jazz didn't know why she was holding herself back from being his real wife. In her heart she knew she loved him.

Cole had mentioned that he was going over to Scottsdale and buy another prize sow for the farm. He wanted her to go with him, but he agreed it wouldn't be a fun trip, so he suggest they plan another trip when the baby was older.

Jazz hated for Cole to be away from the farm. It wasn't that she didn't trust him, but she'd always wondered what Joe was doing on his trips away from the wagon train. "You're going tomorrow then, Cole?" Jazz asked.

"Yes, I have a train ticket to Scottsdale that leaves at noon. We can attend church together."

"Where will you stay?" Jazz asked.

"There's a boardinghouse a mile or so from the stockyard. It will be convenient."

"You'll be hungry on the train. I will make you some sandwiches."

"No need. The train makes a stop, and I can grab something to eat. Please don't go to any trouble for me. And stop fretting. I have made many trips, and I always return home safely."

"I know, but this trip feels different."

"Yes, I will be bringing home a big ugly sow." He laughed.

~

After church, Sam drove Cole and Jazz to the train station. There was nobody else waiting to board, so the place seemed eerie, almost like a ghost town. Jazz heard the train's whistle far off and realized Cole would be leaving. Her hands shook and her stomach felt like it was in knots. She needed to tell him something, but they needed privacy.

"Please help me down. I want to stretch my legs before we start riding back to the farm."

Cole leapt from the wagon and helped her and the baby down. She tugged for him to follow. He tightened his hold on the baby, but Jazz stopped and took Jeffrey from him. "Sam, please hold Jeffrey while I have a few words with Cole." She pulled him a few yards' distance away. "Cole," Jazz's voice faltered as she looked at his worried expression. "I wanted to say that I'm going to miss you." She dared not close her eyes, but she could feel her face burning. "I will be here, waiting for your return."

"Jazz, you have always been here when I arrive home . . . Wait, do you mean what I've been praying for you to mean?"

She lifted her face and smiled. He pulled her toward him. There wasn't anything soft about her small body; even her breasts felt firm up against his chest. He wanted to crush her in his arms, but he didn't want to be the talk of the town, again. Excitement raced through his body as he kissed her goodbye.

The kiss was as familiar as she remembered as she held on to his suitcoat longer than proper. She loved this man, and she was going to show him when he returned.

The train whistle blew as the conductor waved. Cole kissed her forehead. "This is a heck of a time for me to be leaving. I'm going to hold you to your decision." He waved goodbye and barely jumped through the doorway of the passenger car before the train left.

~

Georgia had a nice lunch on the table when Jazz arrived home. She and Lily had stayed home from Sunday services because Lily had a fresh cold. Georgia warned her that she was going to get sick playing in the horses' trough, but the little hardheaded child didn't listen.

"We need to use this time to complete David's room. We put a few things in there when he first came here, but now we should finish it and make it like a real little home," Jazz said as they carried their plates to the sink.

"We have had the windows a long time and now that the weather is hot, he will need to have cool air flowing so he can rest better." Sam said. "Come on, David, we'll measure the windows and cut the wall to insert them."

Jazz and Georgia spent the afternoon pressing the curtains. They pulled out fresh linens and two new pillows. Cole had purchased a rocking chair to set in front of the potbelly stove. A new mattress was the last surprise for David. He had worn out the stuffing in the tick until it was flat.

After the windows were in place and the curtains were hung, Jazz came out with a bolt of cheesecloth. "Sam, in the catalog Cole brought home, I saw cheesecloth covering a frame to go over the glass windows to keep out dust, birds, and other critters like mosquitoes. Do you think you can make a frame to go on the outside of the glass windows? David can still raise the windows up and down but not touch the cheese cloth."

"Mercy, what will people think of next? Sure, I can make the frames, and you can stretch the cloths real tight over them. We'll use small tacks to hold them in place." He smiled at David and then at Jazz. "Let's get busy, man." Sam hurried back into the barn where he'd set up a worktable.

"You know, Miss Jazz, if this works out for David's windows, we can build frames to go over other windows on the house. When Cole returns, I will discuss it with him."

Georgia called everyone in for supper. For the first time, Jazz blessed the meal. She included Cole and each family member. Today had been a nice day, and David now had a real place to retire and enjoy.

After the dishes were cleaned, it was still daylight. Jazz carried Jeffrey outside to the barn to see the goats and the piglets. The two dogs leapt around Jazz's feet. Both dogs loved the baby and always wanted to lick his hands or face.

As she moseyed around the barn to the corral, a man stepped out in front of her. Jazz stopped suddenly and jumped back a few feet. "Who are you?" She wanted to scream for help, but something held her still.

"Even with my beard, you recognize me, don't you, honey?"

"No . . . it can't be you. You're dead." Jazz felt her knees give away, and she tumbled to the ground.

~

"Miss Jazz, Miss Jazz, are you sick?" Lily said, as she saw Jeffrey lying on the ground, playing with his toes and looking at the strange man who stood over him. "Mama, help. Miss Jazz has fallen," Lily screamed as she spun around and raced to the house.

~

David and Sam heard Lily's screams and hurried outside of the barn. Lying on the ground on the side of the barn was Jazz with Jeffrey lying beside her. David picked up the baby while Sam scooped Jazz into his arms and carried her inside the house.

"What happened?" Georgia joined them and asked.

"I saw a man standing beside the fence, but he ain't there now," Lily said, holding onto her mother's apron.

Georgia wiped Jazz's face and spoke softly to her. Jazz woke up, a confused look on her face. Her head thrashed back and forth. "No, it can't be. You're dead . . . dead."

"Who's dead?" Sam asked quietly, peering at David's face.

"I didn't see anyone, did you?" David asked Sam.

Chapter 35

Jazz sat up and removed the cold cloth from her face. Georgia sat straight up in a chair next to her. "Miss Jazz, are you all right now?" she asked.

Jazz felt as if she had been dreaming, but she did remember being outside with the baby. A stranger appeared from the back of the barn, and—"He's alive," she whispered. "I wasn't dreaming. Joe is alive."

"Now, Miss Jazz, maybe you hit your head when you fell. You know that can't be. Your husband was hung by a posse. Men from the wagon train done told you that it was true. Your Joe is gone. He ain't never coming back."

Jazz sat on the side of the bed. "Georgia, I am awake now, and I saw him. He was here. Even with a beard, I recognized him. That's all I remember."

"Why do you think he left when you fainted? He didn't stay to help you. Wonder why?"

"Guess he was afraid. But he'll be back. I feel it in the pit of my stomach." She rubbed her palm across her belly. "I want him to come back," she whispered. "I want to see my Joe again. I loved him, and at times I miss him so much my heart aches. I never wanted to believe he was dead."

"But, Miss Jazz, what about Mr. Cole? He loves you so much, and he's so good to you. What will you tell him?"

"Well, I am glad he's away. I have to see Joe again." Jazz

stood and walked over to the cradle and looked at her son. "Joe doesn't know he has a son, and now he will. I know he will be pleased."

"Even if he is alive, the men said that your Joe is a wanted man. He's a bad man who has robbed and killed. Seeing him again is one thing, but you can't leave with a man like him, not with a baby. Please, Miss Jazz, don't do anything you'll regret."

~

Georgia left the bedroom and hurried into the kitchen to find Sam and David sitting at the kitchen table. "How is she?" Sam quizzed.

"Confused to say the least. She said she saw her dead husband. He just showed up from nowhere. Jazz recognized him, even though he has grown a beard. We must be on guard. He will come back here. She wants to see him. They were married for four years, and he was good to her, but he can't be the same man she loved. We can't let her pack up and go away with him."

"How can we prevent that from happening?" Sam mumbled.

"Pray, I guess, that she'll come to her senses when she sees him again. I just hope he doesn't try and force her to go away with him."

"I'll bust his head if he tries to make her go with him against her will. I'll hurt him bad, if he harms a hair on her head," David said.

~

Early the next morning, Jazz was sitting on the front porch with Jeffrey on her lap. Everyone was busy. Georgia was baking bread, Lily was playing with the leftover dough, David was hoeing the summer garden, and Sam was washing the new colt.

With a mild breeze blowing, her long-lost, dead husband appeared in the distance on horseback. He had a younger man with him. Joe was off his horse in a flash while the man remained on his horse with a rifle resting across his lap.

"Joe," Jazz stuttered, standing and holding a sleeping Jeffrey. "I thought at first I was dreaming, but I knew in my heart I wasn't. I still can't believe you're alive."

David came from the garden with the hoe in his hand while Sam crawled through the corral fence. Both men walked over to the porch.

The man on horseback pointed his rifle at the men, who looked like they would tear Joe to pieces if he touched one hair on Jazz's head.

Joe signaled to his partner. "Orem, lower the rifle. These men are here to protect my loving wife and I'm guessing my baby, too." He smiled at Jazz. "It this my son?"

"Yes. This is the baby we always wanted." She held Jeffrey so Joe could see his son.

"The baby *you* always wanted, sweetheart. I never wanted a kid." He glared at Jazz and rubbed his hand in Jeffery's hair.

Jazz couldn't believe that statement had come out of her dearly beloved husband's mouth. It hurt her heart to hear him say something so unreal. She'd always thought he wanted a family, too.

With her heart pounding, as anger flowed through her body, she peered up at him with narrowed eyes. "How did you escape from the posse? I was told that they had hanged you and left you for dead. I couldn't believe they didn't even have the decency to bury you."

"It was a good thing for me they rode off and left me dangling. Orem—" he gave a nod to the man on horseback, "—came along and cut me down. I was still breathing, but I had a rope burn across my throat that hurt my voice. I sound rough, but at least I can talk." He rubbed the deep scar on his neck. Looking around at the house, Joe said, "It looks like you've landed pretty well on your feet as a young widow."

"You don't have any idea what you put me through. I could

have died because of your behavior. A man crawled into my wagon and at knifepoint demanded that I tell him where the bank money was that you had stolen. I didn't know until then that you were dead. He told me you were a bank robber and a murderer. The man ripped my clothes and threatened to have his way with me, but thank goodness he heard the men returning from a day of hunting." Jazz had almost forgotten that she was lucky to be alive. The hurt and anger poured from her body as she held Jeffrey to her bosom. Finally, she wiped her tears away as angry words spilled out at him.

"I cried and grieved for many months. The people didn't believe I didn't know anything about what you were doing while you were away. The women called me a harlot and worse names I won't repeat. I have never been treated so ugly even when I was a child and had to live on the streets." Jazz used her apron to wipe tears from her eyes.

"The wagon master left me in Yellowstone, homeless and with only a small amount of money I had stored away. I had to go to work to support myself. Everywhere I worked, I got fired because of your reputation. I didn't have it as easy as you like to think. And I moaned your death until . . . well, it doesn't matter now. You aren't dead and I am happy you're alive. Mostly I grieved because I wanted you to see your son, but now you tell me you didn't even want a child. That was another big lie you told me. Anything to get your way at night with me."

Joe hurried to her side and knelt down, attempting to take her hand. "I'm sorry the people were mean to you. You won't ever be mistreated again as long as you are with me. Look at me, sweetheart." He glanced at the sleeping boy in her arms. "I loved you and I still do. I'll give you time to go pack your things while your servant makes Orem and me something to eat." He checked his pocket watch. "Say, we leave at eight o'clock tonight? You know you'll always belong to me." Standing, he motioned for Orem to follow him to the corral where they could water their mounts. "Tell that woman to get busy with the grub," Joe demanded before he left.

Jazz stood and adjusted the sleeping baby in her arms. She walked into the house and nearly ran over Georgia who had been listening at the door.

"You ain't going with him, are you, Miss Jazz?"

"Not tonight, anyway. Who does he think he is? I can't just leave. I have never had a home or people whom I love and care about. Joe and I never had any friends. Even on the wagon train, we were always alone. I never understood why." Jazz laid Jeffrey in his cradle and looked into Georgia's sad face. Her eyes were swollen from crying. "Georgia, I have to talk with Cole. He must understand whatever decision I make. Cole loves Jeffrey so much. It will hurt him if I take the baby away, but I can't leave without him."

"We'd better get busy and put food on the table for your dead husband and his friend," Georgia said, as she trudged over to the stove.

"Sure, after they eat, I will send Joe away until Cole arrives home. Surely, he will understand."

Chapter 36

Joe didn't understand nor did he plan to wait around for Cole to return home. He was a wanted man, and if someone recognized him, he would be shot. But he wouldn't ever give himself up because he had plans to live like a king in Mexico.

"Tonight, after the bank closes, we will go into the back alley, slip in the back window, and have the clerk open the safe. I overheard the bank manager tell the clerk that he would have supper and then come back and help with the end of the month's accounts," Joe said.

"This sounds like a smooth job for sure," Orem said.

"As soon as we tie up the clerk, we will come back here and get Jazz."

"Only Jazz?" Orem asked.

"We don't need a brat tagging along. He will only slow us down, and we'll be riding fast."

"You do know your wife ain't going to want to leave her baby. Mamas are funny when it comes to their young'uns."

"Jazz loves me, and she has always followed my lead. She'll do whatever I say."

~

The smooth bank job didn't go as planned. The bank clerk told Joe and his partner the money was in the safe, and he couldn't open it.

"Well, if you can't open it, then you aren't any use to me." Joe was so angry that he hit the young clerk over the head with the butt of his pistol. He jumped down over the clerk's body and hit him countless times in the face until the young man was unrecognizable. Then he stood and wiped the bloody pistol butt off on his pants.

Orem was in disbelief as he waited at the front door for the bank manager to arrive. He knew Joe had a temper, but there wasn't any reason to beat that young man to death. He had to get away from this madman. "Joe, someone's coming." Orem pointed at the door as he watched the doorknob wiggle. "Someone's trying to unlock the front door," he whispered.

Joe ducked behind the counter as the manager came into the bank and called to his clerk.

"Sorry, fat boy," Joe said, pointing his gun directly at the banker. "There's no one here but you, me, and Orem." He waved his pistol at the banker. "Get over here and open this safe. We ain't got all night."

The banker shook his head. "I can't open the safe. Once it's closed, I can't open it for twelve hours. If you shoot the lock, you'll be sorry because everyone in town will hear."

"No, you're the one who's gonna be sorry," Joe said as he fired his gun and shot the banker in the belly. The older man fell backward and landed next to the bank clerk.

"Joe, heaven help us. Let's get out of here." Orem rushed out the back door and raced to their horses. With Joe on his heels, both of the men rode out of town heading straight to Cole's farm.

~

The townsmen rushed to the bank and were stunned to find the bank clerk brutally beaten to death. The bank manager was still alive.

"Jack," the barber asked, while holding Jack's head in his lap.

"Did you know the men who did this to you?"

"Two men. One, Or . . . em. One . . . beard . . . rough voice," the banker said, as he coughed up blood.

"Get back," Doctor Richards yelled. He ripped the banker's vest and shirt and stuffed a handkerchief over the gunshot wound. "Carry him to my office. It's bad, but I have seen worse."

The barber grabbed the sheriff's arm. "Jack described the two men who did this. It was the same two men who came into my shop yesterday. A young man had a black beard, and when he spoke his voice was rough. He had a red, raw-looking scar around his neck, like a rope burn. The young man called his friend Orem. I remember them well."

"Sure sounds like the same ones. Maybe they were scouting out the bank when they came into town yesterday. One thing I know for sure," said the sheriff, "they didn't get away with any of the town's money. Once Jack closes the safe for the night, he can't open it for twelve hours. He told me that several times."

~

Jazz and Georgia were sitting in the rocking chairs with the front door wide open. There was a cold breeze blowing outside, foreshadowing the coming storm. Georgia was reading to Lily while Jazz fed Jeffrey his last bottle of the day.

Both looked up as horses rode to the front of the house. Loud footsteps pounded on the front porch as Joe stormed inside alone.

"Are you ready to go?" Joe demanded as he looked around the room. He only saw Georgia and her little girl in the living area. "Where are the two men who work here?"

"No, I'm not ready, nor will I be tonight. I have some things that I have to take care of before I make a decision whether I will go with you or not." Jazz appeared at the bedroom door, trying to appear calm. She didn't answer him as to the whereabouts of Sam and David. Blood was all over Joe's pants, but she didn't dare ask. His impatience certainly made her nervous, and she lapsed into silence.

"You don't have a decision to make." Before Jazz could respond, he screamed, "You're going with me. Now, tonight!" The veins in his neck pulsed against the scar. "Grab some personal items, and let's be on our way." His eyes took in the whole property. "Maybe your old man will be willing to pad our bank account with a little nudge. New plan!"

"No. I'm not going anywhere with you . . . tonight. I can't." Attempting to appear calm, Jazz said, "Besides, I will need more than a few things. Jeffrey has a good many things I will need to pack."

"That brat is not going. Now, you get a move on it, or I will kill your friends." He looked at Georgia and then down at Lily. His tone of voice frightened Lily. She jumped away from her mama and ran into the kitchen and out the back door.

"Joe, you don't mean that. If you really love me, you'd never ask me to leave our baby." She was shaking all over. "Look, if you leave now, you'll be able to reach the border and be safe. Please, leave now and we won't tell anyone you were here. Please go." Jazz held Jeffrey so tight, he cried out.

Sam and David walked slowly into the house, followed by Orem, who had his pistol pointed at both men. David was carrying Lily.

"Are you all right?" Sam peered at Jazz as he entered the house.

"She's fine, but you'd better prepare to meet your maker if she doesn't get a move on it. We're leaving, bag or no bag. Tell your boss he'll be hearing from me." Sweat beaded Joe's forehead. He was having difficult clearing his throat, and his voice was rough and shaky. Jazz knew that he'd lost all his patience and would hurt someone soon if she didn't do something.

"All right. I'll go." Jazz turned to Georgia and placed Jeffrey into her arms. "Please, please take care of my baby." She stiffened her back and grabbed her shawl, then walked straight out the front door without glancing at the two men whom she cared for deeply. "Please God, don't let any harm come to my baby and friends," she prayed softly.

As she walked to the saddled horse, lightning appeared in the distance. A storm was coming for sure. She mounted and sat tall in the saddle. Joe came out of the house without any gunfire and leapt on his horse, grabbing her reins. He led them down a road for what seemed like miles to a rundown, two-story house. She shivered and wished she had grabbed more than her shawl when she walked out the door.

"We'll hide out here for a few days," Joe told Orem.

"How did you know this old house was here?" Orem queried.

"I scouted this area while you were sucking up to the bar yesterday." Joe reached for Jazz arm and jerked her off the horse.

"Orem, put the animals under the eaves behind the house for tonight. Tomorrow, we'll prepare a better shelter for them." Joe took Jazz by the hand and kissed the inside of her palm. "Are you ready to share my bed and welcome me home?" The ride had calmed Joe, and he seemed more content than he had back at the farm.

"I'll never be ready to share anything with you. You aren't my Joe, the man I loved and grieved for. I don't really know how to describe the man you have become."

Joe laughed and pushed her inside the house. "Mercy, gal, you sure have grown feisty." He grabbed two lanterns and tossed a few pieces of wood in the fireplace. Taking a flint out of his pocket, he lit the lanterns and dry wood that caught on fire immediately. "Maybe the fire will take the chill out of the room and warm you up a little to me." Joe walked up behind Jazz and sniffed her neck, then wrapped his hands around her breasts. "You're a handful since having a baby."

Jazz spun around and slapped Joe as hard as she could across the face. He grabbed her wrist and pulled her to his chest, only a breath away from his face. He jerked her dress off her shoulder, ripping it to her waist. "I'll make you sorry you slapped me. Don't do it again."

"Who are you?" Jazz asked softly. "You aren't the man I married. You have become a . . . a monster." She lowered her eyes and tried not to let him see her cry.

"Sweetheart, I know you have this ridiculous fear that I'm going to harm you, but I would never do that. In all the time we were married, did I ever hurt you? No, you know I never laid a hand on your sweet body. I'm so happy to have found you before I traveled on to Mexico." He lifted her chin. "Look at me. I need you. And money. I need both in the worse way. That is the reason I tried to rob the bank tonight."

Jazz sucked in her breath. "Is that how you got blood all over your clothes? Did you hurt someone?"

"Listen to me," he said, shaking her shoulders. "I don't want to talk about what happened at the bank. I need money, but I didn't get it." He turned her loose and stared at her for a long minute. "But your husband can get it for me. You are going to ask him to give it to me. Afterwards, we can ride across the border and begin a new life together."

"I can't do that. Cole is not a rich man. He doesn't have money to just give away." Suddenly, it came to Jazz what Joe was planning. "You're going to ask ransom money for me?"

"Call it whatever you want. We need money to live. He has a farm, a store, and livestock he can sell. I don't care how he gets it, but he will bring it to me, or he will never see you again."

"You just said that I was going with you. Which is it? Money for me or money for you and that man traveling with you."

"Quiet!" Joe grabbed his head, rubbing his forehead. "I'm tired and hungry. We'll discuss this more tomorrow." He strode over to his saddlebag and pulled out several cans of beans. Strolling over to the potbellied stove, he put several pieces of wood in it and tossed a small piece of flamed wood inside.

"Get over here and heat these beans. After we eat, we'll go to bed."

Jazz posted her hands on her hips. "I will go to bed alone. Don't think any different. I'm not the timid young woman you married four years ago."

Later, after all three of them had eaten supper, Joe grinned like he had a big secret. Laughing, Joe carried a lantern up the stairs. Hurrying back down, he asked if she needed to go outside for a few minutes of privacy.

While outside, she looked for a way to escape, but Orem stood with a pistol pointed at her. Once she came in from the foul, leaning outhouse, Joe led her up the stairs and shoved her inside a dark room, slamming the door shut. She heard him place a bar across the door.

She leaned into the door, resting her ear up against it. Joe laughed on the other side of it.

"After spending a night up here, maybe you'll be ready to share my bed. After all, I am still your husband." His footsteps stomped down the stairs.

Jazz's eyes soon became accustomed to the dark space. She didn't know if she was in the attic or a bedroom. During the first hour of the night, she felt her way along the wall until she came to a window. Jazz pushed back the heavy cloth that covered the panes and saw faded stars and a cloudy moon in the dark sky. She reached down to lift the window, but it was old and stuck. The only thing she could do was break the glass to get out, but Joe and his friend would hear her.

Why did Joe have to kidnap her? She told him that she wasn't going to live with him. Surely, he didn't want a wife who didn't want him.

With the moonlight shining inside, she twisted around and caught glimpses of her prison. She wiped the glass pane and looked into the darkness outside.

She pulled on her ripped dress. Jazz didn't care about the garment. Her only concern was for her son. If she cried, she might echo misery through the old house.

The wind blew and howling gusts of wind whipped tree branches up against the window. Blinding bolts of lightning lit up the dark sky and faded into loud crashes of thunder. Rain finally spattered the roof, windowpanes, and the outside walls.

At first, she entertained the idea of escape, but there didn't seem to be any hope. Feeling her way over to the door, she couldn't find a handle on the inside. There were large hinges and a couple of cracks in the planks. She remembered Joe dropping a large piece of wood across the door on the opposite side. Jazz placed her ear near the cracks in the door hoping to hear the men talking, but there was only silence. She guessed Joe and the man called Orem were asleep by now.

She bumped into a chair sitting near the window. The rain had stopped, and the clouds faded, allowing stars to shine. The moon shone light into the darkness. She could make out several blankets folded on a chest. Picking up the blankets, she saw that the top one was covered with dust. She stacked the blankets on the floor and prayed there weren't any crawly creatures hiding within. She folded the skirt of her dress as tight as she could under her legs. Weeping and rocking herself, she clutched her knees to her bosom. Fear and fatigue took away her hope. It had been a long time since she had ridden a horse, and her legs burned from rubbing against the horse's hair.

As she finally prepared to lie down, she thought of Cole. *Oh, Cole, I know I will never see you again. And now I won't be able to keep my promise to you. I wish I had told you before you left that I love you.*

Stretching out on the lumpy blankets, she promised herself that she would be stronger tomorrow as she fell into an exhausted sleep.

Chapter 37

Georgia wrung her hands and paced the room. "Sam, you have to go into town and tell the sheriff what has happened. We must get help for Miss Jazz, and Cole won't be home until tomorrow. She would have never gone with her dead husband willingly. Miss Jazz only left because she was afraid for all of us. Did you see the blood on his clothes? He'd already hurt somebody. And there's a good chance he'll kill her if he doesn't get what he wants. Now go. Hurry."

Sam and David rushed to the barn and saddled a horse. "David, you stay out of sight with a loaded shotgun in case that fool man comes back here. You must be on guard all the time," Sam instructed his friend.

"I'll guard those girls with my life. You hurry now and tell the sheriff how he threatened to kill us and means to force Cole to give him money. That Joe fellow is sick in the head. He sure ain't well."

Sam stopped saddling the horse and gave David a hard stare. "How do you know he's sick, you know, in the head? I just figured he's mean."

"Oh, he's a mean one, that's a fact, but I've been around mean men most of my life. They are always the same. That man who claims to be Miss Jazz's husband is different. One minute he's calm and nice; the next he can and will kill. He can be sweet to Miss Jazz, but in a blink of an eye, he'd shoot us all. I know that for sure."

"I'll tell the sheriff. I hope he'll gather a posse and hunt them down. Cole is going to be devastated when he arrives home." Sam raced onto the road that led to town.

~

The sheriff exhaled a breath of desperation. He and his posse had left town to find the bank robbers who had killed the bank clerk and hurt the banker. But the storm had forced them back to town with the tracks of the outlaws washed away. Now most of his men were in the saloon drinking to warm their insides from the chill of the rain. The sheriff was in his office when Sam entered.

"Sheriff," Sam said, exhausted and out of breath. "I need your help. Cole James' wife has been kidnapped by her dead husband and his partner. The man's name is Joe Whitmore, and the other man is Orem something. He took Mrs. James by force, making her leave her baby. He threatened to kill us if she didn't go with him, and he'll probably be demanding money from Cole."

The sheriff bolted to his feet and circled the desk. "Now, wait. You've given me more information in the last few seconds than I can take in. Let me ask the questions. Now, you said something about Mrs. James being kidnapped by her dead husband. Why did you say the man was dead?"

"Some time ago, Joe—that's the man's name—robbed a bank and murdered somebody. A posse hanged him, but he didn't die. Another man came along and saved him. All this time, Mrs. James thought he was dead."

"Yes, I recall her coming into town on a wagon train, and she was in mourning. Yep, I recall some of that tale. So, this man who is supposed to be dead is not dead and is Mrs. James' ex-husband?"

"Yes, sir, you got it. I bet he'll make Mrs. James ask for money from Cole."

"So, you're saying he took Mrs. James to use for ransom?"

"Right." Sam spun around to leave. "Let's go and gather a posse to search them out. Mr. Cole will not be home until tomorrow. He went to Scottsdale to buy a sow."

"Hold on there, old man. We already went after the guy, but the storm soaked my men to the bone. So, we'll be meeting in front of my office at first light. But, the men who've abducted Mrs. James are mighty nasty, so we're going to have to be careful." The sheriff stared at Sam. "This is how it works. If they want ransom money, they're going to send Cole a note. The note will have a drop-off point, so we'll have some idea where they're hiding. We need to wait to hear from the kidnappers."

Sam shook his head with vehemence. "That man, her dead husband, is crazy. One minute he's calm and the next he explodes. He threatened to kill us all, including Georgia's little girl and maybe his own son."

"I saw some of the bank robbers' handiwork. The young bank clerk was brutally beaten—a nice young man with a lovely wife. Sad." The sheriff peered out the window at Main Street. "Look, why don't you go back to Cole's farm and wait until he comes in on the train tomorrow. I'll meet him at the station, and we'll decide what to do. Maybe, the man will send a note to the farm. If he does, bring it to me as fast as you can."

"I can't begin to tell you how evil that man is. He claims to love Mrs. James, but he will kill her if things don't go his way." Sam placed his hat on his head, looking like he had lost the war.

~

As Sam stood under the eaves of the sheriff's office, he peered at the dry-goods store. He needed to tell Cole's mama what was going on with her daughter-in-law. Cole might need the old woman's help with money. The only light in town came from the saloon. It was too late to bother Mrs. James. He'd come back into town tomorrow and wait on Cole. If Cole wanted her to know, he would tell her, thought Sam.

~

Back at the farm, Georgia was sitting in front of the fireplace waiting for Sam to return. After several hours, she met him on the front porch after he talked with David at the barn. "Oh, Sam, what did the sheriff say? Did he form a posse and go looking for Miss Jazz?"

"He did, but the rain stopped him. He is going to wait until Cole arrives home tomorrow because her husband might send a ransom note. The sheriff said the note will give them an idea where they're hiding."

"That boy might take the money and keep on heading to the border with Miss Jazz. He crazy." Georgia leaned into Sam and cried her heart out.

Sam didn't know what do to. He patted Georgia on her back. "You know, Miss Jazz would tell us to pray. Why don't you go to your room and get ready for bed. Pray and then get some rest. Tomorrow will be a long day. We should prepare food—coffee, dried jerky, and some canned peaches to go in Cole's saddlebags. He'll need a bedroll too."

"You're right. He'll be ready to ride out as soon as he gets home. I'll pack a change of clothes for Miss Jazz. She'll need them after he finds her."

Sam turned Georgia toward her room and gave her a small push. "Bed, now. Little Jeffrey will be waking early, ready for a bottle."

Chapter 38

"What?" Cole said with a wavering voice, as he waited for the sheriff to answer. "Do you know if that man has hurt my wife?"

"Sam didn't say anything about her being hurt, only she didn't have a choice but to go with her ex-husband. He threatened to kill everyone on the farm if she didn't leave with him."

"My Lord, I'd better race to the farm and check on my son and my friends. Give me a little while, and I'll be back ready to ride out," Cole said, peering around frantically.

"Wait, Cole, there's something else. Sam said that man and his partner tried to rob the bank. One of them killed the bank clerk. They didn't take any money from the bank. Anyway, the man told your wife he'd be demanding money from you. He said he was going to hold her for ransom. We need to wait until we receive a note from him."

"Is that the reason you're not out searching for them? You're waiting for a ransom note?" he said, pounding his fists on his thighs.

"Listen, the rainstorm washed away their trail. A ransom note will give us some kind of direction. I want to find them as much as you do. This ex-husband of your wife's is a bad man. He doesn't deserve to live." The sheriff pounded his fist against his holster. "Take your sow to your farm and wait for the ransom note. Once it arrives—and I am sure it will come either to your farm or my office—you can gather the money that they're demanding, and we'll go after them."

~

Early the next morning, Joe removed the bar from the door that held Jazz prisoner. She had heard him coming, so she stood waiting. She needed to use the necessary and get something to drink.

"Come, my princess, and have some coffee," Joe said. He stepped aside and allowed her to walk down the stairs.

"I need to go to the outhouse before I drink anything." Jazz looked around the room and found it devoid of furniture except two chairs and a wobbly table, one leg shorter than the other three.

"Follow me. You can have a few minutes of privacy, drink some coffee, and then write a note to that man." Joe opened the door and allowed her to and from the outhouse.

After washing her face and hands from a pail of water in the cabin, she drank a cup of black coffee. Joe moved to her with such an arrogant swagger, she felt he was going to do her harm. She lowered her head so he couldn't see fear in her eyes as he fingered her torn dress.

"Here's paper and pencil. Start writing what I tell you to put down."

He sounded so hateful. She balled her hands into fists and tried to make her heart stay inside her chest. Writing a ransom note was the last thing she wanted to do, but if she wanted to reunite with Cole and Jeffrey, she had no choice. Taking a chair at the table, Jazz reached for the paper and pencil. "What do you want me to write?"

Joe sneered. "Write, '*to my new beloved husband, whom I couldn't wait until Joe was dead at least a year to marry, if you want to see me again, you will bring ten thousand dollars and drop it in a bucket that will be placed on the main road at twelve o'clock in two days. If it is not there, Joe will kill you first and then ride back to the farm and take my son. He'll bring a good price in Mexico.'"*

He smirked at her shocked face, then strode outside.

Jazz held her head in her hands. Joe scared her. At least, Cole would never allow Joe to get his hands on her son. She sighed and wrote out the note that Joe demanded. Too bad Joe could read, or she would have written her whereabouts and other clues. She knew that they couldn't be more than a few miles from town. Jazz reread the note and waited for Joe's return. Where was Cole going to get that much money?

Joe entered the house with his partner on his heels. Snatching the paper from Jazz, he read what she had written to her husband. "Very nice, sweetheart." He turned to his partner. "Orem, ride into town and pay someone to take this note to the dry-goods store, and make sure they give it to Jazz's husband and no one else."

"Sure, I'll take care of it," he said, placing his hat on his head.

~

"Cole, I am so sorry that this has happened. You are my son, and I am happy that you came to me. Of course, I will help you. I need to go to the bank and see how much money I can withdraw. You need to be ready once the ransom note comes. Between your money and mine, surely we will have enough."

Cole reached for his mama and hugged her tight. "Mama, I haven't been this afraid in years. I love my wife and I don't know what I'll do if that man hurts her." Cole kissed his mother on the forehead. His mother wiped away a tear from her cheek. It had been years since Cole had given her a hug, much less a kiss. He smiled and hurried to the back porch.

~

Herman had been standing next to the curtain that led into Mrs. James' bedroom. His heart raced with excitement as he listened to Cole's problem. His lovely wife had been kidnapped and he needed money. Poor thing, he grinned. This was his chance.

Mrs. James came out of her bedroom adjusting her hat over a tight bun, her reticule on her wrist. Herman stepped in front of her. She gasped and grabbed her neck.

"Oh, Milly, I couldn't help but hear Cole telling you that he needs money. This is our opportunity to force him to sell the store to you. Ask him to sign over his half of the store, then it will be my store."

Milly froze in place. She slowly turned around to give her full attention to Herman. "What do you mean, *my store?*" Before he could answer, she marched over to her counter and removed her hat.

"Oh, sweetheart, I didn't mean just mine." Herman searched for the right words. "After we are married, the store will belong to both of us. That's all I meant." He hoped she believed him.

Milly took a good look at the man who had made her feel like a young woman again. She began to see him with new eyes. "Now, I know your game. You don't want me—you want my store. Cole tried to warn me about you, but your sweet words and affection blinded me. You'd better get out that door while you still can." She grabbed a pair of scissors. Holding them like a weapon, she walked toward him.

"Now, Milly, you have it all wrong. What you're saying is not true. I love you."

"Liar, get out. I may have been naïve, but my eyes are open now. You only love my store and the money that it brings in. You almost got away with making an old fool out of me. Don't make me tell you again to get out."

~

Cole walked in the back door but stopped. After overhearing some of the exchange between Herman and his mother, Cole hurried to the cash register and pulled out several bills. "This is the pay you have coming to you. Leave while you can still walk," he said through gritted teeth.

Chapter 39

Orem walked his horse to the edge of town in Yellowstone. A young boy and his mother washed clothes on the side of a shack. The woman was bent over a heavy washboard. The boy who looked to be about ten was dressed in overalls that came up over his ankles, and his shirt was held together with one button. The poor kid reminded Orem of his own childhood.

Climbing down from his horse, he walked to the edge of the woman's yard. "Hey, son," Orem called to the boy. "You want to earn a coin?" He flashed a shiny nickel in the palm of his hand.

"A whole nickel?" the boy looked to his mother.

"Ask what you have to do to earn all that money," she said, her eyes narrowing.

"Do you know the owner of the dry-goods store, Cole James?"

"Sure do. Everybody knows him." The boy glanced at his mother.

"I need you to take this note to him. Put it in his hand. No one else's, understand?"

"Yes, sir. I can do that. Can I, Mama?"

"All right, Timothy, but hurry right back. I need your help." Turning her back to the stranger, the woman walked over to the clothesline.

"Here's the nickel. Now get going." Orem climbed back on his horse and rode slowly out of town.

~

Timothy took off at a full run. He jumped on the boardwalk and dodged several old ladies and men, the nickel tight in his fist. On the stagecoach platform, he sidestepped several passengers and bumped into a carpetbag, causing it to tumble onto the street.

Herman had been waiting for the stage to arrive. It was time to leave Yellowstone and possibly settle in Dallas. He never wanted to see Milly James or her son again. Angry, he grabbed the boy's arm and gave him a good shake. "Look at my bag. You'd better pick it up and wipe the dust off it," Herman said.

"I'm sorry, but I can't. I'm in a hurry. Please turn me loose."

"Where you going in such a hurry that you can't pick up my carpetbag?"

"I got a piece of paper for Mr. James. I need to give it to him so I can earn a nickel." The boy pulled on his arm, struggling to free himself.

Herman grabbed the note out of the boy's hand. The boy leapt to retrieve it from the stranger while Herman held it high in the air and read the contents. Shaking the boy off his arm, he smiled. Herman reached into his vest and held out a penny to the boy. "Here, I will take it over to him. You take this and scat."

The boy's eyes became big and round as he looked at the shiny coin. He grabbed it from Herman's hand. "You must see that he gets it. No one else," the boy said.

"Got it. You move along and forget all about the errand you had to run." Herman smiled as the stagecoach driver yelled, "All aboard." He folded the note in half and placed it in his coat pocket.

Now Herman knew that Cole's wife had been kidnapped and the sheriff and Cole were waiting for a ransom note from the kidnappers. Excitement flowed through his body. Now, he could repay Cole for the way he messed up his plans while he worked at the store. If it wasn't for Mr. Big Britches, he would have soon been the owner of the successful store. Milly was head-over-heels fascinated with him. He had her eating out of his hand. If Cole had kept his nose out of his business, he could have talked his way out of his blunder. Now, he smiled to himself. Mr. Cole James would receive his just reward for a ransom note that would never come.

~

Hour after hour, Cole waited at the store and at the farm for the ransom note to be delivered to him. Some of the men who had formed the posse had to return to their own farms. When and if the note came, the sheriff would need time to round up men in town to help with the rescue of his wife. The more time that passed, the more hopeless it looked.

~

Two days later, Timothy entered the store to purchase some lye for his mother to make soap. Mrs. James went into the storeroom and returned with a small bottle. "Be careful, and don't get that lye on your hands," Mrs. James said.

"Oh, I'm always careful, except the day before yesterday. I was bringing Mr. James a note, and I accidently knocked over a carpetbag, and this man grabbed the note from me. I had earned a nickel to bring that note, but the man said he would give it to him for me. Do you know if that man kept his word?"

Cole was standing in the door that led into the kitchen when he overheard the exchange between his mother and Timothy, the boy who lived outside of town with his mother. "Hey, Timothy. Did you say you were given a note to give to me, but another man said that he would help you by delivering it to me himself?"

"Yes sir. He did give it to you, didn't he? I sure hate to take somebody's money and not do what I was supposed to do."

"Can you tell me what the man looked like who took the note from you?" Cole asked, trying to keep his anger in check.

"Sure can. He was going on the stage somewhere. That was

why he got mad because I knocked his carpetbag in the street, and it got dusty. He was dressed pretty fancy and wore shiny shoes. His hands were clean. He gave me a penny and said he would give you the paper. He did give it to you, didn't he? If he didn't, I shouldn't keep the money, but I already gave it to Mama."

"Don't you fret, son. You did a good job, and you're a good boy."

"That's sure a load off my mind. I'd better hurry back to Mama. She needs this stuff to make soap to wash all those old men's clothes. I sure wish I was rich so she didn't have to work so hard." Timothy turned to leave.

"Wait," Cole said as he walked over to the cash register. He took out a fifty-cent piece and then opened the peppermint jar. He took out four sticks of candy and gave them to him along with the coin. "The candy is for you, and the money is for your mother for raising such an honest boy."

Timothy eyes were as large as a saucer. He thanked Mrs. James and Cole over and over as he backed out the front door of the store.

"Well, Mama, now we know the reason I haven't received a note from Jazz's ex-husband. Herman took the note from Timothy and kept it. He'd better not ever show himself in this part of the country again." Cole took off his apron and marched to the sheriff's office. They were going to have to come up with another plan to find Jazz.

Chapter 40

"Well, Orem, the second day is almost up, and there hasn't been one soul to travel near our drop-off point. What do you think?" Joe asked his partner.

"Ain't got no idea. Maybe that James fellow is having trouble coming up with that much money. Maybe we shouldn't have asked for so much." Orem spit in the open fireplace.

Jazz had been standing over by the stove. The two men had not planned very well. They only brought enough food for two meals. She walked over to the window and stood, avoiding Joe who sat at the table. He made her feel inadequate and miserable. Jazz had loved him with all of her heart, but now she felt only sorrow. Joe was treating her like a stranger. He acted like he didn't remember anything about their past together. She remained demure across the room and only smiled at him when he looked at her.

"Jazz, what do you think your loving husband is doing about now? The two days are nearly up in a couple of hours, and he hasn't been near the drop-off bucket that we placed on the main road."

"I haven't a clue. Wish I could tell you, but I can't even guess," Jazz answered as honestly as she could without making Joe mad.

"I think you'd better write him another note and spell things out the way they are going to be if he doesn't bring the money tomorrow. Come over here now and sit." Joe grabbed paper and a pencil and plunked them down in front of her at the table. "Orem, go saddle your horse and get ready to carry another message. Let's find a big rock and tie the note to it. You'll ride by the sheriff's office and throw it through his front windows. We'll know for sure that they received the message this time." Both men laughed.

~

Cole and the sheriff had their heads together going over a map of the county. Glass came flying across the room as a large rock bounced off the sheriff's desk onto the floor. Both men hit the floor when glass shattered all over the office. Cole flew to the window and then opened the office door. A fast rider was headed out of town. There was no way to catch him now.

The sheriff stood holding the note. "Cole, it looks like we have a drop-off point. You need to deliver the money tomorrow before noon. Can you do that?" A worried frown lined the sheriff's face.

"Yes, I have the money. Thought for sure they would ask for twice this amount. I'm still not sure he will release Jazz. From what Sam said about this man, he's not stable in the mind. Jazz will fight him. I'm sure he will hurt her bad if she does."

~

Joe needed as much insurance and protection that he could get to escape the sheriff's posse. He had been on the run long enough to know that holding a woman hostage wouldn't keep them from coming after him. Cole James wanted his wife returned safe and sound and would do anything to keep Jazz's baby from harm. Joe laughed to himself—he'd never wanted to be a papa. He hated kids, and he was happy every time his own mother lost a new baby. Joe remembered two occasions where he'd put a small amount of rat poison in her food. The doctor could never figure out why she got so sick. Not wanting to share their affections with a baby, he determined that his folks would never have another crying, snot-nosed brat.

As Orem slept on a pallet near the fireplace and Jazz was locked in the attic for the night, Joe saddled his horse and rode to Cole James' farm. He was sure Cole was sleeping at the store. At first light the men planned to head to the designated drop-off.

Joe tied his horse behind the barn and listened for the two men who worked on the farm. The big black man slept in the barn while the older man stayed in the house. Looking around, he gathered brush, limbs, and dry leaves and banked them up against the backside of the barn wall.

Two dogs raced up to him and began barking. Joe remembered the dogs so he had come prepared to control them. He tossed both of the dogs several pieces of dried jerky. The dogs grabbed the treat and rushed under the front porch.

Joe listened to make sure the dogs hadn't disturbed anyone in the house as he pushed more brush against the barn. He eased over to the side of the house and peeked in the window. That woman named Georgia was feeding the baby a bottle, while that little girl was sitting on the floor looking at a book.

Joe went back to the barn and lit a branch covered with leaves and tossed it into the brush. He hid near the back door of the house and waited for the flames to catch the side of the barn on fire.

~

Sam needed to go to the outhouse, so he slipped out the front door without disturbing the girls. He smelled the smoke before he saw it. "Georgia, come out of the house!" He raced to the barn and went inside to wake up David. "Get up and help. The barn is on fire," Sam yelled.

"I'll fetch the water while you lead the animals out."

Sam rushed to the goats and the milk cow. He led them to the corral and headed back inside the barn.

David came back with two buckets of water, gave one to

Sam, and poured a bucket of water on the fire, but it was almost out of control. Georgia came around the corner, carrying a couple of buckets from the well. She handed them to the two men and rushed back to get more.

~

"Mama, that mean man is back!" Lily was breathing hard and pointing at the front door when Georgia rushed up to her.

"Stay away from the barn, baby. I don't want you to get in the way. We have to save the barn," Georgia said, as she hurried around her little girl.

Lily grabbed Georgia's skirt. "Mama, help."

Georgia had carried the last two buckets to Sam, and he was pleased that he had put the fire out. He took a hoe and pulled the last of the burning brush away from the barn wall.

Georgia stood next to him, exhausted and weary, when Lily came around the corner crying. "It's all right, sweetheart," Georgia said. "Sam put the fire out, and the animals are all safe."

"But, Mama, that bad man is in the house."

"Oh, my gosh. Go tell David to grab his gun. Sam, hurry."

Georgia raced inside the house, not afraid of the devil himself, even Jazz's ex-husband. She had to protect the baby, and if it meant facing that awful man, she would. But, the house was empty. She raced into each room, but no one was there. Jeffrey's cradle was empty, and a few of his clean bottles were missing from the kitchen counter.

She eased down on her knees and held her face in her hands. "Oh, Lord," she prayed. "Please don't let any harm come to little Jeffrey. Please let your face shine down over the boy and protect him," she cried as Sam and David entered the house. She bolted to her feet. "That man snuck back over here and set the barn on fire." Georgia wrapped her arms around her waist. "He used the fire to grab our attention away from Jeffrey." She wiped her face with her apron. "Maybe he will carry the baby to Jazz."

Sam took Georgia by the shoulders and said, "He wants as much protection as he can get, so he thinks with the boy in tow, he will be safer."

David walked over to the water barrel and took a big drink of water. "He's running scared, so he wants to hold that boy over Jazz's head. She will do whatever he says as long as he doesn't harm her baby."

"Sam, you have to ride into town and tell Cole and the sheriff that animal has taken the baby. They're going to have to be careful if they catch up with them. That man is a killer."

"I'll go now. David, can you put the animals back in the barn? We were lucky this time," Sam said as rushed to the corral.

~

Sam entered the open doorway of the dingy office. The room held the barest essentials of furniture. The sheriff sat at the desk with his head lying across his arm fast asleep. The night was warm so the sheriff had removed his shirt to catch every breath of breeze.

Sam walked to the desk and shook the sheriff's shoulder. The man jumped straight up, grabbed his pistol, and pointed it straight at Sam.

"Sheriff, it's me, Sam. I came to tell you and Cole that Joe Whitmore came to the farm and took little Jeffrey." The sheriff frowned and wiped the sleep out of his eyes.

"Jeffrey is Cole's and Jazz's baby. That crazy man set the barn on fire, and while we were busy putting it out, he went into the house and took the baby."

"Have you told Cole?" The sheriff asked as he snatched his shirt from the back of his desk chair.

"No, I came straight here. Is Cole at his store?" Sam asked.

"Yelp. Go tell him now and tell him to get over here. We need to make new plans." The sheriff unlocked the chain that held the rifles.

Chapter 41

Jazz rose early to the sound of howling wind and peeked out the window at the heavy gray clouds racing across the sky. She prayed that it wouldn't rain, but soon raindrops beat hard against the windowpanes. A storm was brewing for sure.

During the night, the rain played havoc with her nerves. She should have been resting because today was going to be exhausting and nerve-racking. She prayed that Cole would make a successful drop, and he wouldn't be shot by Joe. Even though, Joe had said that no one would be hurt, she didn't trust anything he had to say.

She sat near the window and leaned her head against the wall thinking about the young man she married. He had changed so much. She never had a reason not to believe or trust him. When he left the train, he always returned in good spirits and with their needed supplies. Joe was a good husband and provider, not a liar or killer. But now, he was proven to be a ruthless killer. She would have never believed it.

A strange noise coming from downstairs made her walk over to the locked door and lean her ear against the cracks. A baby was screaming. Her baby! Those cries were coming from her baby. She would know Jeffrey's cries anywhere.

Pounding on the door, she began yelling at the top of her lungs. "Joe, Joe, open this door. I know you have my baby."

Suddenly, the bar was removed from the door. Orem stood at the top of the stairs holding her baby like a sack of potatoes. "Here, take this wet brat. Shut that wailing up." He turned and practically hopped down the staircase, taking two and three steps at a time.

Jazz held Jeffrey in her arms and cried. "Oh, my baby, I was so afraid I wouldn't ever hold you again. Let's go downstairs and get something dry to go on your bottom. You are soaked through and through."

She eased down the narrow stairs into the open room. Joe and Orem were outside. Rushing over to the window, she watched the two men discussing something. She glanced across the room and saw a few baby bottles sitting on the table. Laying Jeffrey on the wobbly table, she reached under her dress and removed the bottom of her white shift. Tearing the shift, she made a fresh nappy. She removed the wet one and replaced it with the dry material, using the small nappy pins. Jeffrey immediately stopped crying.

Joe came inside the house and smiled. "Finally, peace," he said. "I thought that I had made a big mistake in bringing that brat to you. He cried from the time I picked him up. I wanted to toss him in a ditch." He stared at Jazz without smiling.

She knew he was serious about harming her baby. Not his baby.

"How did you steal Jeffrey away from Georgia? Don't you dare tell me that you hurt her."

"It was like taking candy from a small child. I set the barn on fire, and the woman and the men were too busy putting out the flames to notice that I carried the boy out the back door. No one was hurt."

"Thank God," Jazz said and hugged her baby. "Did the barn burn to the ground?"

"I didn't stay around to watch," he replied with a grin.

"Did you think to bring the baby some nappies and milk?"

"No, I'm not a nursemaid. I did grab a few baby bottles," he said, like he had done something important. "Orem has gone into town to buy some canned milk and material to use for nappies."

"Don't you think he might be recognized by someone?" Jazz

asked, praying silently that someone would remember him.

"Your husband has never seen Orem, and besides, he won't be at the store. He will be with the posse looking for us."

"I see. It is thoughtful of you to think about the baby's needs, but I am surprised. Why did you go and kidnap Jeffrey?" Jazz asked, as she cuddled her son in her arms.

"The posse won't be shooting at us with a baby in our midst. After we collect the money, they will allow us to move on. They know that I will let you return after we cross the Rio Grande into Mexico."

He didn't mention her child. Did he plan on carrying Jeffrey into Mexico? A feeling of dread settled around her heart.

Jeffrey started fretting, so Jazz boiled a small amount of water and poured it in a bottle. After it cooled, she fed him the liquid. He sucked at it greedily.

In less than an hour, Orem returned to the house with a bolt of white muslin and six cans of milk. He whispered to Joe that he had to tie up the old woman store clerk because she was too nosy. She demanded to know who he wanted the items for. The old woman seemed to know he was buying the things for Jazz's baby.

"Why didn't you kill her?" Joe asked.

"Now, Joe, I ain't no woman killer. Besides, I locked the store and turned the open sign over. She won't be found for a long while." Orem turned and walked out of the house.

Joe scowled at Jazz. "Feed that young'un and rip that material into nappies. We're getting ready to move out and pick up the money."

~

Standing in front of the two-story shack, Joe watched as Jazz climbed on a horse. He grabbed her mount's reins and kicked his own horse in the side, then pulled Jazz's up beside his. "If you see any of the posse or your darling husband, you'd better keep quiet. Do I make myself clear?"

Orem had Jeffrey in his arms as they traveled to the drop-off point. The plan was to grab the money and ride across the Rio Grande River. After they were safely across, Joe had still not decided what to do with Jazz. He might let her go, but he wasn't sure what he was going to do with the baby. Joe certainly didn't want him, but his sweet wife needed to pay for marrying so quickly. She didn't wait any time before she crawled in bed with another man. He had a yearning for revenge, and if it meant doing harm to her baby, so be it.

Chapter 42

The sheriff, Cole, Sam, and the posse left town. They had been told to be careful if and when they found the two men, Cole's wife, and baby. "Please don't fire upon the men unless you have a clean shot," the sheriff had ordered.

The men rode several hours and soon entered the forest where a muddy trail had been discovered by a scout. Many tree branches lashed down on the men as their horses slipped from side to side in the mud. The riders were tiring but determined. They continued forward, battling falling trees, branches, and other debris. Their target was a bucket sitting by the pathway. Cole had the money wrapped in a white bank bag.

The sky rumbled. Another summer storm was brewing again. The roads were already filled with mud holes, and it was difficult to pick up horse tracks. They plodded through the forest as clouds chased overhead. Cole prayed that the rain would hold off until they made the drop, and Jazz and the baby were returned to him.

Filled with hopes and fears, the posse rode on until the scout hurried back to Cole, Sam, and the sheriff. "A bucket is sitting beside the road about fifty feet from here."

"Thanks, Bill," the sheriff said, relief on his face. "Well, Cole, are you ready to place the money in the bucket? You know we're being watched. They're going to take the money and ride to the river. We sure need to reach the crossing before they do. Hopefully, we can catch them before they make it into Mexico."

"You and the men go on ahead. I will be directly behind you." Cole said, aware of the eyes watching.

"Sounds like a good plan. We'll hide in the trees at the river's edge," he said. "You go on ahead and we'll move out quietly. See you soon," the sheriff said.

Cole rode slowly down the trail looking for a bucket sitting beside the road. When he came upon a rusty bucket, he reined in his horse and sat still for a few minutes, peering into the woods and bushes for any sign of Joe or his partner.

A haunting laughter came from somewhere near. "Go ahead and put the money in the bucket, and if you try anything silly, I'll have to hurt your wife and child." Joe's voice trailed away.

Cole wanted to ride straight to the voice, but he mentally ordered himself to remain calm. He needed to know if his wife was safe. "Jazz, are you all right?" he yelled.

~

Jazz looked straight at Joe. She wanted to scream for Cole to ride away. Joe was a killer, and he might not allow Cole to ride away after placing the money in the bucket.

"Go ahead and answer him." Joe chuckled. "Say yes. That's all."

"Yes," Jazz said loud enough for her sweet husband to hear.

Cole climbed off his horse and untied the money bag from his saddle horn. He ambled over to the old rusty bucket that had a hole in the bottom and dropped the money into it. Ten thousand dollars was his life savings and all the money his mother could get her hands on. He shook his head, but if this money would make the fool return Jazz and little Jeffrey, it would be worth it. Cole stepped back, his eyes surveying the woods, hoping to catch a glimpse of Joe, but the woods were too thick.

Cole climbed back on his horse, and turned it around, heading back down the way he came. Anger filled him, but what could he do? He would have to wait at the river with the sheriff's posse, which included Sam.

~

Near the bank of the river, Cole joined Sam, the sheriff, and his posse who had hidden their horses in the woods and watched from the cottonwood trees. The river was only about three feet deep in places, but rain from upstream had caused the water to run rapidly with a strong undercurrent. It would take an experienced rider to guide their mount across the Rio Grande. As they waited, they watched several riders continue downstream, looking for higher ground to cross. "I'm sure the two men will be coming by soon," Cole said, as he tied his horse out of sight.

After what seemed like hours, Joe Whitmore appeared near the crossing, holding the baby in his arms while Jazz rode a horse behind his partner. They stopped for a few minutes, looking around for any signs of danger. The one named Orem leapt off his mount and walked to the water's edge.

"Damn, that water is too swift for us to cross here. We'll have to ride a couple miles up the river and try crossing there," Orem yelled over the noise of the roaring water.

"No, we're crossing here. You lead Jazz's horse and I will follow. "Now git!" Joe screamed, juggling the boy.

Orem grabbed Jazz's horse's reins and started in the water. Her horse froze and backed away from Orem's mount. "Come on, you stubborn jackass." He jerked her horse toward the running waters, but his own steed backed away from the water.

Jazz lost her footing, causing her to slip out of the saddle and land in the muddy water. She scrambled onto her feet and wiped her muddy hands on her dress. She glared at Joe as he sat on top of his horse holding Jeffrey as a shield. He was daring the men to shoot at him.

Orem finally coaxed his mount into the river. His horse side-stepped and bolted causing Orem to fall into the river. His head bobbed up and down out of the water as he struggled in the rough water. In a flash, he floated out of sight downstream.

Jazz raced over to Joe, begging him. "Give me my baby," she cried, but he only laughed.

"You want him?" He held Jeffrey high out in front of his body. "You will never have him," his rough voice floated in the strong wind. "Well, my devoted wife, this is payback for you not loving me enough." He glanced back over his shoulder at the posse. "You should have waited for me to come back."

"Please, Joe," Jazz pleaded. "You were supposed to be dead. How did I know to wait? Please, please, give me my baby." She rushed up to him and grabbed his thigh. "Give me my son, and you can cross the river now. You'll be safe."

"Silly girl. You don't deserve to have a baby." Holding Jeffrey high in the air so the posse could see him, he took his boot and kicked Jazz in the chest, sending her flying backward onto the ground. Laughing like a crazy person, he swung the baby back and forth in the air. Moving his horse closer to the water, with one big swing, he attempted to sling the baby into the rapid river when a gunshot rang out.

~

Jazz screamed, "No!" as she hung onto Joe as he moved. With his body sliding off his horse, she saw the white blanket floating in the wind over the wild river. Screaming, she rushed to the river's edge. Seeing the white material go under the water, she screamed "Noooo, as she threw herself into the rushing water. With her screams echoing in the wind, her head went under just as Cole reached the bank where she had jumped in. With nothing to grab onto, she was carried down the rushing river.

Over on the ground, beneath Joe's dead body lay the baby. Joe's body had slowly crumbled to the ground with Jeffrey cuddled in his arms. The sheriff turned Joe over on his back, and the men watched as the baby waved his little arms and kicked his feet. "Thank you, Jesus," he mumbled.

~

Once Cole saw the baby lying on the ground safe, he jumped on Jazz's horse and raced down the edge of the Rio Grande. He looked for any sign of his wife. Terrorizing screams reached his ears several times. His greatest fear was that he wasn't going to be able to find her. After what seemed like miles, he saw her limp body caught on a log stretched across the river. Removing his boots, he jumped into the rapids and swam as fast as he could to her. He lifted her scratched face from the water, pushed stringy, wet strands of hair out of her eyes, and turned her over on her side. He positioned her body over the log and pounded her back while struggling to hold onto the log. She coughed up water from her lungs. "That's right, honey, cough some more," he yelled, over the rushing water.

Finally, her eyes opened as she continued to cough. She tried to speak, but tears and river water flowed down her face. "My baby," she tried to say.

"He's safe," Cole yelled, fighting to hold himself on the log while securing her in his arms. "He's safe, sweetheart."

Grabbing Cole tighter, she cried until she only whimpered. "I love you," she mumbled, as she held onto him for dear life as he waited for the posse to help them to the shore.

Sam and one of the posse members appeared at the bank. In a flash, Sam removed his boots, leaped into the water, and helped Cole brave the rapids and carry Jazz to the riverbank. The three men lifted her limp body onto the bank. Cole climbed onto his horse, and the two men placed Jazz in his arms.

Cole pulled her against his body, tilted her head back, and kissed her hard and thoroughly. It was a kiss they both would remember for a long time to come.

Chapter 43

The sheriff and his posse rode into Yellowstone, tired and hungry but satisfied. Cole James had gotten his wife and child back safe and sound. His mother and he could return their money to the bank and have all the liens removed from the dry-goods store.

The last day had been emotionally draining, but God had protected everyone involved in this dangerous kidnapping. Joe Whitmore was dead, for real this time. When the sheriff posse had hanged him the first time, there was a wanted poster on him for killing several people and robbing a few banks. A reward for five-thousand dollars was on his head. He was believed to be crazy in the head, off balanced, as most folks said, and a ruthless killer. It was hard for people that knew him personally to believe he could do these bad things.

Once the reward money arrived, The sheriff would make sure Jazz Whitmore received it. She could do whatever her heart desired with it. The sheriff walked over to a small cot in the corner of his office and lay down for a much-needed rest.

~

Cole and Sam took Jazz straight to the farm where Georgia, Lily, and David were all waiting. Sam carried the baby cradled in his arms while Jazz lay across Cole's lap. Cole was thankful that Sam had ridden with the posse, but he knew the old man had to be worn to a frazzle.

David was waiting on the porch when the two men rode into the yard. He yelled for Georgia who came running with tears streaming down her cheeks.

~

"Praise the Lord, praise the Lord," she cried over and over as David held the reins of both horses. Sam leaned down and placed a sleeping Jeffrey into Georgia's arms. She cuddled him and watched Sam take Jazz from Cole. All of them went inside the house, while David took care of the animals.

Georgia carried little Jeffrey into the bedroom and laid him on the bed. She unwrapped Cole's bedroll blanket from the little tyke. Jeffrey smiled and kicked his free legs. He placed his fists in his mouth and tried to blow bubbles. Georgia smiled at the sweet baby as she changed his wet nappy. She placed a clean gown over his little body and carried him to the kitchen on her shoulder. She was going to prepare him a fresh bottle of milk and a little mashed potatoes. He already had two teeth.

~

Cole gently placed Jazz in their bed. He smiled down at his lovely wife who was dozing. He rolled her over to unfasten her gown and stripped it from her with the other garments. As she lay naked under the covers, he hurried into the kitchen for a pan of hot water. He glanced at Georgia who was feeding Jeffrey while Lily sat on the floor and played with the little fellow's feet. After setting the hot water on the table, he poured Jazz a small glass of brandy and ran back. "Drink this, sweetheart. It will put some color in your cheeks."

She sat up and obeyed his command. Taking a big gulp of the drink, her face contorted. She coughed and choked on the fiery liquid.

"I should have warned you to just take a sip," he said with a little smile. Cole started pulling pins from her hair, and soon the wet curls were falling loosely over her shoulder. He brushed the curls away from her face, then washed her face and neck with a warm cloth. She had many scratches on her cheeks and neck from floating down the river. A large knot was on her forehead. He squeezed the cloth out and laid it on her head, then went to the door and asked David to go down in the cellar and chop a pan of ice and bring it to him. After he washed her body, Georgia helped him pull a fresh gown over her head.

A soft knock came from the front door. Doctor Richards stood with his hat in one hand and black bag in the other. "The sheriff said I should come and check on Mrs. James. I told him that you probably wouldn't allow me to examine her, but here I am." He stood with a stiff posture.

Cole's shoulders drooped and he sighed. "I'll let you look at her head. Jazz may still have water in her lungs. She's asleep now, but if she awakes, I will assure her that you are here only to help. Thanks for coming," Cole said, leading him into the bedroom.

Cole removed the icy cloth and stood back and watched the doctor listen to Jazz's breathing. He ran his hands over her head and touched the big knot on her forehead.

Jazz flinched and opened her eyes. She cringed and sucked in her breath until her eyes adjusted, and she looked into Doctor Richards' face.

"It's all right, sweetheart." Cole dropped to his knees next to Jazz. "Doctor Richards wants to make sure that you don't have any broken bones and that your lungs are clear of river water. Just lie still and let him check you over. I'm right here."

Doctor Richards asked Cole to help him sit Jazz up so he could listen to her back. He instructed his patient to cough, then said, "I can hear a little rattle in her lungs but not as bad as i thought it would be." Then the doctor asked her to look at his finger and follow it as he moved it from side to side. "Blink a few times. Good." Then he asked her name and the name of the town she lived in. He helped Cole lay Jazz back against two pillows.

Then he turned to Cole. "She must not have swallowed as much water as we all thought. Her lungs have some rattling, which does tells me she has some, but if she coughs several times a day and take the medicine I'll leave, she should be all right in four or five days. I would like her to stay in bed for a few days, then she can walk around inside or outside for about thirty minutes a day. The knot on her head will go down. You did the right thing by icing it. She will have a nice bruise, but she doesn't have any damage to her head or eyes. She is one lucky young lady," he said as he placed the instruments in his bag.

As he walked to the door, he turned to Jazz. "Mrs. James, please follow my instruction and take the medicine I'm leaving with your husband. If you need me for anything else, please send one of your men for me. Good day."

Cole walked the doctor to the door. He took out several bills and gave them to him. "Thank you so much for coming."

~

After a few days, a limb hit the bedroom window. Cole sat straight up, hoping not to awake Jazz. Little Jeffrey was sleeping soundly. He slipped on his trousers and tiptoed into the front room. Georgia was preparing the morning coffee.

"Did the storm wake you, Mr. Cole?" Georgia asked.

"Something hit the window. I'm sure glad it didn't break the glass. I believe the cheesecloth saved it from breaking." He walked to the front door and looked outside. A storm was already blowing everything around in the farmyard. Sam and David were taking the swing down from the porch. Georgia opened the front door and asked the men if they would check on the big sow and the goat. The two puppies were huddled up against the wall on the porch and begged to come inside the house.

"Let the pups inside this morning, Georgia. They're really afraid," Cole said, as he jumped off the porch and ran to the barn.

After closing the shutters in the barn, he hurriedly milked the cow. As he started to the house with the milk, David took the pail from him.

"I'll take care of this, Mr. Cole," David said, as they both entered the house.

"Good Lord, this is a rotten day," Cole said as he poured himself a big cup of steaming coffee. He went to warm his backside as Jazz entered the kitchen. She was swaying from one chair to another before Cole caught her and pushed her down in the rocker.

"Georgia, please bring my disobedient wife a cup of coffee. Since she's up, she needs to eat a hot biscuit or two. Then, back to bed for more needed rest. Doctor's orders."

Sam came rushing in the house. He frowned as he looked back on the stormy morning. "Golly, I hope all this rain doesn't wash up the plants in the summer garden." He bent down and petted the puppies' heads as they rubbed up against his stockinged feet.

"When I was a child, I was afraid of the rain," Jazz said softly. "Especially when it was stormy like this, and I didn't have a cozy place like I have here now." She peered at Cole and gave him a sweet smile.

Cole ambled to his sweet wife's side and held her hand. He raised her palm and kissed the inside of it. "You never have to be afraid again, of anything or anybody. That is a promise. This is your home, and I am your protector."

"Oh, Cole, I feel safe now. I hate what happened with Joe returning from the dead. Who would have ever thought something like that could happen? All this morning, I have been thinking about what I will tell Jeffrey about his father when he asks me. I don't want him to think that I didn't love him, but how can I tell a child that his real father was a terrible person?"

"Sweetheart, I believe when the time comes, you will answer his questions with the truth from your heart. I personally believe that Joe was sick, and he couldn't control his behavior. He was a good husband to you in the beginning. That is all our son needs to learn while he is small. Once he's a grown man, if he hears the truth about Joe's last years, he will be old enough to understand why you withheld the truth from him."

"Oh, Cole, you are a such a nice, loving man. I am thankful that God led me to your store, and you took me in to work for you. I love you," she whispered as she smiled at him.

He was pretty shaken by her expression of love. Tension and anticipation flowed between them. He lifted his gaze to her lips and stayed there as he whispered his affection for her.

Chapter 44

A few days passed and Cole was going to leave Jazz in Georgia's capable hands. He really wasn't ready to leave until he felt that she was back to normal. His mother needed him at the store since Herman wasn't working there anymore. Today, he was going to search for a young man who needed to earn extra money for his family.

Cole entered the store, wrapped his apron over his clothes, and looked and listened for any sound of Mama. He called to her, but after receiving no answer, he took out a large piece of paper and made a sign to place in the window. It read, *Help needed, Young man who desires to work. Apply inside.*

Cole turned the closed sign to open. He called to his mother again at the curtain that closed off her bedroom from the store. No answer, so he filled the cash register with money and began filling the shelves behind the counter.

~

Cole had only been gone about an hour when a wagon pulled into the farm close to the corral. Sam rushed out of the barn and greeted an old woman driving a wagon with a team of mules. A young boy, about eight, was perched upon the seat next to her.

"Good morning, young man," the woman with rosy cheeks and salt-and-pepper hair twisted under a floppy hat called to Sam.

"Hardly young, but good morning to you two. How can I

help you?" Sam asked, while holding onto the lead mule's reins.

"I'm Mrs. Richardson. Is Mr. James at home, or have we missed him?" The old woman asked as she looked toward the barn.

"Now, are you asking about old Mr. James or the young one we all call Cole?" Sam asked.

"I have always done business with old Mr. James. Is his old cranky wife around? I hate having to talk money with that one."

Sam laughed and shook his head. "Mrs. Richardson, I hate to bring you bad news, but old Mr. James has passed away a while ago. His wife runs the dry-goods store in town along with her son, Cole."

"Shoot fire. Just my luck. Mr. James always bought a crate of strawberries from me. He had an old housekeeper that put up jam for here and to sell at the store. I was hoping we could make the same deal."

"Let me help you down, and you can meet Cole's wife. You will like her," Sam said. "You know, Cole is part owner of the store now that his pa has died. I bet he will take some of your produce off your hands. I'm sure Georgia will want some strawberries."

"Who is Georgia?" Mrs. Richardson inquired.

"She and her little girl, Lily, live here and help keep the place running. I bet Lily will show your boy her new puppies," Sam said. The boy smiled and leapt down off the wagon. Sam laughed as he offered his hand to Mrs. Richardson. "Come on, and I will take you inside. Afterwards, David and I will care for your mules while you visit."

~

Jazz and Georgia were pleasantly surprised to meet Mrs. Richardson who told them all about her travels around the countryside selling her produce. "Mr. James was always one of my biggest customers. He bought fruit and other fresh items for this place, and some of my other items for the store—onions, potatoes, strawberries, blueberries, apples, and pears. People would buy him out in a day or two."

"Georgia, do you know how to prepare strawberry jam? I believe I remember. I helped a café owner's wife one time. We must have put up a hundred quart jars." Jazz stood with her arms wrapped around her waist.

"I also sell jars, too, if you need them. Sorry, I don't have enough sugar to sell you, but your man can bring you some from his store, I'm sure."

"That settles it then," Jazz said, as she went to the kitchen pantry and came out carrying cash. "We will take a crate of strawberries, a bag of apples, and several containers of blueberries today." Georgia beamed, and Lily clapped her hands.

"I loves berries," Lily said.

"We will need many jars too," Georgia said. "David, you and Sam help this young man put the jars on the front porch, and later you can carry most of them down into the cellar."

Jazz went into the kitchen and placed four hot biscuits in a brown bag with several boiled eggs for Mrs. Richardson and the little boy. "Here is a little something for your trip into town. Maybe next time you come, you will stay and take a meal with us. We sure enjoyed your visit."

"Thanks for your kind hospitality. Sure, glad I didn't have to deal with old Mrs. James. She never had a nice word to say about my fruit or vegetables, but her husband bought my stuff anyways. You folks are nice and kindhearted. We'll sure enjoy these vittles," she said as she held up the brown bag.

Sam and David walked Mrs. Richardson and the boy out to their wagon. David picked the boy up and practically slung him onto the bench while Sam eased the woman up on the seat. Sam led the mules to the road leading into town.

~

Georgia was buzzing around the food when she pointed at

Jazz.

"All right, Missy, you need to go and take a nice rest. Your face has no color. When you get up, you can help me wash some the strawberries. For now, I am going to make us two strawberry pies to enjoy today. Mr. Cole can bring us some sugar home tomorrow, and we will start making jam. It sure will be good come this winter."

After changing Jeffrey and laying him down on a pallet to play, Georgia made sure Jazz was stretched out on the bed resting. She went into the kitchen, washed and cleaned strawberries, and placed them in bowls for Sam, Lily, and David to enjoy. She sprinkled sugar over the top of them and added some fresh milk.

They were all sitting at the table enjoying their special treat when another horse and carriage pulled into the yard.

~

Mrs. James heard her son coming into the store, so she rushed out back, then down the alley to the train depot. "I want a ticket as far as fifty dollars will take me," she said to Henry Millstone, the station manager.

"Well, Mrs. James, are you planning on taking a trip to anywhere specific?" he laughed. "Where in the world do you want to go?" he said, cocking his head. "As long as I've known you and your husband, neither one of you has ever stepped foot on one of my trains."

"Mind your own business, you old fool, and give me a ticket. I'm in a big hurry."

"Now, Milly, you aren't talking to your husband or son. I won't be treated like you do your customers. If you want a ticket from me, you'd better watch your mouth."

"I'm sorry, Henry. Just give me a ticket." She attempted a smile.

"This money won't take you to California, but for sure, it will carry you all the way to Dallas." Henry said as he laid the ticket in

252

front of her.

As she reached for the ticket, Henry held onto the paper. "Milly, we have known each other for years. Are you in some kind of trouble?"

"Like I said before, Mr. Millstone, mind your own business, not mine." She tried to keep her voice low, but she wanted to hit him over the head with her purse.

The station master looked over his glasses and passed the ticket to her. "Have a safe trip, Milly."

Mrs. James flounced off the train platform and headed to the livery. She called to Mel Carter to hitch her horse and carriage.

"Do you need a driver?" Mel asked, as he started to hitch her rig.

Milly wanted to scream. Men considered all women to be helpless. "No, I can drive myself. Just help me up and get out of the way. I'm in a hurry."

"Will you be gone long?" Mel asked, his brows furrowed.

My Lord, another nosey man who thinks a woman can't get alone by herself. "Mind your own business and don't fret over me. I'm an experienced driver." She flicked the reins and drove her carriage down Main Street weaving from side to side, many horses and riders dashing out of her path.

~

Mel Carter stood watching Mrs. James drive out of town, and he couldn't help but wonder where in the world that pretty, old woman was going so early. He hoped she arrived at her destination without running over anyone.

Chapter 45

David was in the corral when he saw Cole's mama driving a carriage into the front yard. He was surprised to see her driving alone. The horse was snorting and lathered up with white foamy sweat around his mouth and down his chest wall. If he didn't know better, he would have sworn that she had been in a horse race.

He hurried out of the corral, gathered the reins of the horse, and held it still while Mrs. James attempted to get out of the carriage. He noticed her hat was flipped backward and her shawl was covered with dust.

Sam appeared from around the side of the house and offered her assistance to the ground. She waved him away and marched up the porch steps with the two puppies barking at her heels.

With no thank-you to either man, she kicked her boot toward the pups to make them go away. With her fist, she banged on the door. Georgia answered, but Mrs. James pushed her inside without an invitation.

"Good morning, Mrs. James. Did you come to see your son? He has already left for the store. You might have passed him on the road," Georgia said.

"No, I came to see the woman he's married too. Go tell her that I am here," she demanded.

~

Jazz was sitting on the side of the bed, preparing to go to the water closet when she heard voices from the front of the house. She quickly put on her robe and went into the necessary. Hurrying out, Georgia was standing with her back to the door. "Who's here and what is wrong?" Jazz asked, as she ran her hand through her long blond curls.

"Mr. Cole's mama, and she is in a huff of some kind. She is demanding to see you," Georgia said, as she opened the bedroom door.

"Good morning, Mrs. James," Jazz said quietly, hoping that all the loud noise hadn't awakened the baby.

"I will cut right to why I am here. I want you to pack up your things and the baby. There's a train leaving Yellowstone at four o'clock. this afternoon. I want you on it." She sauntered over to Jazz.

"My son may think he loves you, but I know he only feels sorry for you—a young woman put off a wagon train, once married to a killer, bank robber, and heaven knows what else he's done. The whole town is talking about you and your dead husband. A man who came back to life and did horrible things in our town. This story will be told and retold as long as you are living here." She spun around to leave and then spouted more ugly words.

"You aren't fit to be my son's wife. Oh, you're pretty enough, but with your reputation, he will never hold a place in Yellowstone's society. He can never run for mayor, much less be governor of the state. Cole's a smart, ambitious man, but he's tied to a harlot for a wife. For shame, girl. That's all I have to say. I want you on the train at 4:00 p.m. Here is your ticket and some money. You can start yourself a new life somewhere else." She threw the ticket and a stack of bills on the table.

"What will you tell Cole about why I left?" Jazz was in total shock and couldn't believe this woman was demanding she leave her son. She had no idea this woman hated her so much.

"Cole wouldn't expect anything less from the likes of you. He'll be glad to learn that you have left," Mrs. James said as she marched out the front door.

Jeffrey was fretting, so Jazz turned and went into the bedroom. She picked him up and patted his back. "Good morning, my precious boy. It looks like you and I are going on a long trip."

Georgia must have overheard her soft comment to Jeffrey. "Miss Jazz, now you listen to me. You ain't leaving this house. This is your home and you're gonna stay, even if I have to have David and Sam hog-tie you. That old witch can't make you leave Mr. Cole. Lord have mercy, girl. That man loves you so much. He'll just die if you leave."

Jazz laid her son down and put a fresh nappy on him. She headed into the kitchen holding him while Georgia heated a bottle of milk. In a few minutes, she sat down in the rocker and fed Jeffrey.

Finally, Jazz leaned her head back against the rocker and sighed. "Oh, Georgia, I haven't been anything but a headache to Cole since I arrived. For once, maybe his mama might be right. He'll be better off without me and Jeffrey. We have been nothing but a burden to him, for sure."

"Why don't you let me give Jeffrey some oatmeal while you go and lie down for a while? You still need rest."

"All right, I believe I will. I need to think and plan what I'm going to do."

Much later, Jazz got up and went into the kitchen. Two strawberry pies sat near the window cooling. The kitchen smelled wonderful. A big pot of beef stew was simmering on the stove with a large cake of cornbread on the counter. "It looks like you've been busy while I've just been lying about. Why don't we start cleaning some of those strawberries to get ready to make jam tomorrow? We need to wash several dozen jars. How about we all go down to the cellar and bring up the jars and about half of the strawberries. I'll go call in the men to come eat, and then we will tackle that chore. I feel so much better, today."

After David, Sam, and Lily had enjoyed beef stew,

cornbread, and big slices of strawberry pie, they all marched down into the cellar. Georgia followed the men, urging them to be careful to not break any of the jars. They handed the jars to Jazz who stood above them at the cellar door.

~

When they were finished, Jazz quickly lowered the cellar door and slid the big board across it to hold it shut.

"Hey, Jazz," Sam called. "The door shut on us. Open it and secure it with the large stone sitting beside it."

When no answer came, Sam called again. "She must have gone in the house. Light that lantern, and we'll continue to count. She'll be back out in a minute," Georgia said.

After all the jars were set aside to be carried inside the house, Sam called again to Jazz. Still no answer came.

"Something is going on with Jazz," Georgia said. "Do you think she locked us down here so she could get away with little Jeffrey? She said earlier that maybe Cole would be better off without her."

"Did Cole's mama say mean things to her this morning?" David asked. "I don't trust that woman. She was always mean to me when I came around the store."

"Jazz didn't want you to know what she said to her, but yes, she demanded that Jazz leave Cole. I told her that I would never let her leave even if I had to get you two to hog-tie her. Guess she believed me."

"How are we going to get out of here? I've got to pee!" Lily said.

"Listen, someone is over at the barn, but I can't see out," Sam said, then yelled, "Jazz, let us out of here this minute." Still no answer.

~

Jazz hurried to the horse and carriage, then tossed her

carpetbags in the back seat. She placed sleeping Jeffrey on the seat and climbed in. For a few moments, she stared at the cellar door. A light shone through the cracks, which made her feel better. "I love you all," she said as she flicked the reins and drove toward town.

After Mrs. James left the house, Jazz decided the best thing for Cole was for her to leave and let him begin his life over without her. He was such a nice, gentle man who deserved a good girl— one his mama liked. Jazz had tried to be good to Mrs. James, but she only wanted to believe the worse about her, even when the rumors weren't true.

Jazz went straight to the train depot and summoned help from a young man to put her carpetbags on the train-station platform. She gave him a quarter, and he said he would place them on the train for her as soon as it arrived.

Next, she drove the horse and carriage to the livery stable. Mel Carter was standing out front. "Well, my goodness. This is the second Mrs. James that I have helped today. How can I help you?" he asked.

"Please water and feed Cole's horse. When he comes to get his horse, please tell him that his other horse and carriage are here. I would appreciate it very much if you would give him this message. It is private, so please don't open it." She handed him a note.

"Gracious woman, who did you think I am? This note is sealed. I would never open it." Mel Carter frowned.

"I do apologize, Mr. Carter. I didn't mean to imply anything personal against you." Jazz said, her cheeks warming.

"Oh, that's all right, Miss. I am sorry I lost my temper. Sure, I'll give this to Cole as soon as he comes this afternoon." He took the horse and carriage and led it beside the barn.

Jazz boarded the train and took a window seat. Her passenger car was almost empty, so she was able to use the extra seat next to her to lay Jeffrey down. He cooed, kicked his feet, and waved his little hands. Jeffrey was such a good, happy little boy.

The conductor came by and took her ticket and said that the train would be leaving in fifteen minutes. "Can I bring you anything?"

"No thank you," she said nicely, wondering how her loved ones were doing back home in the cellar. Surely, they would be madder than a bunch of wet hens and roosters.

The doors slammed and the train whistle blew, making Jeffrey jump and fret for a second, but he didn't cry. Steam was building up outside her window when suddenly the door to the train car flew open, and Cole stood at the bottom of the steps. She slid back against her seat, hoping he wouldn't see her.

Jumping inside the passenger car, he stood towering over her. "Get up and start moving toward the door, or I will toss you over my shoulder," Cole hollered over the noise of the train.

Jazz quickly scooped up Jeffrey and headed to the door. The train rocked and rattled, then came to an abrupt stop, nearly causing her to fall. Cole held her firmly, but she didn't dare look up at him. The conductor was standing at the bottom of the steps with his arms stretched out to help Jazz with her child. Her two carpetbags lay on the train platform. Just as her feet touched the ground, a firm grip on her upper arm led her to the carriage.

"Climb in." Cole turned to the conductor and took the baby from his arms. "Thank you, George. I will show you my appreciation later."

"You're more than welcome, my son. I'd have never let her on my train if I'd known who she was married to." He laughed and walked toward the first car, then jumped in the doorway and waved at the engineer. The train rattled and spewed steam all around as it moved on down the track.

~

Cole's mother was watching all the activity take place between her son and that woman from the upstairs window of the dry-goods store. He must have received word from some nosy

259

body that his wife was leaving, and now he would know that she was the reason. He would never speak to her again. *Can't anything go my way?*

Chapter 46

Cole didn't say a word to Jazz as they drove past the crowd that had gathered. He'd already heard that many of the men had placed bets on how he was going to treat her when he got his hands on her. Some bet that he would take her in his arms and confess how sorry he was, and others bet that he would take a strap to her right in front of everyone. Of course, Cole wasn't supposed to know about the bets.

He could tell several ladies were thrilled beyond words that he had taken her off the train and was carrying her home— Mrs. Harrington, the minister's wife, Ruby Goodman, from the tailor's shop, Thelma, the saloon gal, and even Mrs. Browning, the boardinghouse owner.

Once they were out of hearing, Cole finally spoke. "So, my dear wife, did you think that a short note would satisfy me and make me understand why you left your new home and me? Oh, let me refresh your memory," It read something like this:

> *My dearest Cole, very nice, I hate to have to leave, but I must. You have been so good to me and my son, and I will always be grateful. You are a wonderful man, and like your mama said, you can have a better life without me. I shall always remember you, Love, Jazz.*

Did I leave anything out?" he asked, but she didn't answer. "We have a lot to discuss when we get home. Yes, I mean home. My home, your home, and Jeffrey's home. I will do most of the talking, and if you don't like what I have to say, then too bad. You are married to me and we have a son to raise. End of story.

"But Cole, you can't make me stay."

"Don't try me, my sweet wife. I am in no mood to hear you out. I only want to know one thing from you. Where in the world was Georgia, Sam, and David? Not to even mention Lily when you were packing. I can't believe that they just let you up and leave."

~

"Everyone stand back against the wall. I am going to break us out." David waited until Sam, Georgia, and Lily were in the back of the cellar. He reached up on one of the beams holding the cellar roof and started swinging his large frame.

"Careful, don't bring the house down on top of us, David," Sam said, and he wasn't joking.

"I got this," David said as he continued to swing his large frame back and forth. Suddenly he pulled his legs up and kicked at the closed door. A board broke into pieces, and daylight shone through. He dropped to the floor, climbed the ladder, then snapped the board loose. Lifting the door he crawled out of the cellar. As he was sitting on the side of the entrance, the sound of a horse and carriage came from the front yard. "Someone is here," David said, leaning his face down in the cellar. I am going to see who it is. Sam, help the girls out."

David raced around to the front yard and saw Cole driving his carriage. Beside him sat the most beautiful girl in the world, Jazz. He ran up beside the carriage. "Oh, mercy me, Miss Jazz. I'm so happy you're home."

"David, how did you get out of the cellar?" Before he could answer, Cole turned to her. "You locked him in the cellar?"

"It's okay. We ain't hurt, none of us, but I'm so glad you

came back."

~

Cole jumped down from the carriage and hurried over to the cellar. Georgia poked her head up from the cellar and then came Lily. "Go on up, little Miss, so I can get out," Sam yelled.

Cole couldn't believe his eyes as he watched his devoted friends climb out of the cellar with broad smiles on their faces. Instead of being mad at Jazz, they were thrilled to see her and little Jeffrey.

David helped Jazz down from the carriage and held little Jeffrey high in the air. Jeffrey cooed and dripped slobber down on David's chest. The giant only laughed and hugged the baby tighter.

Jazz hurried over to Georgia and Lily. They hugged each other. Sam was the last to climb from the cellar, and he waved at Cole as he hurried to grab Jazz and swing her around.

"Gal, we're sure glad to see you," Sam said.

As everyone headed inside the house, Cole stopped Jazz. "You had better be glad that it wasn't me locked in that cellar, because I wouldn't be smiling. And you wouldn't be able to sit for a week after I finished blistering your behind."

~

Jazz didn't respond but smiled at her beloved family members who must have understood her actions. They wouldn't have ever allowed her to leave for the train station.

Georgia helped Jazz put her carpetbags back in her bedroom. Jeffrey had finished his bottle and fell asleep in David's arms. Jazz took him and placed him back in his cradle. "Jazz, I am so happy that you are home. We were afraid for you, traveling all alone to wherever. I know you had no idea where you were going. Oh, child, I cried most of the day. Please don't ever listen to Cole's mama again. He loves you and he would never let his mama hurt you."

A soft knock came from the bedroom door. Georgia opened it and allowed Cole to enter.

"Thank you, Georgia. We will be out for supper in a little while." Jazz watched Georgia close the door and leave them alone.

Cole sat down on the bed and looked at Jazz. "Come sit beside me and let's talk. I am ready to listen to you. Why did you tell me that you loved me, and then you packed up and tried to leave?"

Jazz slowly walked to the bed and sat down. She sighed and wiped tears from her face. "This whole situation is insane. Your mama hates the sight of me. All I want is a home for me and my son. You think you know me, but you really don't. I've never had a home until I moved in with you. I lived on the streets until Joe came into my life." She shrugged. "I'm a nobody from nowhere."

He pressed his hand over hers. "No, you're not. Don't talk like that."

"I'm what people call white trash. Never knew my daddy, and my mama was a washwoman during the day and a lady of the evening when it got dark. That's how she made ends meet. My background would make great headlines for the newspaper when you run for governor. You would be dead in the water before the first ballot was ever cast." Jazz couldn't hold the tears back any longer. Cole waited until she cried herself out.

"Now, sweetheart, I am going to speak. First I want to say that you've managed to have quite a high opinion of yourself, haven't you? Look at me, Jazz. Can't you trust me?"

When she didn't answer, he asked, "Do you want a divorce?"

Jazz's head snapped up and looked up at him. She couldn't believe he had asked her that question. Was he really wanting his freedom? Jazz never thought of divorce. All she wished for was Cole's arms around her to hold her tight. But divorce? Jazz never liked it when her mama fought with a man. Jazz vowed never to say unkind words to her man. That was probably the reason she never had problems with Joe. Whenever she disagreed with him, she let him have his way. Now, sitting here, not a foot away, she was arguing with the man she loved.

"Jazz, this has been a long, hard day, and we'd best come to grips with things. Now you will listen to me." He took her hand and rubbed it between his two big hands.

"My mama has no say in my life. I can't believe that she would come here and talk to you like she did. She will be sorry that her words hurt you. Oh, don't worry. I'm not going to hurt her, even though I would like to strangle her. Honestly, I have no idea where she got the idea that I wanted to be the mayor of Yellowstone or the governor of Texas. She is delusional, that's for sure," he said, chuckling.

"But she's your mama. How can we go on when she hates me so much?"

"You let me worry about her. She will not come between us again." He tipped her chin to look into his eyes. "Promise me you will never leave me again."

She read honesty in his eyes. Determination. He was speaking the truth. Could she trust him? Flashes from the past came back. Of Joe. Of her mother. Of all the people in her life, Cole was the one—the only one—she could trust. Jazz nodded, then said with as much determination as she could muster, "I trust you, and I will never leave you."

"Well now, before we continue this conversation, I have to eat something. I am famished." He stood and led her to the kitchen. "Georgia, I would love a piece of strawberry pie. The pies look delicious."

"Did that Mrs. Richardson come by the store this morning? She came by here, and Jazz bought a crate of strawberries and other fruit. We also purchased a lot of jars to put up strawberry jam," Georgia asked.

"Yes, she did, and she told me all about meeting with all of you. She said that you were all very kind, and she enjoyed her visit. Thank you for buying her produce. That old woman works hard." Cole smiled broadly as he bit into the fresh pie.

After the dishes were washed and put away, he told Jazz to tell everyone goodnight. She stared at him but decided not to argue. He sounded like a father speaking to a small child, but he didn't mean for it to sound like that.

Jazz checked on Jeffrey, who was in a deep sleep. David and Lily had taken him outside and showed him the barn animals. Apparently, he'd pulled on the puppies' ears, let the goat lick his fingers, and kicked at the piglets. After he ate his supper, he could hardly hold his eyes open.

Jazz went into the water closet and changed into a white gown on which she had sewn yellow daisies across the bodice. As she walked to the bed, Cole held her in front of him. He leaned in and gave her a deep kiss. The kiss left her dazed. She staggered back and would have lost her balance if the back of her legs hadn't touched the bed. She wrapped her arms around his neck and leaned into him. Whispering his name, she placed a kiss on his throat, her lips soft and sweet. One kiss became another as they stood there sharing wild, fierce kisses. Jazz's lips met his with devouring impatience.

He pushed her back away.

"Is something wrong?" She had submitted to his kisses with small gasps of pleasure. "Don't you want me?"

"Yes, unfortunately too much, and I ache all over to take you to bed and love you until the sun comes up. I promised myself that I wouldn't touch you until I was sure you were well. Now, I am standing here about to burst my breeches 'cause I want you so much. You nearly drowned, but I'm not sure you have recovered completely." He pushed her hair away from her ghostly pale face.

"Please, Cole. I'm fine. Doctor Richards said I should be recovered in about four or five days. It has been almost a week, and I feel fine. Do you remember while you were leaving for Dallas, I promised you that I would be waiting for you to come home? Well, you're home. I'm home. Please let me grant my promise to you. I love you and I want to be your wife." She held out her hand and slowly pulled him down on the bed.

This was a start of a new life—their lives together, really together. With her arms wrapped around his muscular arms, she looked into his eyes, knowing that this was the time for endless lovemaking. Neither wanted to move. This had been a hard, emotional day for both of them. For just this moment, she held onto him like a lifeline, their breathing as one.

Much later, as the lantern oil flickered, Jazz went to sleep with her head cradled against Cole's shoulder, her hair tangled across his chest.

Epilogue

"Hurry, everyone. We don't want to be late for church today. Georgia and David, leave your service a few minutes early so you won't be late for Jeffrey's baptism. We can't have the small service until you both arrive."

"How many times do I have to tell you that those people ain't going to like it one bit that David and I are in their church?" Georgia said as she looked at David in his new white shirt Jazz had made special for him. It fit him perfectly and he looked so handsome.

Jazz smiled and posted a hand on her hip. "I told you I spoke to Preacher Harrington, and he said you could come, and no one had better object. We will be in God's house, and all God's children are welcome. Besides, this is a special service for our family only."

"All right, but have you invited Cole's mama to attend? She might just show up and cause a ruckus and embarrass everyone. I don't want any trouble to spoil little Jeffrey's special day." Georgia was almost sick to her stomach with worry.

"I promise you, Georgia, nothing is going to spoil this wonderful day. You look beautiful in your new dress. I love the ribbon in your hair, too. Now let's get Lily and be on our way. Cole has already carried Jeffrey to the carriage."

Cole let David drive the flatbed wagon a good ways ahead of their carriage. They waved at David and Georgia as they turned off the main road headed to their church in the woods.

On the way, Jazz asked Cole if he thought his mother would attend the baptism for Jeffrey.

"I asked her to come. She didn't answer me, and like I said before, I didn't beg her to come. I personally know that you bend over backwards being nice to her whenever you come into the store. Also, I know you gave her a lovely shawl for her birthday. Well, sweetheart, there isn't much that gets by me in this town. She never mentioned it to me, but I have seen her wearing it."

She brushed tendrils of hair away from her face. "Cole, I only want her to be a part of our family. She's an unhappy woman. I know Miss Ruby has invited her to tea, and she did accept her invitation. Maybe they will be friends again. Miss Ruby told me that your parents were good friends with her and your pa a long time ago."

"I'm glad that Mrs. Goodman is reaching out to Mama, but it does take two to make a friendship."

"I did offer to help decorate the display in your big window for fall. She didn't refuse my offer, so I plan to do that when it gets closer to Thanksgiving. Is that all right with you?"

"Of course, I miss you working in the store, but I know how much time our son takes, and now with the new baby coming— well, you'll have your hands full."

"Remember, you promised not to tell anyone about our baby. I want Jeffrey's day to be all about him. Later, he will have to share many things, I'm sure." She laughed as she moved closer to Cole.

At the beginning of the church service, Reverend Harrington said he had an important message. "A special donation has been made to the church with one purpose in mind. The money donated will be left up to me to help needy families and widows. I wish I could tell you who donated this money, but the family wishes to remain anonymous. They only pray that the recipients will use the money wisely to help make their lives a little easier. Let us pray for the generosity of others and grateful hearts." Reverend Harrington said amen and then gave his congregation a big smile. He sat down as the pianist played a hymn while everyone sang more joyfully than usual.

The service seemed to go on and on. Jazz was too excited about having Jeffrey baptized and named after Cole. He loved her baby so much.

Finally, the service ended, and Reverend Harrington announced that there would be a baptism after the service, and everyone was invited to attend. As soon as the words spilled out of his mouth, his hand went to his mouth. Too late.

Cole patted Jazz's hand, and both walked to the front of the church waiting for Reverend Harrington to finish shaking his congregation's hands as a few members departed the church.

From the back of the church, Mrs. James strode in on the arm of Mr. Mel Carter, the livery owner. They appeared to be a couple. Jazz smiled broadly at them and punched Cole in the side. "Go and greet your mama. Tell her how pleased we are that she came."

~

The side door opened, and Georgia and David stood staring at all the people in the church. Murmuring came from several people, but Jazz hurried over to her two friends and led them to the front pew next to Cole's mama. Jazz leaned down and kissed both of them on the cheek and thanked them for being brave warriors. "Jeffrey, Cole, and I will always remember your presence today."

Reverend Harrington hurried to the front and stood at the altar. After a lengthy prayer of love and forgiveness, he asked Cole and Jazz a question. "Who gives this child for baptism?"

"We do, his parents, Cole and Jazz James." More murmuring came from the congregation.

"Do you, Cole and Jazz, promise to instruct this child in the truth of God's word; in the way of salvation through Jesus Christ; to pray and to teach him to pray and to train him by your example through worship and through the nurture of the church?"

"We do."

Reverend Harrington then asked, "What Christian name is this child to be called?"

"Jeffrey Coleman James," Cole enunciated each word.

Reverend Harrington sprinkled water over Jeffrey's head, which brought loud screams.

The last words of the service were drowned out by the baby's hysterical cries. Jazz jiggled Jeffrey up and down, back and forth to quiet him down, but nothing helped until David stood and took the baby, then swayed him on his hip by the sidewall. Silence ushered in as Jeffrey felt secure in the big man's arms.

Mrs. James walked over to her son at the end of the service. "I see you tagged your middle name to the baby."

"Yes, we named our son after me, his father, in every way. I love him as if he were my own. I hope you won't forget that Jeffrey is now your grandchild."

Mel spoke up, "That is wonderful, Cole. I never had any children— something I wished for all my life." He leaned over and whispered, "Since we have just a minute, I wanted to ask if you care if I called on your mama. I've had fond feelings for her a long time."

"No, I don't mind at all." Cole nearly laughed out loud. "In fact, I am pleased. Maybe something will come of it, and you can help her to see what real love is. God has blessed me with a wonderful wife, a son, and great friends of all colors. Mama is blind in many ways. Maybe you can help her see people and life the way God intended."

Mel smiled broadly and shook Cole's hand. "I'll do my best."

"Jazz wants her to be in our life—my mama, her friend, and grandmother, in that order. Just maybe you're the man to help her find a way to accomplish all this. Good luck."

The End.

Other Forget me not books by

Linda Sealy Knowles

Journey to Heaven Knows Where

Hannah's Way

The Secret

Bud's Journey Home

Always Jess

Kathleen of Sweetwater

Abbey's new Life

Joy's Cowboy

Sunflower Brides

Trapped by Love

The Gamble

A Stranger's Love

Anna - A Lawman's Problem

Linda Sealy Knowles is originally from Saraland/Satsuma, Alabama. Linda wrote her first novel in 2013, and since then she has written fourteen. Who would have ever thought that she would write so many love stories? After completing a story, she is joyful and sad at the same time. Her characters are like family and wonderful friends, and it's sad to write, The End. God has blessed Linda, and she enjoys sharing her stories with her readers.

Made in the USA
Columbia, SC
11 June 2022

61486256R00152